THE BCMC

The BCMC

The Big City Motor Cop

*To Bill,
Best wishes to old motor cops!*

Gary Smith

10/02/09

Gary Smith

Copyright © 2009 by Gary Smith.

Library of Congress Control Number: 2009906380
ISBN: Hardcover 978-1-4415-4998-3
Softcover 978-1-4415-4997-6

All rights reserved. No part of this book may be reproduced or transmitted in any form or by any means, electronic or mechanical, including photocopying, recording, or by any information storage and retrieval system, without permission in writing from the copyright owner.

This is a work of fiction. Names, characters, places and incidents either are the product of the author's imagination or are used fictitiously, and any resemblance to any actual persons, living or dead, events, or locales is entirely coincidental.

This book was printed in the United States of America.

To order additional copies of this book, contact:
Xlibris Corporation
1-888-795-4274
www.Xlibris.com
Orders@Xlibris.com
64601

CONTENTS

Acknowledgments 7
Prologue 9

Chapter One	Los Angeles, 1963	13
Chapter Two	The Beginning, 1961	20
Chapter Three	The BCMCs	26
Chapter Four	Learning to Fly, 1961	30
Chapter Five	Fall, 1961	35
Chapter Six	Los Angeles, Highland Park Division, 1962	39
Chapter Seven	Crazy Streets, 1963	46
Chapter Eight	Crazy People, 1964	52
Chapter Nine	The Drunken Streets, 1964	55
Chapter Ten	Freeway Cop, 1964	60
Chapter Eleven	The Academy Steak Fry	66
Chapter Twelve	Back on the Streets, 1965	69
Chapter Thirteen	The Farm and Back, 1965	76
Chapter Fourteen	The Little Redhaired Girl, 1965	82
Chapter Fifteen	Trouble and More Trouble, 1965	88
Chapter Sixteen	The Second Day in Hell, Watts, 1965	96
Chapter Seventeen	The End and Aftermath, Watts, 1965	104
Chapter Eighteen	The Lone Ranger Rides Again	110
Chapter Nineteen	Code B	119
Chapter Twenty	Being There	124
Chapter Twenty-One	Yee Haw!	130
Chapter Twenty-Two	Married Life and Death	137
Chapter Twenty-Three	The Little Nipper	143
ChApter Twenty-Four	Some Fun and Some Not	149
Chapter Twenty-Five	Earthquake!	157
Chapter Twenty-Six	New Bikes	160
Chapter Twenty-Seven	Motor School and Pain	163
Chapter Twenty-Eight	Back Again	176
Chapter Twenty-Nine	Justice?	182

Epilogue 185

ACKNOWLEDGMENTS

Thanks and warm regards to and for the many BCMCs who contributed to the rich heritage of the Los Angeles Police motor squad. Many are now End of Watch and no longer with us. To the ones who are still here, I salute you and wish you all well. I wish to thank Linda, for living this part of my life with me and dealing with the fears and trials with which officers' wives must deal.

Many thanks go to Ruthie, who has been my inspiration to move ahead in the progress of this book, as well as of my life.

Cover design by Rick Campbell, Creative, Portland, Oregon

PROLOGUE

The excitement in the voice from the TV news helicopter pilot sank into the brain of the middle-aged man seated on the edge of his couch. His eyes glued to the TV screen, the man clenched his fists as he watched crowds of black people running in the streets of Los Angeles, attacking the drivers of passing cars. As he watched, a small car was stopped by a group of young black kids. He mumbled to himself, then yelled out loud "Get the hell out of there you idiot!" His voice rumbled through his gritted teeth. The raging crowd pulled the helpless Asian woman out of the car and started to beat and kick her. As she rolled around on the pavement trying to protect her face from the kicks, the newsman in the helicopter gave a running commentary of the incident.

"Where are the police?" the helicopter pilot kept saying. The man watching at the other end of the broadcast felt his guts turning over and wondered too.

As the middle-aged man continued to watch the television reports, the looting and beatings continued. He sat frustrated, unable to do anything else but watch and swear.

"The crowd has now stopped a large truck and is pulling the driver out of the cab," said the helicopter newsman. "They are beating him with sticks and anything they can pick up. This is attempted murder! Where are the police? There are no police in sight anywhere!" he yelled into the microphone.

The middle-aged man sat in his house and watched as the helpless truck driver was struck with bottles and bricks. His blood splattered on the ground. A man walked out into the street and pulled a sawed-off rifle or shotgun from a bag and fired a shot at the downed and helpless man.

"You son of a bitch!" the man watching the TV heard himself yell. His clenched fist pounded the arm of his couch in frustration.

"Honey, why are you watching that?" asked the man's wife from the other room. "You'll just get all frustrated, and there's nothing you can do about it," she said.

The rioting in Los Angeles had been going on for about twelve hours and seemed to be spreading out to the far reaches of the suburbs. The television had been gushing with news about the verdict handed down on the Rodney King beating case. The four officers accused of excessive force had been found not guilty on all counts, except one count on one officer, and that was a minor one. The Mayor of Los Angeles and other local and even national political figures were making public statements about how the justice system had let the people down. A riot was not surprising under the circumstances. Still, what do riots solve? thought the man as he watched.

"I can't believe what I'm seeing," he moaned to his wife. "Not one police car in the area. They had better move in soon, or they'll lose the city." The man sank back in his couch as his wife came into the living room. "If they don't act now with a show of force, things will get out of hand. Didn't they learn anything from the Watts Riots in 1965?" he said in a loud voice.

Pete Felix had been retired from the Los Angeles Police Department for twelve years now. He had put in almost twenty-three years as a cop and had enjoyed most of it. Now he was out of it. Well, physically, he was out of it. Mentally, cops are always cops. Pete had taken a new and different direction from what most cops take on retirement. Most of Pete's old buddies had gone into security or detective work or worked movie jobs as retired motorcycle officers. Retired motor cops who worked on movie locations made good money but Pete wanted out of uniform and out of police work altogether, partly because he was tired of the political changes going on in the department and partly because of Noel, his wife. She worried, and like all police wives, she wondered how long it would be before she received that phone call in the night about her husband.

It had been hard for Pete to leave, but he could see it had to be. Now, at fifty-six, Pete still enjoyed good health and still had most of his hair. His sideburns had turned salt-and-pepper gray, which blended into his brown hair in a way that looked distinguished, Pete thought. He had put on weight since his retirement and change of career. Gone was the lean-and-mean look that most cops try to maintain. Pete had kept up an exercise program until his retirement. His last duty assignment on the department had allowed him time after work to run the hills around the police academy on a regular basis. Since he had taken the job in private enterprise, he had let himself go, and his weight had climbed to about two hundred pounds from his original 185. At a height of five nine, Pete looked very stocky, but most people were surprised at the hardness of his bulk. He didn't really care too much what anybody thought, anyway.

Although Pete had lost his boyish figure, he had never lost his sense of humor. That humor had made him somewhat of a legend during his police career. Some of his antics had gotten him into trouble on many occasions. But humor had also gotten him out of trouble just as many times.

On his retirement, Pete had taken a job in the corporate offices of a major motorcycle company working in safety promotions. He had been a motorcycle instructor while on the police department and had obtained a credential to teach school on the California community college level in the subjects of police science and traffic safety. He had also been certified as a motorcycle instructor by the Motorcycle Safety Foundation, the national motorcycle riding program. His new job had allowed him to do one of the things he loved most: riding motorcycles as well as moving into a new career field of private enterprise.

It had not been easy for Pete to retire. He'd been a cop all of his adult life! Mannerisms and skills learned over a period of twenty-three years were not easily forgotten. Sometimes he thought he'd never be able to think like a "civilian." He couldn't seem to shake off the ways he'd learned to rely on for his survival on the streets of Los Angeles, California. Maybe he never could. Noel lost patience with him on many occasions because of his negative attitude about people and some of their ways.

"Everyone is an asshole until they prove otherwise," Pete had said many times. His wife didn't like that attitude, but, in many cases, it had proved to be reliable for him.

As he watched the city, to which he had dedicated a good portion of his life and some of his blood, appear to be going up in smoke, he sighed and got up to pour himself another drink and decided to drink it all away.

"Fuck it! It's not my problem anymore."

CHAPTER ONE

LOS ANGELES, 1963

The siren on the Harley-Davidson police motorcycle screamed its shrill, high-pitched wailing notes into the rider's helmet at about 100 decibels, but Pete Felix didn't hear it. His mind and body were totally focused on the speeding car and the traffic ahead of him. The motorcycle's engine roared as Pete shifted down to second gear to slow for the approaching intersection. His mind kept telling him to grab the radio microphone and broadcast his direction of travel to communications so other cops could follow his pursuit and assist him in capturing his suspects. But every time he tried to take his hands from the handlebar to reach for the mike, a car pulled out in front of him or the next intersection would be speeding toward him.

Bam! The Harley bottomed out as it bounced over the dips on both sides of the gutters. Pete's mind was operating at top speed to keep up with all the events that were happening to him. Sixty miles an hour in a district of Los Angeles designated for twenty-five-mile-an-hour traffic. He knew a crash at that speed would mean almost certain death or, at best, some life-threatening injuries. He gritted his teeth, put his head down, and hung on as he twisted the throttle on the right handlebar wide open.

Little rivers of sweat rolled down the nose of Cleophus Johnson as his hands clutched the steering wheel of the 1961 Buick. He and his partner, Robert Davis, skidded the fleeing vehicle through the intersection of Vermont and Vernon Avenues, running the red light. They had just missed a southbound vehicle by inches as they ran the red light at about sixty miles per hour. The Buick bounced a couple of feet in the air with sparks and gray rubber smoke coming from under the car.

"Shit, man," yelled Robert, "cool it or you'll kill us for sure!"

"Fuck you, man. I ain't goin' back to the joint behind no chicken shit grand theft auto." Cleophus had been out of San Quentin only thirty days; and if he was going back to prison, it had to be for something worthwhile like robbery, his usual means of support, or at least burglary, his secondary means of support.

Both men had long criminal records dating back to their early childhood. They knew the LAPD well from many personal contacts with them. They knew all the ways the Los Angeles cops operated and how to con them. Cleophus also knew how to keep his parole officer happy and had stayed out of jail longer than the last time he was out. But this was a motorcycle cop on their tail. They were unpredictable. Cleophus had met some who were very friendly. The kind you could con. But others were different. Most of them seemed older and more streetwise, and they didn't take any shit from ex-cons. Anyway, he wasn't about to stop and find out how this motor cop was going to react to two ex-cons in a stolen car and who were leading him on a dangerous chase through the darkened streets of south central Los Angeles.

Sweat was also blowing off Pete's nose. The wind whistling over the plastic windshield of the police motorcycle distorted the cheeks of the officer. He finally grabbed the microphone from its clip on the handlebar.

"Thirteen Mary Thirty-two is still westbound on Vernon, just passed Vermont in pursuit of a 1961 Buick convertible, red in color, driven by two male Negro suspects. The vehicle is wanted for speed and possible GTA."

Pete tried to control the volume of his voice as he spoke into the mike. It was hard to do because he couldn't hear his own voice over the roar of the big Harley engine. If he yelled into the mike too loudly, the distortion might muffle his voice so badly that his location might not be audible. At a time like this, he wanted everyone to know where he was, especially his partner, who was somewhere behind him in the darkness. Pete couldn't take the time to look in his rearview mirrors to see if he was there or not. He hoped he was.

The chase had gone on for what seemed like ten minutes. Actually, it had been only about five minutes since Pete and his partner had seen the red Buick convertible speeding north on Central Avenue from Santa Barbara Boulevard. As the motor cops turned on the red lights on the front of their motorcycles to stop the car for a ticket, they noticed the two men in the front seat talking rapidly to each other, as if deciding what to do. Pete and his partner Ron Byron knew what that meant. The speeders were deciding whether or not to "rabbit," as cops called it. They rabbited.

Pete knew as soon as a pursuit was announced on the police radio, all other activities were suspended, and the chase became priority for Communications Division, who operated from the Police Facilities Building (PAB) downtown. That was a comforting feeling to the field officers, but didn't ensure that the pursuit would come to a successful ending. Most police pursuits ended in a traffic accident involving the suspect, the officer, or an innocent party who gets in the way.

Like most cops, Pete hated pursuits. When pursuing in a police car, officers had the protection of the surrounding metal automobile and the seat belts to improve their chances of survival should a crash occur during a pursuit. Motor cops didn't enjoy that protection. A fiberglass helmet, a pair of high-top leather boots, and a leather jacket were Pete's only protection. His main source of safety was his brain, his riding capabilities, and his experience.

As the next intersection approached, Pete peered into the darkness ahead of his headlight to see the color of the signal light at Western Avenue. The light was green for westbound traffic. The red Buick made a left turn and sped south on Western. Pete swore as the light went amber. By the time he got there, it would be red for him. He knew he would have to slow down before going through the intersection, even though he had his red lights and siren on. Experience had taught him that the siren on a police vehicle is usually not heard by approaching traffic, especially when many people have their radios blasting while they drive. Pete's right boot hit the brake pedal at the same time he squeezed the front hand brake. The heavy motorcycle slowed, but only a little. Pete frantically increased pressure on the foot brake until he thought he would push the pedal through the footboard, and still, the bike only slowed slightly. The brake shoes were hot and fading fast. This can't go on much longer, he thought. I'm going to have to stop them or pull out of the chase. That meant he would lose, and the suspects would probably get away. "Shit!" he said out loud.

The chase continued to Slauson Avenue and turned west. Pete remembered the long stretch of straight street that went uphill toward the boundary between Los Angeles City and Los Angeles County at Overhill Street. He'd make his move there. Now all he had to figure out was what that move would be. He couldn't shoot at them since there had been no direct assault on him or anyone else from the time Pete and Ron had tried to stop them.

The car had been verified as a "77th Division stolen" by communications during the pursuit, but that was still not enough to use deadly force. Had Pete's life and other lives been endangered by the suspects' failure to stop? Sure, but that wasn't enough reason to kill the bastards, according to the courts. All these thoughts flashed through Pete's mind as the pursuit was coming to its climax.

Now they were westbound on Slauson, starting up the long hill toward the city limits. Pete saw his chance. He twisted the throttle wide open and gained on the Buick, which was by now smoking badly and overheating. Pete pulled up about fifty feet behind the fleeing vehicle. He could see the heads of the two occupants swiveling around as they realized the cops had caught up to them and the car they were driving was about to blow up.

"Fuck this shit," Pete muttered as he twisted the spark advance handle of the Harley's left handlebar and then cut the ignition switch on the bike. He then held the throttle open for two or three seconds to allow more gasoline to flow into the hot carburetor. Then he turned the ignition back on.

Pow! The backfire from the Harley's exhaust pipe shot a spout of flame at least a foot out of the muffler. The sound was deafening, like a cannon shot.

Both men in the fleeing car ducked as the "shot" echoed between the apartment buildings that lined this part of the street.

"Motherfucker, he shootin' at us!" screamed Robert to his partner.

By this time, Cleophus had decided that going back to the joint was better than being shot up by some crazy motor cop. *Bam!* Another "shot" rang out. Cleophus and Robert saw the motor cop pull up on the left side of their car with a pistol in his hand, and it was pointed at them.

"He gonna shoot us, man! Stop the motherfuckin' car, man!" yelled Robert. Cleophus slammed on the brakes, and the Buick started to skid.

Pete's brakes were now so hot that they had ceased to exist. As the Buick skidded and slowed, he was unable to stop and rode right on by the suspect's vehicle, pointing his revolver at the car as he passed by. He thought how dangerous it could be if the suspects were armed, and also how stupid he must look. There he was in front of the suspect's vehicle, totally exposed.

Fortunately, the two suspects were not about to raise their heads above the door level and get their heads shot off by some crazy motor cop. Ron Byron pulled up behind the suspect's vehicle and jumped off his motorcycle, gun in hand.

"Okay, you assholes, get your hands up and come out of that car!"

"Please don' shoot, man! We gives up!"

Both suspects were out of the car and handcuffed when the rest of the cavalry arrived a few minutes later. As the suspects were about to be loaded into the police car to be transported to jail, Cleophus's pride couldn't take it anymore.

"Man, you pigs would never caught me if that crazy motherfucker hadn't shot at us. You ain' s'posed to be shootin' at auto thieves, is you?"

"I didn't fire a shot, asshole. I just backfired my motorcycle, and you dudes just pulled over."

"Shit!" whined Robert. "You mean you didn't shoot at us?"

Pete smiled that smile criminals hate to see when a cop is sending them back where they belong: to prison.

"You don't think I would do anything to endanger the lives of any of our good citizens, now do you, sir?"

"You all nothin' but pigs," snarled Cleophus as the door of the car slammed shut. Pete leaned down and got the last word in.

"Yeah, but when I go home and take off this uniform, I'll look just like everyone else. But you'll always be an asshole!"

A mild Los Angeles night breeze stirred through the dirty palm trees that lined the streets of Los Angeles as Pete and Ron pulled their Harleys into the stalls marked for police motorcycles, next to the decaying brick building that housed the offices of the Seventy-seventh Police Division, where they patrolled. Both officers wore the uniform of an LAPD motor officer: dark blue, almost black, shirt with shoulder patches, and insignia that identified a traffic officer from the regular street cops. From the right shoulder hung a chain attached to a police whistle tucked into the right breast pocket. The dark blue riding breeches had white stripes down the sides into black leather riding boots, which were polished to a high-glossy shine.

Pete took off his white-and-black safety helmet and reached to unfasten his saddlebags. "You know what I like about pursuits?"

"What?" answered Ron.

"Nothin'!"

"Yeah, I thought you were gonna lose it when you bounced over those gutters."

"So did I. It's hard to turn it off when you're chasing these assholes." The two cops walked into the station and were greeted by one of the patrol cops they knew.

"Look out. Here comes Fric and Frac," warned the officer. Several other cops looked up from their desks as the motor cops came into the room. Pete and Ron had earned a reputation among their fellow officers for being humorous and somewhat wild.

"Internal Affairs is probably right behind them too," commented the short, stocky officer at a corner table.

"Hey, fireplug, why don't you go down to the property room and check out a neck?" yelled Ron.

Another cop turned to his partner and said, "Ya know, I tried to get on motors once, but they found out my mother and father were married and washed me out."

The ensuing laughter attracted the attention of the watch commander, who stuck his head out of his office.

"Hold it down out there. This isn't a recreation hall!"

"It isn't?" said Pete softly. "Then why are we having so much fun?" The two cops snickered as they climbed the stairs toward the coffee room where they were going to have a sumptuous lunch consisting of hot links and Diet Pepsi.

Pete enjoyed having Ron as a partner. Most motors teams picked their partners on night watch. If you didn't have a partner, you'd be assigned to anyone who needed one. Not all motor cops were fun to work with like Ron, thought Pete. They had been in the same motor school class and had become instant friends while training for Traffic Enforcement Division. Several months later, they had teamed up as partners.

Ron and Pete were about the same age. A little taller and more muscular than Pete, Ron had a similar sense of humor, and the team soon became known as Fric and Frac, after some old show business comedy team from the past. The two cops loved the attention, and any gathering of officers offered another opportunity for Fric and Frac to try and outdo each other in entertaining the troops.

They had made department history on one occasion when the department psychologist was giving a lecture how to handle psycho cases to a class of new police recruits at the academy. As the psychologist was making a point about how serious this type of police work was, Fric and Frac skipped through the classroom holding hands. Although the incident got both their asses in hot water, it made them a legend in the eyes of their fellow officers.

Pete Felix was not very tall, by police standards. Five feet eight was the minimum height limit for LAPD officers, and he had just made it by one-half inch in 1958, when he came on the job. Because he had always been small and thin, he had learned to use his brain, rather then brawn, to defend himself from bigger and older kids. He had developed a sense of humor that helped him in his childhood and now made him well-liked by most who knew him. This view was not universally held by his supervisors, however, and Pete was frequently in trouble for his attempts at humor at roll call meetings.

At age twenty-seven, he'd already been an LAPD cop a little more than four years. Like all other motor cops, he'd done his time in a patrol car before coming to motors. The motor squad would not take anyone who didn't have at least one year on the job, but Pete didn't know anyone who made it on motors with less than two years under his belt.

"Man, I feel like I been rode hard and hung up wet," remarked Pete, as he plopped heavily into a chair. He felt drug out and weak all of a sudden. The coffee room was empty, except for another motor cop doing a report. Charlie Behan had come on motors with the pair and was a chubby, happy-go-lucky type of guy that both Pete and Ron liked.

"Hey, you guys, I heard your pursuit on the radio. Pretty hairy, huh? Kinda takes the starch out of your shorts, don't it?"

"No shit!" Pete opened his Diet Pepsi and took a big swig. The cool, bubbly liquid felt good in his hot throat. "My asshole sucked so tight to my seat, I thought we'd need an Abalone knife to pry me loose! Ah! Now all I need is a couple of these hot links and some clean underwear, and I'll be all set for the rest of the evening!"

"You keep eatin' those hot links and mustard, and you'll end up shittin' in one of those colostomy bags someday."

"Thanks, Charlie. But you know what a perfect asshole I am, so I don't worry about it."

"Those pursuits are really a strain on the brain. Remember when we were in the motor school? We all thought the instructors were being hard on us," recalled Charlie. "Little did we know..." Charlie shook his head as his sentence trailed off and went back to his report. Pete and his partner ate their lunches and talked about the training they had gone through to become motor cops. Their minds flashed back to the beginning.

CHAPTER TWO

THE BEGINNING, 1961

The LAPD motor squad was one of the largest in the world, its Traffic Enforcement Division (TED), fielding over four hundred men assigned to patrol the streets of Los Angeles. TED headquarters were located in the Police Administration Building (PAB) at 150 North Los Angeles Street in downtown Los Angeles. The same building also houses Central Patrol Division and many other divisions including Robbery Division, Homicide, Forgery, Scientific Investigation Division (SID), Records and Identification Division (R&I), and many other police administrative offices. It was the hub of the Los Angeles Police Department.

Pete had walked by the TED offices when he was a patrol cop at Central Division and had noticed the motor cops all looked sharp and seemed to have a spirit that was different from their fellow officers who didn't ride motorcycles. Whenever Pete talked about going on motors, he always got an opinion about the motor squad.

Some said, "Those prima donnas on motors are a bunch of assholes. All they do is write little old ladies jaywalking tickets—when they're not shopping, that is." Others advised, "If you spend too much time on motors, it will affect your chances of promotion later on the job" or "The brass have got it into their heads that motor cops are crazy, and if you stay on motors too long, you'll be crazy too. If you go on motors, you should only stay two or three years and then move on to some other job for varied experience." Everyone had their own ideas about the motor squad, but Pete wanted to be a part of these crazy motor cops from the beginning.

That mid-January day, 1961, had dawned cold and crisp. Pete remembered it was cold enough to put frost on the grass of the golf course he'd passed as he headed for the motor school training area in Griffith Park near the new Los Angeles Zoo.

As he looked around, the candidates all looked a lot older than him, he'd thought. There were several guys he'd known from patrol. They were all nervous. The instructors were all seasoned motor cops. An old wrinkled sergeant—who, from the looks of his nose, must have been a prizefighter at some time in his life—was in charge of the training program. Sergeant Patton briefed the fledgling motor cops shortly after they arrived.

"LAPD has the best motor squad in the world," the leather-skinned old sergeant bragged as he addressed the new troops. "We have fourteen days to teach you how to ride a police motorcycle, so you won't get killed out on the street. We don't have time for screwing around or for slow learners."

As they listened, the men shifted their feet and looked at the ground, afraid to look at each other, in case they looked scared. Most of them were. The old sergeant continued, "Anyone who doesn't hack it the first couple of days will be sent back to your original job assignment." They all knew that the saying "Here today, gone tomorrow" had special meaning for the would-be motor cops because it was true. Anyone who didn't catch on very quickly went right back to their old job. No one wanted that.

The uniform for the motor school was Levi's, over-the-ankle shoes or boots, long sleeved shirts, and gloves. Since the weather was cold, jackets were heavy. Motorcycle helmets were provided by the department. The motorcycles to be used were old Harley-Davidsons that had been retired from service and stripped of all nonessential equipment for the training, leaving only the bare motorcycle. No saddlebags or radio equipment—just the frame, a motor, a gas tank, and fenders.

The bikes were early 1950's vintage and still had the old-fashioned rocker-type foot clutch. Pete had never ridden one before. The motorcycles he had ridden had been equipped with hand clutches and a foot shift. The newer-model Harleys had them, but the new motor cops trained on the older models.

On these ancient motorcycles, gears were shifted by a lever on the left side of the gas tank with the left hand while operating the clutch with the left foot. It seemed very awkward to Pete, especially when starting up and making a left turn at the same time. Since the left foot was operating the clutch, you couldn't put your left foot down to steady the motorcycle if you were off balance. It had to be done right the first time, or you could go out of control; and that's just what a lot of guys did the first day.

The candidates were systematically put through every torture the instructors could think of to do with a motorcycle. They were required to ride slowly through a maze of rubber cones without putting a foot down and maintaining complete control of the motorcycle using the clutch and brake. They rode off the pavement in the dirt on a motorcycle not designed to be ridden there.

Pete decided the goal of the motor school instructors was to kill or maim the candidates. "Why else would the instructors have us doing this stuff?" he'd whined to several of the other cops as they stood around, feeling the soreness of their muscles and looking at the bruises on their legs. Frequent falls had put bruises on all parts of Pete's body. By the end of each day, the men had to force their fingers open because they were molded into the form of handlebar grips. The instructors seemed to love it, though. It was their way of making sure that only the best made it through.

Pete had been riding motorcycles since high school and owned his own bike. He had been riding to work for nearly two years. The riding experience was invaluable. Other officers had none. Some picked up on the riding skills quickly, and some didn't. The department did not have much patience with slow learners at motor school. You either made it in the first few days, or you were back where you came from. It was that simple.

The first day, two men washed out. One guy lost control of his motor and nearly ran over an instructor. That was highly frowned upon. Pete felt sorry for the ones who washed out, but it was better not to ride at all than get killed in a motorcycle accident. After the first few days had weeded out the slow learners, the "training" really got serious.

"All right, you, guys," yelled the instructor Buck Rockwood, "line up on the dirt road, facing this direction." He pointed to the side of the road that ran along a large field of tumbleweeds about five feet high. The men fired up their motors and complied, lining the motorcycles up side by side on the dirt road, facing at a right angle to the direction of the road.

"I wonder what they've dreamed up now to try to kill us." Pete commented to Ron Byron, seated on the bike next to him. Pete and Ron had started to hang around together during the school. Pete respected Ron's riding ability and liked his sense of humor.

"They're probably going to make us spin around in circles on our motors until we ride up our own assholes," quipped Ron. The guys around laughed almost halfheartedly because they didn't think the scenario was too far from reality. They had all been amazed at the tremendous pressure put on them by the instructors. None had dreamed this training would be so rigorous. Now they began to realize why motor officers felt they were different from the rest of the department.

They sat on their idling motorcycles and waited for the next order. Pete wondered what that order would be. They had to turn left or right on the dirt road, he thought. It was the only place to go.

"Okay," yelled Rockwood, "I want you all to ride across that field to the road on the other side!" The men were stunned and glanced around at the others. Pete's mind raced. There wasn't anything in front of them but a wall of tumbleweeds higher than their heads. No trails—nothing. The field appeared to be about a hundred yards wide. The men hesitated.

"Fire 'em up!" Rockwood yelled. The men on the bikes revved the engines and waited. The noise was deafening as more than twenty motorcycles roared. The men all raised their hands to indicate their readiness. The instructor stood in front of the line of motors.

"Go! Go! Go!" he screamed over the roar of the engines and pointing toward the field of tumbleweeds. Off they went into the wall of tumbleweeds. Pete squinted his eyes and dived in, shifting to second gear. The rough branches of the tumbleweeds scratched his face, and dust filled his mouth and nose. On both sides of him, he could hear the roar of the other motors, but couldn't see anything but dust and weeds.

Several bikes went down almost immediately. He heard the characteristic roar of an out-of-control engine, spinning the rear wheel of a motorcycle that was lying on its side.

As Pete plunged on into the unknown and unseen, he wondered what purpose this training would have on his career. Never mind that, he told himself. Now he was just hanging on and trying to be one of the guys to come out on the other side of the field.

After what seemed like about two minutes, Pete broke out of the sea of tumbleweeds on the other side of the field. Ron was already there, laughing and dusting himself off. The instructors were laughing too. When Pete got off his motor and thought about the "exercise" he had just performed, he also started to laugh. Why not? The other few trainees straggled in over the next several minutes.

"Let's go back and pick up the whipdicks that didn't make it through," ordered one of the instructors. Five men had not come through the weeds. One had hit a hidden log and had the wind knocked out of him. He was okay. The others had just gotten bogged down in the tumbleweeds and had been unable to start their motors again. By some miracle, no one was hurt.

Later, at lunch break, Pete and Ron sat together on a picnic bench, eating and talking.

"So you're from Iowa?" asked Ron. "I moved here from Indiana when I was a kid. I guess most people who live in California came from somewhere else."

"Yeah, I came out here to take the police test and stayed. It took me a little while to get used to this crazy place. But, after a while, it kinda grows on ya."

"Back in the Midwest, they call California 'The Land of Fruits and Nuts.'"

"After working the streets in LA for a couple of years, you might think that's true."

"Okay, kiddies, saddle up!" yelled the old sergeant in charge.

Most of the training the fledgling motor cops underwent was relevant to their future job of enforcing traffic laws from a motorcycle. The men were taught that motorcycles allowed traffic officers more mobility in the congested traffic of the big city. There were always complaints from budget experts who said motorcycles were too expensive and unnecessary because police automobiles do the job just as well. Those who worked the streets knew better.

The inefficient use of police motorcycles was mainly blamed on the fact that only one officer used that motorcycle, whereas a car could be used by all shifts of patrol. The justification for only one officer per motorcycle lay in the concept of "twenty-four-hour emergency response." This meant that all motor officers were on twenty-four-hour call for any emergency. The first large contingency of cops on any big emergency scene was usually the motor cops. The squad theoretically could be mobilized on a few hours' notice because the motor cops all rode their motorcycles home and kept them there.

The training Pete and the other men were getting was starting to pay off. Most of the men could now negotiate the mazes of rubber cones, laid out by the instructors, almost perfectly, without putting their feet down.

Braking exercises taught the officers that both front and rear brakes should be used to stop in the shortest distance. Skid control was taught by requiring the students to lock up the rear wheel of the motorcycle and skid to a stop. The police instructors were very critical of stories commonly accepted by motorcycle riders about accidents.

"You hear motor riders talking about their accident," said Bob Smith, one of the instructors. "They say, 'I didn't have any choice but to lay the bike down.' What he's really saying is, 'I didn't use my brakes properly and went on my ass.'" The men crowding around the instructor laughed. He continued.

"When you're confronted with the choice of hitting a car while you are upright and braking or hitting a car while you are down, sliding on your ass, take the first choice!" he said emphatically. "Think about it," he urged. "The friction of your rubber tires on the pavement is much more than the friction of your metal crash bars on the pavement, aren't they? It takes guts and control to keep the bike upright and straight while you keep the binders on to get the slowest impact. Most people panic and throw it away or try to turn while braking and go on their ass and get more seriously hurt than if they had stayed on the brakes until impact." It was a lesson Pete never forgot.

Pete honed his skills so that, although the rear tire was skidding, he could maintain control and stay upright. By practicing what the instructors taught, keeping his head up and looking straight ahead while holding the handlebars straight, he kept himself from falling to the right or left. He could even keep control while skidding sideways. Pete knew that all of this was vital to his survival on the street.

He was beginning to see a similarity between the fighter pilots in World War Two and motor cops. To be either, it required excellent eyesight, split-second timing and coordination, as well as willingness to take risks. To many cops, just being a cop was more-than-enough risk for them. Riding a motorcycle *and* being a cop was too much. For Pete, riding a motorcycle was the next thing to "flying" while on the ground. He loved every minute of it. After two weeks of riding for eight hours a day, most of the candidates wondered why they even wanted to be a motor cop, but he loved it.

The third, and final, week, the men spent in the classroom studying the Vehicle Code—the "bible" of traffic enforcement officers. Then, the surviving members of the motor class of January 1961 graduated. With no fanfare, they were each assigned to a thirty-day training period on night watch in the metropolitan Los Angeles area. And so it had begun for Pete.

CHAPTER THREE

THE BCMCs

The new motor uniform felt uncomfortable on Pete. How do they expect us to ride in all this stiff gear? he wondered as he examined himself in the full-length mirror in the locker room. The riding boots were stiff and new. The leather jacket was stiff and uncomfortable, and the whole outfit felt like it weighed about thirty pounds. The riding breeches were tight from the knees down and were patterned after the old army cavalry uniform breeches. The trousers bloused out at the thighs and narrowed at the knees with a zipper from the ankle up to mid-calf, allowing the riding boots to slip snugly over them.

Pete liked the look of the uniform but thought the riding breeches seemed to be for traditional reasons than for riding comfort. The high boots were for safety purposes, they were told. The shirt was regular LAPD, except for the shoulder patches. They had a small patch under the larger traffic patch, which depicted a "wheel with an arrow" through it, indicating a motor officer.

"Let's go. It's time," said Ron, as he walked out the door toward the coffee room.

As the new motor officers filtered into the coffee room, the older officers cracked jokes about the new, ill-fitting uniforms on the novitiates.

"Hey, kid, where'd you get the finger-tip-length leather jacket?" asked a leather-faced old cop as he sucked on his pipe, his boot-sheathed leg propped up on a table.

The victim looked at his jacket and missed the joke completely, not realizing how the new leather had not been broken in yet. Later, Pete and the other cops realized that leather jackets wrinkle at the elbows and fit better, so the sleeves don't look too long on the wearer.

Another salty officer leaned over close to Ron and asked, "Do you have any nude photos of your wife?"

"No!" answered Ron emphatically.

"Would you like to buy some?" asked the older cop. The gang in the coffee room broke out into loud laughter. Ron swallowed his anger and gritted his teeth.

"Fuck you, old man," he whispered as he smiled at him. The old guy chuckled. Pete knew this was a test the veteran cops used to pressure the newcomers to see if they could take the guff.

Pete's two years in patrol told him the older cops put all the new guys through an acid test of humor, but still, it was hard to take. Most of the new guys pass the test because they want to be "one of the troops."

After grabbing their coffee, Pete and Ron walked into the roll call room across the hall. They looked around for a place to sit. Most of the seats were taken. Pete sat his coffee down on the long tabletop and was about to put his books down.

"Hey, kid, that's my seat," said a gruff voice behind him. Pete looked up into the frowning face of a very large cop.

"Sorry, I didn't know there were assigned seats," Pete said as he moved his stuff over to another table. The older cop sat down and busied himself with his paperwork.

"Some guys are touchy," said Pete in a whisper as his buddy sat down beside him in the roll call room on their first day on motors. "I just got chewed out for sitting in the wrong seat!" Ron smiled and shook his head.

Norm Cooperman, one of the oldsters on motors, turned around from the next row. "Some of the BCMCs have favorite places at roll call they like to sit. Just hang around, and you'll see where not to sit."

"BCMC? What's that?"

"Big city motor cop," drawled Dick McCory. The officer who spoke was rather short and well-rounded, and Pete noticed the two hash marks on his sleeve, indicating at least ten years on the job. McCory was one of the jokers on the squad, always trying to outdo others in dreaming up things to piss off the supervisors who conducted roll call.

"Hey, Beach Ball, what are you gonna do with that firecracker?" asked someone from the other side of the aisle, calling McCory by his nickname. The Beach Ball broke out with an evil smile as he fingered the M-80 in hand.

Pete had heard about motors roll calls from other cops, but this was his first experience. The old-timers liked to impress the new guys by showing their disdain for supervision.

Many of the supervisors also had nicknames given to them by the men. Names like "the Animal" and "Cabbage Head" belonged to lieutenants. Allan

James, one of the least-liked sergeants on night watch, was called The Honey Hornet because he was always buzzing around, trying to please his bosses.

It was almost time for the watch commander to arrive and conduct roll call. The watch commander is a lieutenant or, if the lieutenant is off, a sergeant. The lieutenant on this watch was Lieutenant Holman, one of the few supervisors the troops liked. He seemed to still have a sense of humor about the job and liked a good laugh once in a while. He didn't have a nickname.

Pete noticed the Beach Ball and one of the other cops were doing something under the desk where the supervisors sat at roll call. Some of the guys up front were chuckling. Others just shook their heads and continued to fill out their logs from the previous shift. Their task completed, the two officers returned to their respective seats.

"Seven minutes," said the Beach Ball, pointing at his watch and nudging the cop next to him. Pete wondered what the hell was going on. Ron winked as if he knew something was up.

The door opened, and the lieutenant came in with the Honey Hornet close behind, carrying the notifications and information for the watch.

"If the lieutenant stopped real quick, the Honey Hornet's nose would go right up Holman's ass," mumbled Cooperman. Some snickering was heard among the troops.

"Roll call!" The Honey Hornet started to call names, and the officers answered up. "Jones?"

"Here."

"McKinney?"

"Present, sir," came the cynical answer.

"You clowns work 6M12 tonight." Pete looked at the assignment sheet. The beat was Hollywood Boulevard. The regular beat guys were apparently off.

"Oh my goodness! Hollywierd! Thanks so much, Sergeant, sir," McKinney answered in a lisping voice. The troops chuckled. Pete and Ron were still in shock. A couple of officers kept looking at their watches and smiling at one another. The roll call continued with the additions to the "hot sheet" of stolen and wanted vehicles.

Boom! A muffled, but powerful, explosion came from the small stage where the supervisors sat as the M-80 went off. The desk behind where the lieutenant and sergeant were seated lifted off the ground a few inches, then toppled off the stage to the floor. Smoke rose toward the ceiling. The two men on the small stage sat motionless in shock. No one spoke. The pause seemed to last for a minute or two; then, slowly, the lieutenant and the sergeant got up and stepped off the stage. They picked up the desk and returned it to its original position on the stage, then took their seats, and calmly picked up where they left off. Everyone acted as if nothing had happened. No one commented until after roll call.

"I told you," bragged Beach Ball, "seven minutes almost to the second!"

"Did you see the look on the fucking Honey Hornet's face?" laughed Cooperman. "I bet if the lieutenant hadn't been there, he'd have really freaked out."

Pete's curiosity got the better of him. "How'd you time that to go off in seven minutes?" he asked the roly-poly officer walking next to him. Beach Ball chuckled.

"You take the fuse of the firecracker and push it through a burning cigarette. When the cigarette burns down to the fuse... *Boom!*" They all walked out to the motor parking area laughing and talking about the expression on the supervisors' faces when the firecracker had gone off.

The whole scene reminded Pete again of a movie he'd seen about pilots in World War Two. They had the same type of humor and esprit de corps. In fact, several of the men on the squad were World War II pilots, Pete learned later. He knew he was going to like being a BCMC.

CHAPTER FOUR

LEARNING TO FLY, 1961

"Man, I used to think riding a police motorcycle would be just like riding any other motorcycle," Pete mumbled as he walked into the Hollywood police station coffee room with his training officer. The new BCMC had quickly discovered that riding a motorcycle in the heavy Los Angeles traffic—and looking for traffic violations at the same time—was not an easy task. It seemed like every car on the street was trying to hit him.

The first few days on the street were a revelation to him. He began to think all the bad-mouth he had heard about motor cops from his buddies in patrol was misdirected, and motor cops were probably the most misunderstood officers on the job. Most of the cops who complained about motor cops were guys who probably wanted to be one but couldn't, he reasoned.

Riding took a lot of coordination and practice. To complicate matters, the new motor cops were assigned "new" motorcycles after the motor school. New, that is, compared to what they had ridden in the school. These "new" bikes had foot shifts rather than the old hand shifters on which they had trained. The new foot shifters made it easier to brake and maneuver the bikes on the street, but split-second timing was still required every minute of every hour of every day on duty. It made Pete feel good just to be a big city motor cop.

Then he found out about people. People hate traffic cops. He discovered when traffic cops stopped drivers for a violation, no matter how guilty they might be, most drivers will never admit it.

"How come you're picking on me, officer? Why aren't you out there catching the *real* criminals?" were frequent complaints that Pete and his fellow traffic enforcement pals heard from the irate drivers on the wrong end of the officer's pen.

"Don't let it get to you, kid," advised long-time motor cop John Sudinski, who had been assigned to break Pete in on the streets of Hollywood. Pete and his teacher dropped their leather jackets over the backs of chairs in the Hollywood police station, where they were taking a break to plan their evening strategy.

"I don't see how you put up with it," whined Pete. "It's starting to get to me."

"Don't let it bug you, kid," said the veteran motor cop as he sat down with his steaming cup of what they called machine coffee. "What people don't understand is that the biggest problem in all of law enforcement is *traffic*. It's not what most people think of as 'real crime.' Yet more people get killed in traffic accidents than all the murders and robberies combined!"

At first, Pete thought he was kidding, but Sudinski's face was stone serious.

"These whipdicks on the street don't care if there are nearly fifty thousand people killed in this country every year in traffic accidents, most of which could have been prevented. They look at accidents as some kind of natural way to thin out the population or something. It's like a natural thing to them."

"I never thought of it that way before," said the novice traffic cop.

"So, when Mr. J. Willie Roundass goes out and runs stoplights and drives ten or fifteen miles over the speed limit, he thinks it can never happen to him, until he crashes his car into some other dumb shit and kills his silly self!" John couldn't stop now. He was on a roll. "You see, kid, to the average person, driving a car is like breathing. They don't think about it. It just happens every day. They don't take it seriously. That's why they try to blame all the traffic problems on someone or something else." John was really building up steam now, and little beads of sweat broke out on his forehead.

"You ever notice on the radio in the morning how they announce the accidents on the freeway?" Pete looked at John inquisitively and shook his head. "The newsmen say, 'A car went off the road' or 'Two vehicles collided,' right?" Pete nodded.

"Yeah. So?"

"The cars did it, not the people!" yelled Sudinski, waving his arms in the air. "They don't say what really happened!" Pete was spellbound by Sudinski's oration.

"How would this sound on radio station T-R-U-T-H in the morning?" Sudinski held his nose and imitated a news broadcaster. "The Harbor Freeway is totally blocked this morning, ladies and gentlemen, because some dipshit, driving with his head up his ass, ran into the car in front of him. Traffic on the Hollywood Freeway is slowing because Billy Joe Gumbutt, who was picking his nose instead of looking where he was going, had to lock up his brakes when traffic ahead stopped, and he swerved off the fucking road into the ivy!'" Two motor cops came into the coffee room.

"Hubba Hubba," said one officer, which Pete presumed was some sort of a greeting.

"Uh-oh, look out! Sudinski's on his soapbox," wailed Hubba Hubba Burke, one of the few men with enough time on the job to pull a Hollywood beat.

"Fuck you, Burke! You wouldn't know what a good ticket was if you saw one! The only tickets you write are fruits for jaywalking across Hollywood Boulevard." It was obvious there was no love lost between the two men. Sudinski thought Burke was an asshole, and Burke thought Sudinski was a loudmouth. Pete figured they were probably both right, but he liked both of them because they were from the old school of motor cops: totally salty.

They were a vanishing breed on LAPD. Most of them were veterans, and some were actually war heroes. Pete had heard of one motor cop whose bomber had been shot down over Germany. He was captured, and when the Germans found out he came from a German-American family, they broke his arms and legs.

Yeah, the old motor cops were a breed unto themselves. Later, Pete pondered what Sudinski had said and the way people think of traffic problems. It made him understand how important his job really was. He was not just a cop writing tickets for "minor" violations, but he was doing something to help people. They just didn't know it.

New motor cops had to spend at least one month working with a more experienced officer before they could be assigned their own beat. Beats were handed out according to seniority, so the fledgling cops got the ones the older guys didn't want. Most cops thought the seniority system was good because the longer you spent on the job, the more rewarding it was. That made sense to Pete, but it also meant that officers with little seniority had to work night watch and all the undesirable beats for a few years. Pete didn't care about that either because right now he was having too much fun just being there.

"Most people think traffic cops hide behind billboards and wait for someone to speed by," said Sudinski. He and Pete had just parked their motorcycles on the southwest corner of Hollywood and Vine, facing north toward the intersection. Hollywood and Vine! thought Pete. The kids in Des Moines should see me now!

"This is what we call 'sitting in,'" taught John. "The department has rules about how traffic cops do their job. One is, when you work traffic, you must be in plain sight at all times." Pete had heard all this before in patrol, but he listened intently to his teacher.

"You can sit in now and then and, as long as you don't abuse it, it's a good way to work traffic. You sit still, and let the violation come to you," confided John. "Like that one," said Sudinski, as he kicked the start pedal roared away toward the intersection. Pete hadn't seen anything, but he fired up and went after his partner.

Pete had a hard time catching his partner, who was by now weaving in and out of westbound traffic on Hollywood Boulevard. His mind tried to keep up with the speed of his motorcycle as he sped down Hollywood Boulevard, and he talked to himself as he rode.

"Look out for that car! Brake. Shift! Oops! Try to keep up, but don't kill yourself."

When Pete caught up with John, he had just pulled the car over at Highland Avenue. Pete parked his motor in back of John's and turned on his rear flashing lights to ward off other cars. By this time, John already had the driver's license and was starting to write the citation.

"What kept you, kid?" he asked, with a twinkle in his eye. Pete watched in amazement as Sudinski wrote out the ticket and was walking up to the car to get a signature. He was so fast Pete could hardly believe it. Patrol officers sometimes take between five and ten minutes to complete a citation. John was fast.

"What did he do? I didn't even see it," Pete asked as the violator drove away.

"Hell, the guy blew the light at Vine by twenty feet."

Pete thought he'd better start paying more attention. He found out that motor cops can carry on a conversation and at the same time look for violations. Soon Pete started to pick up on it himself. Then he started seeing violations in his sleep.

Pete worked Hollywood Boulevard for a week. It was fun and made him think about his life as a kid in Iowa. How different things were now. Exciting things were happening to him. It was like a dream come true.

Yesterday he had sat next to Slapsy Maxie Rosenbloom and had coffee. Rosenbloom was a former boxing champ in the twenties and thirties and had owned a famous restaurant in New York in the forties. He had greeted Pete warmly, and they talked while they had coffee. Pete enjoyed the privileges of being a policeman. You could talk to anyone, and they would listen. He loved his job.

Later that day, John Sudinski was writing a ticket on the boulevard while Pete stood by. A car stopped, and the driver waved. Pete went over to the car.

"There's an injured cat laying in the street a block or so back there. I think someone ran over it," said the driver. Pete thanked him and waved him on.

"I'll take care of it, partner," said Pete as he threw his leg over the saddle of his Harley and fired up. Pete's partner waved his hand in approval.

Riding west on Hollywood, he saw a police car stop on the south side of the street. Pete made a U and parked behind the black-and-white. A patrol officer was picking up the body of the cat.

"I got it," said the patrol cop as he placed the cat's corpse in his trunk. "People are more concerned about a fucking cat than they are about a human," grumbled the cop.

"Yeah, ain't it the truth?" agreed the young motor cop.

At roll call the next day, Pete filled out his daily field activities report (DFAR) for the night before. On the log, he entered the incident about the dead cat, since all police activities must be reported on the DFAR. He listed it as a "citizen's call," and for the "disposition" of the call, he wrote, "Picked up pussy on Hollywood Boulevard." He chuckled, as he turned in his log, thinking he was being slyly humorous.

The following day, old sergeant Patton, the head of the motor school training program Pete had just finished, asked him to stay after roll call. The old sergeant dropped Pete's log from the day before in front of him.

"Did you write this?" he asked.

"Yeah, Sarge, it was kind of a joke," said Pete with a halfhearted smile. The sergeant wasn't smiling.

"Don't you know this is a public record? Anyone might read this, all the way up to the supreme court!" The sergeant's voice increased in volume. Pete's heart started to beat faster. "You can't just write anything you want to on a daily log, Felix. I got my ass chewed because of this log! The lieutenant wanted to know why I let you through the motor school."

"Gee, I'm sorry, Sarge. It was only a joke. It won't happen again."

"It better not, kid, or you'll find your ass back in patrol!"

Pete's ears were burning as he walked slowly out to his motor where his new training officer was waiting for him. Norm Cooperman was nearly as old as the sergeant. When Pete told him what had happened, Norm doubled over with laughter.

"I love it," he said, wiping his eyes of tears. "That old fart and those assholes in the office got no sense of humor. Fuck 'em, kid. Don't worry. They ain't gonna kick you off motors over that. They're just puttin' pressure on you, so they can control you later." Norm was still laughing as he kicked the pedal that started his motor. Pete felt a little better at having impressed the old-timer, but he thought he'd better be cool for a while until the heat was off him.

CHAPTER FIVE

FALL, 1961

Pete knew that Bel Air was a ritzy part of Los Angeles nestled in the hills above the campus of UCLA, north of Sunset Boulevard. He'd never been there and knew only that a lot of movie stars lived there. It was fall of 1961, and he'd been on the motor squad for nearly six months. So far, he had kept the motorcycle on the rubber and had survived Los Angeles's traffic.

Suddenly, hell broke loose in beautiful Bel Air: Fire! Bushfires engulfed the hills. The winter rains and the summer sun had made the hills around Los Angeles green for several months; then the grass and undergrowth faded, dried out, and became a tinderbox for fire. It seemed like fires in the fall were as much a part of the life cycle in southern California as the floods and tornadoes were to the Midwest of Pete's birth. Pete considered weather as one of the prices you pay to live anywhere, but fire was different.

The motor squad was the first to be called up. After all, it was their job. They were the "emergency response" division. Pete went to the roll call briefing with excited interest. It was his first emergency call-up.

The men sat around the room, chatting in low tones. There were more men in the room than he had ever seen before on a shift. He estimated it was the combined midwatch and night watch. The lieutenant came in, and the room became quiet.

"The fires are spreading out over the hills, and there have already been homes lost. It doesn't look good. Our job tonight will be to assist the fire departments and protect property of those who've had to abandon their homes." Sounded pretty simple.

The briefing ended, and the men were put on a twelve-hour shift. Their instructions were to report to the command post at a school near the UCLA campus. The men would ride there in a group.

As the BCMCs, about forty in number, hit the Hollywood Freeway, all traffic came to a stop. The officers rode two abreast, and the lines stretched out for about a half-mile on the freeway. Pete felt the vibrations of the motorcycle engines as they rumbled toward the huge cloud of smoke that filled the sky ahead of them. It looked like the world was on fire.

A chill went up Pete's spine as he looked in his rearview mirrors and saw the group of motor cops riding with him. They were all straight in the saddle, and Pete couldn't help thinking of cavalrymen as they headed out to help the people of Bel Air—and Pete was one of them. He was excited and proud. The cops all turned on their red front lights and rear amber flashers, making the procession even more impressive.

When they arrived at the command post, the cops were assembled in a staging area. As the calls for assistance came in, officers were assigned to various jobs around the fire. Smoke was heavy in the air, and fire equipment was everywhere. Darkness was starting to fall, and the sky was glowing with red as the hills and homes burned.

"Felix, I want you to go with these people into the evacuated area and help them retrieve some personal property," ordered the lieutenant. Pete immediately recognized one of the people as the actor Keenan Wynn. He was accompanied by a man and a woman who he did not recognize. Pete had heard that Mr. Wynn was an avid motorcycle rider and had seen pictures of him riding in races. He shook hands with Wynn and introduced himself.

"I'm Pete Felix. What are we going to do up there?" he asked the movie actor with the worried face. Pete noticed the actor had a hearing aid in one ear.

"I've got to get some papers out of my house before it burns. They're very important to me." Wynn gave Pete the directions to his house in the hills.

"Okay, follow me. We stop before we run over any fire hoses," Pete cautioned. "I'll make sure it's okay with the firemen. If we just run over them, it may cause a hose to rupture and leave a fireman without water." The small group nodded in agreement. They started off into the smoky streets of Bel Air.

The night was cool and crisp as Pete threaded his way through the fire apparatus toward their destination. Smoke filled the air, and water filled the streets. At one point, there was a maze of fire hoses to cross. After clearing it with the fire captain in charge, they started to go over the hoses. The tires of Pete's motorcycle were wet and slipped off a large diameter hose. The motorcycle went down, falling on its side. Pete was only traveling about two miles per hour, so he just stepped off and let the bike fall. The two men following Pete quickly got out of the car and helped him put the motor back up on its wheels. No damage done.

"You all right?" asked the movie star.

"I'm fine. Ready to go again?" They started off again up the hill into the fire area. The smoke got thicker, and sparks began to fill the air. Pete hoped they wouldn't burn holes in his $22 motor breeches. His leather jacket would protect his shirt, he thought. The small procession made its way through the winding streets of the hilly residential area. The fire had not yet reached this area but was very close. Pete could feel the heat increasing outside his uniform.

The whole scene looked surreal. The sky was red with flames and smoke. Sirens wailed in the distance as the wind whipped sparks around his motorcycle. Scenes from an old movie he had seen years ago filled his mind. A volcanic eruption had spelled doom for *The Last Days of Pompeii*.

The sound of the horn from the car behind him brought Pete back to reality. They had reached their destination. They parked outside and went into the house. The home was very expensive and nicely decorated. What a waste if it burned, he thought. Wynn seemed like the nice type, and Pete hated to see him lose his property; but time was running out.

"I don't want to rush, you folks, but my ass is NOT fireproof," reminded Pete. The group finished their mission and headed back down the hill. The flames were licking the houses behind the Wynn home as they left. Pete felt sorry for the people who were losing everything they owned and wondered why anyone would build a home in these fire hazard areas. People don't think that far ahead, he guessed. Or maybe they think it can never happen to them. Pete filed the information away in his memory for future use in buying a home.

The trip back down the hill was uneventful, and when the group returned to the command post, Mr. Wynn thanked Pete warmly for his help. Pete knew it was not the time to take advantage of the poor man with trivial conversation about motorcycles, so Pete shook hands and said good-bye.

The fires seemed to be coming under control as the cold night passed. Pete and about twenty other officers were assigned to a staging area away from the fires to wait in reserve, in case they were needed. They spent the rest of the night sitting in a school bus, waiting for an assignment that didn't come. During the long cold night, the men amused themselves by telling dirty stories. It was one of those "can you top this" contests among the cops, and by the end of the night, Pete's sides ached from laughing so hard at the funny stories that were told. The first liar didn't have a chance in that bus. Pete got off a couple of good stories himself, and as the dawn came up, the cops were ready to get the hell out of there.

The fires were dying out and would soon be under control. Over five hundred homes were lost in one of the worst fires in the history of the whole country, but Pete was glad he had been there and had decided that firemen must be supermen. They had worked their asses off. Pete wouldn't have traded places with any of them, though. They can have that job! he thought.

CHAPTER SIX

LOS ANGELES, HIGHLAND PARK DIVISION, 1962

There had not been much happening in Pete's social life since he got on motors. He'd been dating two or three women, but nothing had come of any of them. There were plenty of women around, but Pete was not finding the ones who were his type, whatever that was.

The BCMCs pulled into the parking lot of the bowling alley on Eagle Rock Boulevard and kicked down their side stands.

"Why are we eating at this roach stand?" asked Ron in his cynical voice. "Let's boogie on down to the main jail and have a good meal."

"Because I've got something I want to do here."

"You mean someone. Okay, what's her name?"

"I want to say hello to Morrie."

Morrie, the owner (Pete couldn't remember his last name), was good to the cops on the beat, and they all seemed to like him. He was a Jewish man from the east who talked with a strong New York City accent and smoked big cigars. Morrie was from the old school of businessmen who took care of the cops and expected them to take care of him and his business. Generally, the cops did take care of Morrie, not so much because he fed them, but because they also liked Morrie. He had a great sense of humor and shared many of the same feelings about criminals. Morrie had lived in New York where the cops were not as conscientious as they were here in Los Angeles.

"Back in New York," Morrie had said, "you pay the cops for nothin', and they don't do shit. Here, you don't pay off the cops; just feed 'em, and they bust their ass for you."

Pete had found that to be true. He had discovered the cops differ widely from one city to the other like night from day. Some cities' cops are better than the others. Overall, the LAPD was one of the cleanest, if not the cleanest, police departments in the country.

Cops spend a lot of time in restaurants. The bowling alley wasn't a fancy place by any means, but the food was good and half-price to cops on the beat. But the food was not the main attraction for him.

Pete had a soft spot in his heart for waitresses. He thought their job and his were somewhat similar. Both had to deal with people every day. It seemed to Pete that neither profession was treated with much respect by the public. Waitresses seemed to feel the same about cops.

Evelyn Barone was a dark-haired Italian girl who worked at the bowling alley restaurant. Evie was the main attraction. He liked her style. She was not real pretty, by Hollywood standards, but nice. Her figure leaned a little toward the plump side, but Pete thought it looked good on her. She always had nice things to say when Pete was around, but he'd also seen her operate when customers acted rudely to her. She didn't mess around when it came to putting the jerks in their place. She was able to handle herself, and Pete liked that.

He had heard the story of how one evening some members of a visiting college football team came into the bowling alley for food and a beer. As Evie was bending over their table, cleaning up, the center for the team, a hulking dude of about 270 pounds, bent over and bit her on the ass. Evie grabbed a beer bottle and smacked the guy over the head and laid him out cold.

"You better get this asshole out of here before I kill him," she told the other shocked members of the team. They left, dragging the half-conscious team member with them. My kind of woman, Pete thought. His partner thought otherwise.

"This chick is trouble, man. I can feel it comin'." The two cops had stopped at Highland Park Station to use the landline (cop talk for phone). "What do you see in a woman that knocks guys out like Rocky Marciano?"

Pete felt stupid defending his newfound feminine interest. "I like a woman who can take care of herself. It's something unique in today's world."

"A chick named Rocky who knocks guys out? Not my idea of a sweetheart, unless you're gonna be her boxing manager." Ron wouldn't let up. "I can see the headlines now . . . ITALIAN MARE KO'S STALLIONS."

Pete could see it was a losing battle. "Look, skullhead," chided Pete, referring to Ron's balding pate, "if you don't knock it off about Evie, I'll put the toe of my boot so far up your ass your breath will smell like shoe polish!"

"Okay, okay, I just hate to see a big city motor cop step on his dick."

"Don't be so worried about my dick, partner." Pete headed for the door. When he reached it, he turned to Ron. He knew Ron was only trying to keep his partner out of trouble. Pete appreciated that.

"Anyway, I've stepped on my dick so many times already it's got Neolite stamped on it." Ron smiled and shook his head. The two cops headed back to the beat.

Pete had coffee with Evie a couple of times after that and found out she had a daughter about twelve years old. He surmised the daughter was illegitimate. Not that Pete cared, but he began to wonder where this relationship was going. As he learned more about Evie, he wondered how much more he *didn't* know about her.

The 1962 World's Fair was being held in Seattle, and Pete was due for a vacation.

"Let's drive up to Seattle and take it in," he said. Evie readily accepted, and they were off in Evie's car.

Early on, Pete had noticed a small tattoo of the word "cap" on Evie's left breast near her collarbone, but had never mentioned it.

"What's the tattoo for?" Pete had asked as they drove along Highway 101, heading for Washington.

"It's my old boyfriend's nickname," she told him. "He's the father of my kid, Sherry." She started to tell him about her former life.

"I got into a bad crowd when I was younger," Evie revealed. As she talked, Pete was more aware of her age. He thought she must be about thirty or thirty-two, about two or three years older than he. As she talked about her past life, he wondered where he fit in. He knew he cared for her and she for him, but there were obviously a lot about Evie he didn't know.

"Anyway, we split up; and he went his way, and I went mine. Cap taught me how to ride a motorcycle, and it was fun being in a motorcycle gang for a while. Now I just work my ass off to support my daughter and live with my father," she had said.

Pete had been to her house and met her father. He was a grouchy old fart. The house was old and messy too. They lived in an old neighborhood in Highland Park that had seen much better days.

When they arrived in Seattle, the town was jumping and filled with people in a festive mood. All the hotels in town were full for months before the fair, but they had found a private residence that wanted to rent the upstairs rooms. The home was nice and had a view of Green Lake from the bedroom window.

"This is the room," said the middle-aged woman, as she opened the door.

The room was small but cozy, and the view made up for any cramped feelings Pete had. Seattle was a beautiful town, and the lake down the street was equally attractive and added to the romance of the moment.

"You'll have the whole upstairs to yourselves. And your own bathroom. My husband is in LA on business and won't be back for another week. It'll be nice to have company, especially a policeman."

"Thank you, Mrs. Steel. We're looking forward to a nice visit too." Pete could hardly wait until the woman went downstairs. As nice as she was, Pete had other plans. As soon as the footsteps reached the bottom of the stairs, Pete took Evie in his arms and kissed her. He held her close as his tongue found hers in a long wet kiss. He felt his pulse quicken as her hand slid down over his hip and into his crotch. Her hand then pulled his shirt out of his pants and slid onto his stomach. As her fingernails caressed his abdomen, his muscles tightened involuntarily, causing him to make a noise as if he's been hit in the stomach.

"Okay, that's it. Into the shower with you," he said.

"Come join me?" Pete suddenly realized he had never showered with a woman before. Big city motor cop! he mocked himself in thought. It made him chuckle as he shed his clothes. As they undressed, they watched each other. She was not a tall woman. Her hips were well-rounded, and her olive-tinted skin was smooth and silky to touch. Pete ran his hands down over her shoulders and cupped her breasts. They were not huge but big enough. Bigger, in fact, than Pete had guessed they would be. Her large dark nipples were hard and pouting out, exciting Pete even more. They stepped into the large shower and took a long time washing each other and teasing. By the time they got into bed, Pete was ready to climb the walls.

Pete had made up his mind that he would take it slow and really try to impress Evie with his masculine lovemaking ability. Forget that. Once he was inside her, his mind went blank. When he regained his senses, they were lying beside each other, gasping for breath.

As they lay talking, Evie revealed it had been many years since she had a climax. Pete resolved to remedy her problem during their stay. After about fifteen minutes, he returned for round two. This time, he got control of himself and made his best effort to kill her with climax. For a while, based on her reaction, he thought he had.

Exhausted, Pete fell back on his pillow. He reached over and turned on the radio next to the bed. He found a classical music station and turned it down low. They lay there for a while, and then Pete drifted off to sleep, feeling the warmth of her body next to him. The next day, Pete was in love.

The rest of that week, they went out every night and hit the nightspots of Seattle. There were lots of good music and many celebrities in town. Pete enjoyed himself, and he and Evie had fun together. That was one thing they did have in common. They liked to have fun.

As they lay in bed each night talking together, Pete thought about the job and his future and the unanswered questions about Evie. Was she for him? What was she really like? He didn't know, really. He reached over and turned on the radio beside the bed and tuned in the classical music station. The music was soft, and Evie snuggled up next to him. Pete didn't want to think right now anyway. He just wanted to feel being alive.

Back in Los Angeles and back into to the work mode again, Pete was working a Highland Park beat and, after end of watch, thought he'd wait for Evie near her house until she got off work at midnight. As he parked his motor at the curb, he noticed a man sitting in a car parked across the street about half a block away. It was nearly eleven thirty, and police instinct told him to investigate. He fired up and rode over and parked behind the car.

"Hi, what's up?" asked Pete as he walked up to the side of the car, his right hand resting on the butt of his pistol.

"Nothing, officer. Just waiting for a friend," replied the man. Pete saw the guy was about forty years old and well-dressed. He seemed out of place sitting here in his new Buick in this neighborhood.

"There are a lot of burglaries around here, you know. So we have to check things out," said Pete. "Let's see your ID, please." The guy produced a driver's license, and Pete made a mental note of the name.

"Eddie Solomon, huh? Still live at this address in Glendale?" asked Pete, keeping the man's every movement in his peripheral vision.

"Yeah. Anything wrong?" asked Eddie.

"No. Just checking." Pete had the uneasy feeling that Eddie and he were waiting for the same person. Pete decided to leave since it was well after end of watch, and the rules of the motor squad required officers to take the motorcycle home. It wasn't worth getting involved in anything now. He gave the man his ID back and drove home, wondering what this guy was to Evie.

"Who is Eddie Solomon?" Pete asked the next time he saw Evie. Her face got a funny look, and she was stuck for an answer for a minute.

"He's a guy I know from many years ago. He lives in Glendale. Why?" She wanted to know.

"Why was he waiting for you the other night?"

"He comes over to see me sometimes. There's nothing between us, though."

"Really? Why would he be waiting for you late at night, Evie?"

"Hey! I don't have to account to you for everything, do I?"

"No, I guess not," said Pete and left. As he rode away, his heart sank when he thought of how he had fallen for Evie, and now, he was finding out that she may not be what he thought she was. He resolved to find out.

The Highland Park Division police station was old and well-worn by the years. There was a rumor that the station was soon to be replaced by a new one. Pete went upstairs to the detective offices. He knew a couple of guys that worked there, one of whom had graduated from the academy with him.

"Hey, Pete! What's up? How's motors treating you?" asked Gilbert Fernandez as Pete clumped into the office.

"Best job on the department," answered Pete as they shook hands. Pete hadn't seen Gilbert since he'd transferred to work juvenile in Highland Park Division. Pete couldn't think of why anyone in their right mind would want to work juvenile. He couldn't stand the smart-ass little bastards. In the conservative atmosphere of postwar Iowa, where Pete had been brought up, kids were taught to respect the law and old people. California was a real challenge to that philosophy. It was all he could do not to grab a smart-ass teenager by the throat and squeeze until their eyes popped out. How the juvenile officers kept from doing it, he didn't have a clue. After Pete filled Gilbert in on the latest in his life, he changed the subject.

"You know, I've been seeing this woman that lives in Highland Park, and I'd like to see what her background is and if you guys have anything on her in the files," asked Pete, feeling like a jerk asking for the information, but he had to know. Gilbert took Pete to the Field Interrogation files.

"Let's see what we have here," mumbled Gilbert as he fingered through the hundreds of FI cards that had been filled out by the patrol officers. FI cards were filled out when officers in the field interviewed suspects but did not arrest them. The card contains information on where and when the suspect was interviewed and under what circumstances. The cards were then filed by date and last name and kept for a specified period of time. Officers may use the files to determine whether a person was interviewed on a certain day at a certain place to see if a suspect was in town or near the scene of a crime. As Gilbert searched the file, an older officer entered the room.

"Can I help you, guys?" asked the Highland Park detective.

"Yeah, Herb. Ever hear of a chick named Evelyn Barone?" asked Gilbert.

"Evie? Sure. She's been around Highland Park since she was a kid," said Herb. "I've busted her several times." Pete's heart stopped.

"For what?" He didn't really want to hear the answer but knew he must.

"Selling dope to kids at the bowling alley. She was also busted for child endangering for allowing her twelve-year-old daughter to smoke marijuana." Pete must have looked strange.

"You okay, kid?" asked the detective.

"Yeah, sure," said Pete, getting his cool again. He couldn't believe what he had heard, yet why would the detective lie? The FI files also turned up some interesting interviews on Evie and her daughter, Sherry.

As Pete left the station, he felt so weak he could hardly kick start his motor. Knowing how the department felt about cops being involved with criminals, things did not look good for Pete. He decided to stop seeing Evie.

CHAPTER SEVEN

CRAZY STREETS, 1963

"Okay, you clowns, fall out in the parking lot for inspection," said Lieutenant Barney Hertzer (a.k.a. the Animal). The Animal was not one of the men's favorite supervisors, but he had been around forever. Friday was inspection day for the BCMCs, and the Animal had a fetish for inspections. Boots and guns were his big things. Boots had to fit right and be just the right height on the leg bone. The "Hertzer bone," the men called it. They were none of those cheap low-cut imitations, and they must be spit shined perfectly. Pistols had to pass a rigid cleanliness requirement.

"Well, I wonder if it will be guns or boots today," griped Norm Cooperman, as the men filed slowly toward the parking area. "The man is crazy," Cooperman continued. "Ever watch him inspect the motorcycles? All he looks at is the rear fender. If that's clean, you've got it made. I just hope he doesn't want to look at guns today."

"What's the big deal about that?" asked Ron, as they trudged along the hallway from the roll call room.

"He's also got a quirk about gun inspections. Some of the guys like to rattle his cage by pulling the trigger and clicking the hammer of their pistols during inspection."

"So what?" Pete interjected. "After the cylinder is open and the bullets are out, there's no danger."

"It's a thing with the Animal, and all the guys know it; so when there's a gun inspection, there's always one joker that just can't resist pulling the trigger, just to get the Animal pissed off."

As the men lined up for inspection, they waited for the command. What will it be today? Gun inspection? Handcuffs? Boots?

"Prepare for gun inspection!" yelled Honey Hornet. The Animal stood at the head of the troops, waiting.

"Inspection... Arms!" All the men removed their pistols from the holsters, opened the cylinders, and dumped the bullets into their left hands. Then the officers held their pistols at port arms in their right hands.

The Animal started down the rows, checking each man's pistol. He looked in the barrel and then the cylinder, then handed the weapon briskly back to the owner. As he neared the end of the first rank—*click*—the hammer of a pistol fell.

"Who did that!" yelled The Animal. "Who did that?" he yelled again. The men were stone silent.

"Okay, if that's the way you want it, we'll all come back here after end of watch for another gun inspection," he ordered and dismissed the men. They walked away grumbling among themselves.

"Damn it," groaned Cooperman, "I knew we'd never make it through the inspection. There's always one asshole that can't resist pulling the damn trigger. I don't know about you, guys, but I don't like to come back here just because some idiot cop pisses off an officious watch commander. I got better things to do than be treated like a fucking kid." He slid his ticket book into the saddlebag and turned to Pete.

"I've got an idea," he said to Pete, who was to be his partner for the night. "Let's go have coffee and talk this over."

Later that night, the phone in the watch commander's office rang. The Animal answered, "Traffic Enforcement Division, Lieutenant Hertzer." The clear sound came over the phone from the other end—*click...click...click*—the sound of a pistol's hammer falling. The Animal's face reddened, and his hands started to shake. He knew the call couldn't be traced. On the other end of the line, Norm Cooperman and Pete Felix were laughing so hard they could hardly stand up. It made the trip into the station for the midnight gun inspection almost worthwhile.

The following Friday, one of the "loyal" sergeants tried to impress the BCMCs by having his own gun inspection. During the inspection, someone threw a firecracker behind him. It went off just as he looked into the barrel of an officer's pistol. He jumped about three feet into the air. The whole night watch nearly died laughing. That was the end of gun inspections for a while.

To Pete, all the clowning around at roll call was a lot of fun. He thought it broke the tension among the men and made going out onto the streets a little easier to take.

Pete decided to take the freeway out to his beat in south Los Angeles. As he entered the freeway, he saw a car traveling at a high rate of speed. Pete positioned his motorcycle to the right and slightly to the rear of the speeding vehicle to get "a clock" on it from the driver's blind spot. Then he saw a second car following the first car he was clocking. Pete's speedometer was indicating seventy-three miles per hour in a fifty-five-mile zone.

Not bad, he thought. He decided to stop both cars and cite the lead car for speeding and the car in the rear for following too closely at a distance of about twenty-five feet. Definitely too close at that speed, he thought, and two birds are better than one anyway.

He pulled alongside the two vehicles and motioned them both over to the right shoulder. Pete waited until both drivers got out and started back to his location. He noticed the driver of the lead car was a white man. The driver of the second car was black.

"Gentlemen, may I see your driver's licenses, please," Pete asked. As they started getting out their IDs, Pete explained the situation to both drivers.

"Sir, I clocked you at seventy-three in a fifty-five-mile zone. And you, sir"—he nodded at the black man—"were going the same speed as he was, and you were following him too closely." The black man looked at Pete and scratched his head.

"How could I be goin' the same speed as him if he ahead of me?" he asked. Pete stopped writing and looked at the man to see if he was serious. He was. Pete decided to explain it, so the man could not possibly misunderstand.

"You were right behind that guy, right?"

"Right."

"And he wasn't pulling away from you, was he?"

"Nope."

"And you weren't gaining on him, were you?"

"Nope."

"Then you had to be going the same speed, didn't you?" Pete knew he was triumphant.

"How could I be goin' the same speed as him? He ahead of me!" Pete couldn't believe his ears. He thought he'd try again.

"Look, man, if you're right behind him and keeping up with him, you're going the same speed!"

"Look'a here, officer, if we goin' somewhere, he git there first, doan he? Then he be goin' faster than me!" Pete could see that this was going nowhere, so he decided to take another approach.

"Well, you were too close to him, weren't you?" Pete was grasping at straws now.

"I guess so. Gimme the ticket." Pete did.

The streets were crowded with protesters lately. The BCMCs of LAPD tried to deal with it all. Pete thought a lot about what they were protesting: the war in Vietnam, civil rights, police brutality, and just about any other cause that interested the vocal minority these days. Pete agreed with their right to express their feelings, but somehow, he thought it was a part of a plan to destroy the country from within.

Charges of police brutality had always been around. Police can't function unless they take away rights from people accused of crime. That's what cops do. They forcibly incarcerate persons suspected of committing crimes and take away their right to walk the streets freely. Pete believed the public at large were very naive about the system of justice in this country. Nobody wants to go to jail and most don't go quietly, so enforcing the law requires force. The amount of force is dependent on the amount of resistance of the one being arrested.

At a party one night, Pete's date let it be known that he was a policeman. Pete had found out very quickly that the fewer people who know you are a cop, the better. Especially at parties. It never failed to attract someone who either wanted to bad-mouth cops or complain about the bum ticket they got.

This night, he became involved in a discussion with a group of people regarding the use of force by police. The leader of the discussion seemed to fit a stereotype Pete had come to visualize in his mind. In his limited experience as a cop, he had run into a number of these types, and he hated them. This guy fit the stereotype like a glove. Wearing a tweed jacket with leather elbow patches, loafer-type shoes, and khaki pants, he puffed on his pipe and stroked his beard as he spoke.

Probably drives a Volvo or a Saab, he thought as he studied the loud mouth from the edge of the small group who listened intently. Probably a college professor or social worker or school teacher, he mumbled to himself. Pete hated the school-teacher types most of all. Why they seemed to have an abiding hatred for policemen, he didn't know. Maybe it went back to the reason they picked the profession in the first place. They really resented authority. Some of these people should come out in the street and experience the realities of life instead of spending their time in classrooms matching wits with people half their age. Even a hawk is an eagle among crows.

"I see no need for the use of brutality by police in any circumstance," said the Teacher. "Police should be trained to do their job without resorting to such barbaric tactics. After all, this is 1963, not the Old West." The Teacher sucked on his pipe and tried to look very intellectual as he stared right at Pete. Pete looked the man over and decided that the Teacher was about to put on his act for the benefit of the rest of the people around him, using him as the goat. Much as he disliked arguing with these people, he couldn't resist defending the street cop's position whenever it was attacked. Pete had been there. He jumped in before the Teacher could make his next move.

"Tell you what, let's perform an experiment," said Pete. "You be the cop, and I'll be the human." The crowd chuckled. "Well, what about it?" Pete pushed the Teacher verbally.

"Why not?" agreed the Teacher. "I like role play." He nodded. Pete set the scenario.

"Okay, you're a cop walking your beat, and you see me popping the hubcaps off a parked car, a misdemeanor theft. As you approach me, I see you coming and throw the hubcaps into the bushes. There is no one else around." The Teacher nodded his head and sucked on his pipe. The bystanders were now listening intently. Pete continued.

"You are sworn to uphold the law, right?" asked Pete.

"That is correct," answered the Teacher.

"You are well-trained, and your job is to arrest me for the theft you just saw me commit. How would you do it?"

"I would come up and tell you I just saw you stealing hubcaps and that you are under arrest."

"And then I say, 'No, I didn't. I was just looking at the wheels on that car.' Now what do you do?" asked Pete. "You have accused me of the crime, and I have denied it. Now what do you do?"

"I would inform you of your rights and tell you that you were under arrest," the Teacher proclaimed.

"And then I say, 'But I didn't do anything, so you can't arrest me.' Remember, this is just you and me out there," reminded Pete. The Teacher was beginning to see where Pete's scenario was taking him and started to stutter a little.

"Well, I . . . I would tell the man again that I saw him stealing and that I must arrest him," repeated the now-nervous Teacher.

"Okay," said Pete, "but I deny the allegation and say I didn't take any hubcaps, and you can't prove anything because it's my word against yours. Then I say, 'Well, I gotta go now, so I'm leaving.' Now what do you do?"

"I tell him not to leave because he's under arrest."

"And I tell you that I'm not and that I'm leaving right now," said Pete in a loud voice. Other people were now joining the group around Pete and the Teacher. The man in the tweed jacket was now starting to sweat a little on his nose.

"I start to walk away," said Pete. "Now what do you do? Are going to let me walk away after you've told me I'm under arrest? Are you going to violate your oath to uphold the law?" Pete pressed in for the kill.

"I would grab hold of your arm and try to keep you from leaving while I explain to you that you can't leave," stated the Teacher, as he reached out and took Pete's arm. Pete quickly pulled his arm away and yelled.

"Don't put your hands on me, pig! I'm not doing anything, and I'm not going anywhere!" The people that had just come over to see what was happening were shocked and waited to see what would happen next.

"Well," Pete pushed, "what are you going to do now? I'm leaving!" He started to walk away, turning his back on the man. The Teacher was thinking fast but hadn't come up with the only answer possible in this circumstance.

The teacher grabbed Pete's arm and hung on tight. Pete tried to pull away, and they struggled in the center of the room. Then the Teacher stopped and backed off.

"This is ridiculous," he said. The crowd was quiet. Pete jumped in and made his point.

"You see, at some point, force has to be used. You are a cop, and you can't just let suspects walk away from a crime! You just arrested him! Are you going to let him go because he says he didn't do it? It's not your job to decide that. That's the court's job. But how will he get to court if you let him go because you will not use force on him? Remember, you saw him stealing the hubcaps. You know he's guilty. You have the power, given to you by the people you protect, to use force, if it's necessary, to bring this guy in. Was it necessary? You used it when you put your hand on me to stop me from leaving the scene. If I don't respond to that amount of force, you may have to use more, up to and including physical violence, to take me in. You have no other choice if you want to do the job the people have entrusted you with!"

The crowd was mesmerized by now. Pete turned to them. "And what about you who just walked over to see what was happening? Did you know what was actually happening? Did you see the suspect commit the crime? Did you hear the officer put the suspect under arrest? No! All you heard and saw was a cop trying to grab hold of a poor guy who is saying he didn't do anything, right! Police brutality in the making," said Pete. Then the group was silent.

"Well, I guess I never looked at it that way before," admitted the Teacher once again, puffing on his pipe.

"Maybe there *is* hope for you." Pete laughed. "Come on, I'll buy you a drink." Pete put his arm around the Teacher, and they walked over to the bar. As they walked, Pete thought maybe he was starting to sound just like John Sudinski on his fucking soapbox.

CHAPTER EIGHT

CRAZY PEOPLE, 1964

Pete didn't mind dealing with people most of the time; but people were, as John Sudinski had said in his soapbox talk, a pain in the ass. They did dumb things and got into really dumb situations and asked really dumb questions. Sometimes the cops got back at them by giving dumb answers. Pete was standing behind a car, writing a ticket, when a car pulled up; and the driver rolled down the window.

"Hey, officer!" he yelled, interrupting Pete's line of thought. "How do I get to Disneyland from here?" Annoyed, Pete yelled back.

"You can't get there from here."

"Well, how do I get there then?" asked the stunned citizen.

"You'll have to go back where you started from." The man looked at Pete and then drove off with a quizzical look on his face.

Pete and Ron had a black man stopped for a citation later that night, and Pete was writing it out. When he finished, Pete handed the citation book to the man to sign.

"I ain't signin' this! I don't agree with it," said the young man in his late twenties. He looked intelligent and was well-dressed.

"Well, sir," said Pete, going into the routine that cops do when someone refused to sign a citation, "you see on the line above where you sign, it says 'Without admitting guilt'? That means you don't have to agree with anything I say on the ticket, and when you sign it, you're not admitting anything. You are signing a promise that you will appear and take care of the ticket. You can plead not guilty and have a trial if you want to, but you have to sign the ticket; or I must arrest you and impound your car and take you to jail." Pete was taking extra time with the man, mostly because he didn't want to have to book the dude and tow his car over a ticket. Standard procedure required a sergeant to be called to the scene to advise the arrestee and approve the booking. He just didn't feel like going to all that trouble.

"I ain't signin' nothing," said the dude.

"What's the problem? I just told you that you're not admitting guilt when you sign."

"That's a lie!" said the man.

"What do you mean 'It's a lie'?" Now Pete was getting mad. "How do you know it's a lie?"

"Because I'm studying law in college," came the answer. Pete and Ron looked at each other.

"Why are you studying law? Are you going to be a lawyer?" asked Pete.

"No, I'm gonna go into politics," answered the man.

"Well, you'll probably get elected because you don't know what the fuck you're talking about!" prophesied Pete. He picked up his microphone to call a tow truck and a sergeant.

Pete walked down the hall from the roll call room to the property room to renew his supply of ticket books. The door from the police parking area opened, and two officers in plain clothes walked in with a suspect in handcuffs. The female prisoner's dark brown hair was down over her face. As she threw her head back to flip the hair from her eyes, Pete saw it was Evie.

It had been several months since Pete had seen her. He had purposely avoided her since the incident at Highland Park records when he learned about her arrest record. Even so, his heart fell when he saw her in shackles.

"Evie!" he said, as he walked over to the officers. "What the hell is happening?" The arresting officers looked at Pete and stopped.

"You know this little lady?" asked one of the detectives.

"Yeah. She's a friend of mine." Pete heard his own voice as if from a distance.

"What's the charge?" he heard himself asking.

"Two Eleven."

Robbery! thought Pete. Impossible!

"Suspect from the 211 at the Pioneer Market a couple of nights ago," continued the officer.

"Can I talk to her for a minute?" asked Pete.

"Yeah. Go ahead." The two officers backed off about twenty feet, so they could have some privacy. How pitiful she looked, he thought. Her eye makeup was smeared from crying, and her hair was a mess.

"I didn't do it, Pete. Honest! All I did was loan my car to a friend. They said that someone used my car in a robbery! But I didn't have anything to do with it, I swear." Her voice was whining, and she was trying to lean on Pete. He pulled away unconsciously. He knew his fears had come true and that Evie and he were through. Even if she were innocent of the actual robbery, it was obvious that she had friends Pete would not have liked.

"I'm sorry, Evie. There's nothing I can do at this point. You'll have to go through the system. Let me talk to the officers." Pete left Evie and walked over to the older-looking officer.

"What's the story?" Pete asked. The officer had several items in a plastic evidence bag.

"Robbery. The 211 went down a couple of nights ago at the Pioneer Market. Seems like someone rips off that place at least once a week! Someone got the license number of the getaway car. We ran it and came up with this chick's address. We go to the house with a warrant and find money in a shoe box in the closet and a bunch of marijuana too."

Pete's thoughts raced back to the World's Fair and the time he spent with this woman. Those were good times, but now, he was seeing a different person: not a loving, attractive woman anymore, just a suspect in handcuffs, crying on her way to jail.

Pete didn't hear from Evie for a long time after that. One day he was in Highland Park Station, thinking about her. He went to the FI files and looked up her name. Nothing. Then he looked under her daughter's name, and a card came up.

"Sherry Barone . . . same . . . address," Pete read out loud. "Suspicion of drug use . . . . juvenile . . . parents . . . mother deceased." The shock of what he had just read sunk in to his guts.

"Deceased!" he said it again. "Oh God!"

Pete went to the phone and called the coroner's office. Using a confidential number officers use for information, the coroner's office told him that Evelyn Barone had died of a gunshot wound to the head. The shooter was listed as her common-law husband. His name was Eddie Solomon. He realized he had heard that name before. He was the guy he had encountered the night he was waiting for Evie on the street.

He also learned she had just given birth to a child about a month before. The suspect had been arrested and convicted and was serving time. He got four years.

"Four years?" he mumbled. "Four . . ." his voice trailed off.

The impact of his new information whirled around in his head. Memories flashed back of Evie and him laughing about stupid things. Standing on the shore, watching the ships move across the sound at Seattle. "Shit," said Pete and went over to Ron's and got drunk. He never told his story to anyone but to his partner.

CHAPTER NINE

THE DRUNKEN STREETS, 1964

Even though many cops rode motorcycles, most cops were not motorcycle-riding enthusiasts. Pete noticed that most motor cops disliked bikers, and he shared their dislike for the hard-core Hells Angels type of motorcyclist, but was sympathetic to those who rode motorcycles, in general. Pete's great love *was* riding motorcycles.

He had always remembered the motorcycle cop who lived in the apartment house where he lived as a kid. He loved to watch the cop climb on his bike and smell the exhaust fumes as the big motorcycle roared to life. Later, when Pete was about fourteen, a neighbor kid had taught him to ride a motorbike, and he was hooked on motorcycles for life.

Pete now owned a Triumph TR6 twin-cylinder bike that he rode off duty. One of his favorite ways to spend a weekend was to get together with some other guys and head out to the desert to ride off-road.

He loved the cold clear desert air on the dry lake in the early morning. The guys would arrive and unload their bikes. Blasting across the dry lake and accelerating in a wide arc that seemed to last forever were Pete's ideas of fun. He did all his own maintenance and had rebuilt his bike's engine to be more powerful in the dirt.

"Just a bunch of whipdick cops riding around in the sand," John Sudinski said. "It's not bad enough that we ride these damn things all day; you dumb bastards want to ride them on your days off too!" John was obviously not a motorcycle enthusiast.

Pete and Ron Byron were still teamed up. They got a beat in Highland Park, where Pete had always liked to work.

Ron liked to agitate people and always seemed to have some quick comeback for every occasion, which helped make the day more interesting for Pete.

Also a motorcycle enthusiast, Ron rode an English Matchless in the dirt, and he and Pete went out to the desert as often as they could.

One thing Pete and Ron learned about being a motor cop is every day is a new ball game. Pete looked forward to each day with a sense of anticipation and excitement.

The evening was balmy and warm as Pete and Ron left the PAB for their beat on North Figueroa Street. As they rode up the Pasadena Freeway to Avenue Twenty-six, Pete was feeling the motorcycle under him and listening to the roar of the Harley's exhaust. As he and his partner exited the tunnels that lead into the northern part of metropolitan Los Angeles, Pete felt a little chill go up his back.

What a great way to make a living, he thought. Getting paid for riding motorcycles and helping to "protect and serve" the people of the city. He knew it sounded corny and probably would never admit it publicly, but he really did feel a sense of loyalty to his job. Not to the city, but to the people in it and to himself. He knew the things he did sometimes helped people out. He knew that sometimes the tickets he wrote to grumbling citizens helped to slow the tide of traffic accidents. And, who knows, maybe saved a life or two here and there.

"Deuces"—the cops called them. It was short for the 23102 section of the California Vehicle Code for driving under the influence of alcohol or drugs. Cops had shortened it to "2310-deuce" or just deuce.

Pete liked to get drunk drivers off the street. He had never forgotten the incident when he had rolled on an ambulance call for a traffic accident. When he arrived, the accident investigation unit was already there, and the ambulance had just left. As Pete walked up to the officers at the scene, he sensed the tension immediately.

"What happened?" Pete had asked. The officers told him the story.

"That deuce asshole cuffed in the backseat was driving westbound," said the officer, "traveling about fifty when he hits the dips in the intersection back there," pointing to the east. "He bounces off the ground, loses control, hits the south curb, blows both front tires," related the officer, getting more excited as he talked. "He skids across the lawn and hits that porch over there. A Korean woman and her two little girls are sitting on the porch, minding their own business." Now the cop was very agitated. "He hits the woman and the two little girls and smashes them into the wall like a couple of ripe tomatoes. Now he sits in his car and tells us that his attorney will get him out of this, and it ain't nothin'." The officer was really upset, and Pete could understand why. The picture he painted was not a pretty one.

"I could very easily walk over there and blow that motherfucker's brains out and sleep like a baby tonight," said the officer's partner as he fondled the handle of his pistol. The more Pete thought about it, the more he agreed with him.

Now, riding south on Figueroa Street, they both saw the car at the same time. They slowed and took a good look at the car trying to parallel park, facing north. The old Chrysler hit the left rear fender of another car parked at the curb. As Ron and Pete made a U-turn and headed back toward the Chrysler, the driver made another attempt to park again. Again, the fender of the parked car was hit. As soon as the cops parked, Pete walked up to the car window.

"Having a little trouble parking your car, ma'am?" asked Pete.

"Oh!" The woman behind the wheel jumped and yelled. The startled middle-aged woman driver looked the worse for wear. Her hair was messy, and she had a strong odor of booze on her breath.

"No, officer, I'm not."

"Then why are you hitting that car's fender?" Pete reached in and turned off the ignition. "Please get out and go over to my partner on the sidewalk," ordered Pete. The woman looked skinny and shriveled up. Pete visualized her smoking twelve packs of cigarettes a day and drinking a gallon of vodka. She staggered over to the sidewalk, and Ron started to ask her the questions regarding her sobriety. Pete got behind the wheel of the car and sat down on the pillow the woman used to sit on so she could see over the steering wheel. He finished parking her car at the curb and got out into the cool evening air. His pants were wet. Pete reached back without thinking and grabbed a handful of soaking wet pants. He flared up.

"Don't tell me you—" Pete only got out the first few words, and the woman began to wail.

"I couldn't help it. You scared me when you pulled up!" she wailed.

Since an accident was involved, an accident investigation unit was called. When the AI officer got there, he found Pete walking around, mumbling and grumbling to himself, and his partner chuckling.

During the interview that followed, the young AI officer asked the woman if she had any physical defects. Before she could answer, Pete yelled the answered for her.

"Yeah! She pisses her pants!" The woman started to wail again. The AI officer shook his head and continued the report. Pete rode around with his butt hanging off the edge of the seat for a while until his pants dried out.

Pete and Ron were having a slow night tonight. Nothing shaking anywhere.

"All units in the vicinity, unit Thirteen T Twenty-Nine is in pursuit northbound on the Harbor Freeway, passing Vernon," the radio announced.

Pete and Ron were working Figueroa Street between Santa Barbara and Pico Boulevards. They had just stopped at a drive-in and gotten coffee.

"Hey, Pete, he's headed our way," said Ron with a big smile on his face. "Shall we enter the race?"

"Let's," said Pete, and they fired up and headed east on Thirty-seventh Street toward the Harbor Freeway.

As the two rolled east, they listened to the progress of the pursuit on the radio. All other broadcasts came to a halt when a pursuit starts. The "hotshot" operator took over until the chase was ended. The radio informed them that the vehicle being chased was a stolen car and was wanted for robbery. That bit of news made the two young cops even more anxious to get involved.

"All units, the suspect is out of the vehicle at Exposition and on foot, running northbound. The suspect is a male, Negro, tall, and thin," the operator advised all listeners. Pete was concentrating on the intersection ahead at Flower Street when Ron suddenly turned right and went south. At that same moment, Pete saw the suspect running across the street ahead of him. He yelled at his partner, but Ron didn't hear him. Pete wondered where the hell his partner was going. Now he was by himself.

The suspect was taking giant steps and looked like he was pacing himself for a long run, as he headed north on Flower. There were no other cops in sight anywhere. Pete made a left turn and rode up alongside the man running on the sidewalk.

"Stop, motherfucker!" yelled Pete. He could easily keep pace with the suspect but could not pull his pistol and keep both hands on the handlebars at the same time. The running man swerved left into a parking lot and began to stride toward a narrow gate in a block wall fence. Pete knew that if the dude made it through the gate, he would be home free and Pete could not follow. The thought made him mad.

"Stop or I'll shoot, asshole," Pete yelled, knowing he couldn't shoot without his gun in his hand. Frustrating, thought Pete. I want this guy, he said to himself. If the son of a bitch gets through that gate, I'll lose him! It's now or never, he thought as he accelerated toward the back of the running man. He aimed the front wheel of the Harley between the legs of the suspect. As soon as he made contact, Pete hit the foot brake and spun the motorcycle down on its left side. The running dude wasn't running anymore. He was going up in the air. Pete's mind had shifted into slow motion as he watched the man slowly upended and thrown about six feet into the air. Pete was off the motor and on top of the man before he could regain his composure. A voice yelled from close by.

"He's mine!" Pete looked up and saw a very tired black officer huffing and puffing toward them. Apparently, he had been one of the original pursuing officers. Pete rolled off the man, and the pursuing officer jumped on and beat the living shit out of the suspect. Pete watched with interest. He didn't blame the cop. Nothing is more frustrating than chasing someone who is getting away from you.

As the officers were putting the suspect into the police car, guess who the suspect was mad at? The cop who beat him up? Wrong. He was pissed at Pete. Oh, well, thought Pete, it was an interesting chase, and I probably couldn't do that again in a million years. He had flipped the guy in the air and didn't even scratch his motor.

CHAPTER TEN

FREEWAY COP, 1964

Pete, like most people, believed the freeways of Los Angeles were very dangerous for a motorcycle officer to work until he talked to some of the officers assigned to the freeways. They seemed to love it. Pete wondered why. He thought he had better find out soon because he was about to be assigned to work freeways on night watch starting the next month. He had mixed emotions about the assignment. Of course, he had no choice in the matter actually, since he had little seniority as a BCMC.

Pete knew one of the freeway cops. Al Predhom was a tall lanky man about thirty-five years old. He had been on freeway duty for about five years. Most of the time, it was by his own choice. Pete wanted to know why.

"Well, there are several reasons," Al explained one evening in the coffee room of Highland Park Station. "First, it's the safest place to be on the public streets." Pete looked puzzled.

"How could that be, Al?" he asked. "Everyone is going so fast and all."

"But," added Al, holding his index finger up to make his point, "all in the same direction. Most accidents occur at intersections, right?"

"Well, yeah, now that you mention it."

"There ain't none on the freeway, man," informed Al. Pete had never really thought of that. "Speed is only unsafe when you hit something," continued Al. "So don't hit anything. The main reason people crash on the freeway is because they don't pay attention to what's ahead. How can they? Most of them have their head up their ass anyway," Al stated philosophically. "Look ahead down the road and be aware of what's going on around you in your peripheral vision, and you can drive safer on the freeway than anywhere else!" It seemed logical to Pete when he put it that way. Al continued,

"When you work freeways, you know what you're going to do every day. Your main objective is to keep the traffic flowing. You take a sweep up and down your beat at least once an hour and stop for all stalled vehicles. You handle the accidents until AI gets there, you write a few tickets, and it's end of watch," he explained with a wave of his hand. "Then you go home, have a beer, and play with the kid's mama."

Pete could see why some motor cops would like the routine but wondered if he would after spending a couple of years on streets. The street is where it's happening. Life is never dull there. There's always something new. It was what Pete enjoyed about the job, almost as much as riding the motorcycles.

"Okay, you turkeys, roll call!" yelled night watch sergeant Gross. Gross was an old-timer and had the nick name of "the Bird Dog." The Bird Dog got his name because he was always out looking for you on the beat. If he didn't find you on one pass, he would call you on the radio. He spent a little too much time in the field, according to the freeway cops. That's why they named him Bird Dog.

It was Pete's first night on freeways, and he was a little anxious. At the same time, it was exciting starting a new job.

"Felix, you work with Reicher on the San Berdoo," said Gross, referring to the San Bernardino Freeway, which leads out of downtown Los Angeles to the San Gabriel area. It traveled through East Los Angeles and was a short, but very busy, beat compared to others. As his name was called, Pete nodded to Richie Reicher who nodded back. After roll call, Reicher and Pete shook hands and walked out to the motor parking area.

"How long you been on motors, Pete?" asked Reicher. Pete answered the usual questions about his experience on the job, as they walked to their motors.

"I spent two years in patrol and been on motors about a year and a half on night watch."

"Well, Pete," said Richie, "working freeways is a little different than riding the surface streets. I'll ride on the left, and you ride alongside of me. Stay close and do what I do, okay?"

"Roger."

They fired up and headed for the beat. They entered the freeway from the Vignes Street on ramp, and Richie accelerated rapidly up to about sixty miles per hour. Pete tried to stick to his right side like glue. He noticed that the motorcycles were riding about three feet apart. Although motor cops on the surface street beats rode side by side, it was different at high speed on the freeways. It seemed close at that speed, but he hung in, trying to impress Reicher with his riding ability. While Richie was riding relaxed and smoothly, Pete was having a hard time just keeping even with his partner around the curves in the freeway. As they cruised out the San Bernardino Freeway, the center divider fence whizzed by in a long blur. Pete imagined he could hear the sound of the fence racing by, but the sound of the two throbbing Harleys drowned out all other sounds. Once in a while, Pete would hear the police radio attached to the handlebars in front of him, but he was concentrating more on staying up with Richie than listening to the radio.

As the sound of the motorcycles throbbed in his ears and the cool evening air rushed by his windshield, Pete began to get the hang of riding with his partner. He started to relax and understand why many cops liked the freeway beats. Riding along at sixty miles an hour, two or three feet between bikes, smoothly rounding the curves in the freeway made Pete think of dancing. It was similar in a way. Two people moving in unison in a rhythmic fashion. A little tingle went up his spine like it always did when Pete was enjoying something unique and exciting.

A freeway cop's job while riding "shotgun" was to protect his partner when he was pulling over violators. Pete learned when Richie flipped on his rear flashers, it meant he was about to stop a violator. Pete then would flip on his flashers and drop back behind Richie to protect his rear from the traffic. It took teamwork to get a violator pulled over safely to the shoulder of the freeway.

Sometimes people did funny things when the red lights came on behind them, like slam on the brakes. Pete learned to stay far enough behind to react to whatever the violator might do. Most freeway officers will pull alongside the car they are trying to stop and get the driver's attention. People usually notice when a cop pulls up next to them anyway. When the driver looked at the officer, the officer motioned for the driver to pull over. That usually did the trick, and it put the officer alongside of the car and not to the rear, in case the driver did brake abruptly.

Once the driver seemed to understand, the cop then pulled back behind and to the side and followed the violator over. Meanwhile, he's depending on his partner to "block" for him. When officers work alone, the job is riskier, and the officer has to be even more careful.

After dark, traffic thinned out, and Pete and Richie concentrated on tickets instead of traffic flow. As they rounded the curve just before the Mission Road off-ramp, they saw a car stopped in the middle of the center or fast lane. Both cops braked hard to slow and investigate the hazard. The car was parked in the middle of the lane with all lights out. The driver was standing behind the car, jacking up the rear of the vehicle. As Pete and his partner rolled up, Pete could "feel" the traffic coming up from behind and imagined the impact.

"What the hell are you doing?" yelled Richie as he sat on his motorcycle directly behind the car. Pete had pulled up behind Richie with his rear lights flashing, knowing they were not enough to keep some jerk from running into them at any second.

"I'm changing a tire, obviously," was the answer from the Jacking Jerk. "What does it look like?"

"Sir, run the jack down, get in you car, and pull that hurdy-gurdy off the freeway right now!" yelled Richie. The hair on the back of Pete's neck was standing out straight as he waited for the impact of the car he just knew was coming any second.

"I'm not going to drive on my flat tire and ruin it," yelled the Jacking Jerk.

"Mister, if you don't move it, I will," Richie threatened.

"You can't do that."

"Watch me," yelled Richie.

Richie was now off his motor and had grabbed the keys out of the trunk lid. He threw the jack handle into the trunk of the car, slammed the lid shut, and jumped into the driver's seat. The car started, and Richie drove it off the jack and over to the shoulder on the flat tire. The Jacking Jerk screamed and jumped up and down as he followed his car over to the side of the freeway.

After getting the car and the motorcycles safely out of the traffic lanes, Richie pulled out his ticket book and signed the guy up for stopping on the freeway and creating a hazard. No amount of explanation at the scene made the Jerk understand that you cannot just stop in a traffic lane and endanger your life and others just to save a tire from further damage. It never occurred to the Jerk what danger he was really in. Pete shook his head in amazement at the lack of common sense people exhibited sometimes.

The next day in the coffee room, Pete and Richie told the story to the small group of freeway cops in the room. As usual, someone had a story to top theirs. Dick Rutsa told of an incident he had encountered just the day before.

"I'm working the 'Slot' on the Santa Ana Freeway and see this car stopped on the apex between the split of the San Berdoo and the Santa Ana southbound, so I stop to check it out. I see a woman standing behind the open door on the passenger side of the car. When I walk up to see if I can help, I see this guy hunkered down behind the door, takin' a shit! So I say, 'What the hell are you doing?' and the lady says, 'Well, officer, he had to go.' She's real upset that I should even ask!" Rutsa was laughing so hard now he could hardly finish the story. The other cops were also bent over with laughter.

"So the guy finishes and wipes his ass with some Kleenex and throws it on the ground. So I signed him up for illegal dumping! You should have heard them yell then!" The group was in tears by now. Pete determined that, on the freeways, you can expect anything.

Freeway accidents are usually fender benders that don't cause much damage. When an accident is bad, it can be really bad. Pete was working the Pasadena Freeway when the call came out about an "ambulance/injury accident on the Pasadena Freeway at Avenue Twenty-six."

Most of the freeway cops didn't like the Pasadena Freeway because it was the first Los Angeles freeway. In use since 1939, the freeway has few of the modern safety features of later freeways, like wide shoulders and emergency pull-off areas. On top of that, the freeway was one curve after the other all the way to Pasadena.

As Pete neared the location of the call, he heard calls go out for additional ambulances and the coroner's office. This meant bad news. As Pete worked his way through the evening traffic that was starting to back up from the accident, he steeled himself for what he knew would be an unpleasant experience. Then he saw the car.

The station wagon had smashed into the base of an overcrossing. The speed of the vehicle at the point of impact must have been at least ninety to one hundred miles per hour. The car or, more accurately, the pile of metal that once was a car was blocking the right lane. Traffic was backed up because of the rubbernecking of passersby. It seemed everyone wanted to look at the accident, but no one wanted to see it.

Pete parked and went to see what he could do to assist with the traffic problem. The bodies of the car's occupants were being removed by the fire department. What a mess. The resistible force of the car had met the immovable bridge. The impact had driven the engine backward into the passenger compartment of the car, tearing up the occupants terribly. In fact, the officers at the scene could not tell how many people were in the car until they started to count the arms and legs. They ended up counting eight legs and eight arms and surmised there must have been four victims. But only three heads were found.

"Okay, let's fan out and find the head," ordered the sergeant in charge. Pete couldn't believe his ears. Find the head? A human head is missing? Shit! The sergeant explained briefly when he saw the expression on the faces of the stunned officers.

"Look you guys, we can't leave a human head lying somewhere in the ivy now, can we? Visualize some citizen stopping to change a flat, and he finds the head! It's our job, and we ain't leaving here until we find it." He sounded very emphatic, thought Pete. So they all started looking under shrubs and through the ivy for the head. The traffic on the freeway was now at a standstill, watching the action and wondering what the hell was going on.

"I found it," yelled a happy officer. All eyes were on the cop, as he walked down the shoulder of the freeway, holding the missing item by the hair. Several drivers passed out on the spot.

They wanted to see the shit so bad; now let 'em look, Pete thought. The whole incident really bothered Pete, and he had trouble getting to sleep that night.

The next day in the coffee room, before roll call, the cops chattered among themselves about the accident. The discussion revolved around ways to carry a human head. Several suggestions were put forward.

"The best way is by the hair, just like Mettler did it," stated one officer.

"What if the head looks like Byron's?" came the question. "There's nothin' to grab onto!"

"How about the 'bowler's grip'," suggested another man, as he put his thumb in his mouth and his two fingers in his nose. The men laughed.

"I would prefer the ear hold myself," chimed in another. More laughter.

Valdez came up with his solution. "Why not dribble the fucking thing like a soccer ball?" he said, as he demonstrated his suggestion with his feet. More laughter.

Pete sat stunned at what was happening. He had lain awake half the night thinking about the head, and now these guys were laughing about it. Then it began to dawn on him why. It's the only thing cops can do for self-preservation. If they didn't laugh, they would have to cry; and they can't cry about these things. Then Pete began to see just how important humor was to a BCMC—or to any cop. Without it, they can't survive.

He also realized why cops hang around mostly with other cops. If they acted like that in front of civilians, they would think cops were a bunch of sadistic, crazy men.

Maybe we are, he thought, as he followed the rest of the officers into the roll call room. They were now silent as they walked, each dealing with his own thoughts and emotions.

CHAPTER ELEVEN

THE ACADEMY STEAK FRY

The annual TED Steak Fry was always a fun event that most of the BCMCs attended. A stag affair, the gathering offered the cops a chance to see other officers not on their shift or in their area. The guys who worked the outlying divisions, like the San Pedro and the San Fernando Valley, hardly ever got together. The event was traditionally held at the Police Academy in the gym.

Built in the mid-1930s, mostly by prisoner labor, the Los Angeles Police Academy nestled in the hills of Elysian Park, just north of downtown Los Angeles. The old buildings have been the training place for thousands of Los Angeles cops. The Academy maintained a restaurant and bar there also. The restaurant was open to the public; and many fire, police, and other city personnel used it. The bar was open to the public also but was frequented only by cops and their friends.

Most cops had a feeling of nostalgia about the old place. It was like returning home for many. Others wouldn't care if they never saw the place again.

Pete liked the place. It seemed warm and friendly to him. It was also a bit of the old Los Angeles, which had almost ceased to exist. A piece of history of the town. It even had a familiar smell about it. One you couldn't quite trace, but unique to the place.

Pete walked in the rock garden to the rear of the buildings. The odor of ferns and palms brought back memories of his days in training. Even though it had only been a few years since Pete had trained there, it felt like a long time to him. So many things had happened to him in his brief career as a BCMC.

He recalled older cops saying the experience you got in five years working in Los Angeles as a cop was the equivalent of a lifetime on smaller departments. Pete understood that well.

A steak fry meant steaks, baked potatoes, and baked onions. The steaks were top-grade New York cuts from the local meat market, which were available at a very decent discount to the cops. Same deal on baked potatoes and onions.

The first time Pete heard about baked onions, it didn't sound appetizing. Later, he changed his mind. They were delicious. The sweet, mild flavor of the onions went really well with the meat and potatoes.

The cooking was done in the rock garden by officers who liked to do that kind of stuff. The bar was set up in the classroom area, and the dining tables were in the gym. The bar was a very popular place at steak fries.

"Hey, Pete," yelled Ron Byron as Pete came into the bar area, "come on, and I'll buy you a drink." Of course, the drinks were free at steak fries. Ron had a drink in each hand. The well-known objective of a steak fry was to drink as much as you could, as fast as you could, before you ate.

The smell of the steaks cooking filled the air. Some of the cooking was also being done in the kitchen area just off the classroom.

"Man, I haven't seen some of these guys in years," said Beach Ball. "Hey, Nipple Head!" he yelled at a bald officer across the room. "You look like you're losing weight. Your waist is the same, but your shoulders look narrower!" The group around them laughed as Nipple Head flipped the finger at his antagonist.

The cops stood around and enjoyed the booze and stories while the dinner cooked. Pete and Ron stood apart from the main group.

"What's up, man? When are we going desert riding again?" asked Ron.

"Man, I don't have time for anything anymore. I feel like a cat trying to cover up shit on a marble floor!"

"I hope you're over that 'Rocky' thing. I was a little worried about you, partner."

"Yeah, well, life goes on in the big city. Say, do you smell smoke?"

"Yeah. The steaks are cooking, you dumb shit."

"Well, the smoke is coming into the room," said Pete as he pointed up to the ceiling. There was indeed smoke starting to collect at the ceiling level.

No one had really paid much attention until the smoke slowly got lower and enveloped the heads of the taller officers.

"Hey, the kitchen is on fire," yelled an officer, as he entered the room. The BCMCs looked at one another, waiting for someone to make a move.

"What about our steaks?" somebody yelled as several cops started to head for the door.

"Hey, let's move the bar outside," yelled someone else. That sounded like a good idea. They all pitched in. Some carried tables, and others carried the bottles of booze. By this time, most of the cops were feeling no pain and were not about to let a little fire spoil their evening.

"Put the bar over there so we can watch the Fire Laddies put out the fire," ordered one officer. The bar was quickly set up on the patio outside the building. Sirens could be heard coming up the hill from town. As the first fire engine rolled up, a great cheer rose from the crowd of drunken cops.

Pete was satisfied to stand back and watch as the firefighters unloaded their equipment. Other cops were willing to help their brother civil servants fight to save the beloved Academy. Several of the drunken cops rushed to the fire engines and helped pull the hoses off the trucks. One cop grabbed a hose and ran forward toward the fire that now had started to engulf the classroom area. As he ran with the hose, the other officers cheered and raised their glasses. The hose became fouled and jerked to stop, causing the cop pulling it to do a prat fall, worthy of any Charlie Chaplin movie.

"Yea!" cheered yelled the crowd of drunken cops.

Several firemen got ready to enter the fire with their breathing apparatus. The outfit included little bells that rang every few seconds so that the firefighters could hear one another's location, even in heavy smoke. The firefighters headed into the smoke and flames.

"Ding, ding," went the little bells every few seconds. As the firemen got into the burning building, they stopped to look over the situation. When they turned around, there was a cop standing there, holding a drink in one hand and a cigar in the other.

"I wanna see how you guys do this shit," the cop slurred as he stood in the burning building with tears rolling down his cheeks from the smoke. He had followed them into the fire.

The fire was quickly extinguished, with the help of the drunken cops and the steak fry continued, although the steaks were ruined. But the bar stayed open, and everyone had a great time, which was the main thing anyway.

CHAPTER TWELVE

BACK ON THE STREETS, 1965

Pete smoothly maneuvered his rumbling Harley-Davidson north on the Pasadena Freeway. The November afternoon was one of those rare cool, clear California days that really made living in the Southland worthwhile. The mountains above Pasadena were in clear view, and the air was free from the smog that plagued the Los Angeles Basin most days of the year.

He was enjoying the ride and feeling the vibration of the big motorcycle under him. As the air rushed by, he drew it into his nostrils, smelling the damp odor of the water running in the arroyo that parallels the freeway from South Pasadena to Avenue Nineteen, where it dumps into the Los Angeles River. Pete liked the smell. It was damp and fresh smelling.

The roadway unfolded to the front wheel of the motorcycle like a ribbon of concrete. As the BCMC rolled down "his" freeway, he had a feeling of well-being. He was satisfied with his life; not that it was all roses and doughnuts for Pete, but he was in charge of himself. He had a job he loved. He felt his job was useful and unique. How many guys get to do the job I do and meet the people I meet and get paid to do it? thought Pete.

He glanced at his speedometer as he entered a short straight portion of the freeway. It read sixty miles per hour. He looked ahead at the approaching curve at Avenue 64 and felt the urge to go as fast as he could through the curve. He slowly increased the throttle on the right handlebar. The big motor gained speed. As he entered the curve, he leaned to his right, into the turn. The lines between the lanes blurred with the speed as he felt the centrifugal force push his butt into the seat of the motorcycle. Faster! The more speed he turned on, the farther he leaned over until he seemed to be looking at the surface of the pavement from a few inches away. He felt the footboard on the right side of the bike start to scrape the concrete.

Pete's heart was pumping, and the adrenaline was now flowing. Hold it in there, Pete told himself as the big Harley tried to deviate from the path he had chosen.

The curve straightened out, and Pete rolled back upright, feeling like he wanted to yell out loud. Yeah! He rolled up the freeway soaking up the good feelings from the few brief seconds of pleasure he had just had in the curve. His thoughts were interrupted by the approach of the off-ramp at Bridewell Street, where his beat ended and he must exit.

Pete shifted down and applied the brakes as he slowed to exit. That was great, he complimented himself. He would miss working freeways, but he really liked the variety of working the surface streets. The freeways were boring after a while. Too predictable, he thought.

His stint on freeways over, Pete returned to the surface streets after New Year's. The new year of 1965 promised to be a real challenge. The civil rights movement had stirred up raw feelings in many people around the country. Riots had occurred in several cities, and people were choosing up sides on the issues of the day. Cops could choose sides but couldn't express those feelings while exercising their duty.

In the City of Angels, the tension was high, but not as high as other cities around the country. Pete thought it was because Los Angeles was a very liberal city with few racial problems. He had worked the bowels of the city and seen the worst Los Angeles had to offer. It seemed tame by comparison to other cities like Detroit, Chicago, and New York. Those towns were all old and run-down. People in the inner city didn't have the chances that people out here had.

People in California could go into almost any part of town with little to fear from racial prejudice. There were still places of resistance to blacks, but not like other places.

Pete knew inside the police department the attitude was not what the news media and the civil rights agitators would have people believe. Cops generally did their job without much concern for race, but there were always a few incidents that occurred that stirred the pot to the boiling point. If a black man got shot by a white cop, the press would usually print all the crap that the local agitators had to say.

"If it had been a white man, he wouldn't have been shot" and so on. The reality was that people got shot by cops because they were criminals and not because they were one color or another. Sometimes it tested an officer's patience to the limit to be accused of all the racial ills of the community when he's just trying to do his job.

When you wore the uniform, you inherited the problems. Pete and Ron were working 77th Division on night watch. The confrontation was inevitable.

"Man, the oniest reason you stopped me is 'cause I's black," yelled the irate man in front of Ron Byron. "I ain' did shit! You fascist pigs be pickin' on me fo' nothin'," he yelled as Ron calmly wrote the ticket. The black dude kept yelling at the top of his lungs and waving his arms around.

As Ron handed the man the ticket, the man got up in Ron's face and screamed.

"Fascist pig!" yelled the black man.

Ron leaned over and spoke quietly, "If you don't shut your loud mouth, I'm gonna hit your head with my baton so hard it'll ring like a ten-penny nail hit with a greasy ball-peen hammer." The man stopped yelling and looked at the smiling cop, whose face was close to his. "You'll have a bump on yo' head so high you'll have to use a stepladder to grease it."

The black man's face quivered for a second; then he broke out with laughter. "Man, after a threat like that, I ain't gonna say shit." He laughed. He signed the ticket and went away, shaking his head and chuckling to himself.

"Why do they blame us for everything that happens to them?" asked Ron when they arrived at the station for lunch. "I try to be as fair as I can and not let my personal beliefs interfere with police work, but it's hard," he said, as he popped two hot links into the microwave oven in the coffee room.

"The only thing I could think of that would really piss him off made him laugh."

"I think humor is the only thing that can keep all of us from going bonkers," said Pete.

"But shit!" whined Ron. "I pay my taxes and manage the Little League team and go to church, but when I put on that uniform, none of that counts, does it?"

"Forget it, Ron. We can't change the way things are, no matter how much we try. We just do our job and get the assholes off the street," he philosophized. "Even white people hate your guts when you give them a ticket. When was the last time you heard someone ask for a traffic ticket, partner? The people want us to enforce the laws but only on other people! 'Not on me! Get that other asshole just passed me!' How many times have you heard that?"

"Too many." Ron smeared mustard over his hot links. "I'll be shittin' my brains out in about an hour, but I love these hot links," he whined.

Later that night, the two partners were sitting in at the intersection of Eighty-fifth and Vermont when the radio flared up. "Twelve A Seventy-Nine, Twelve A Seventy-Nine, a 415 fight in the front yard at 1847 West Ninetieth Street. Twelve A Seventy-Nine Code 2."

"Want to roll on that, Pete? We're only a couple of blocks away."

"Sure. Let's go." They fired up and headed in the direction of the call. The two partners had agreed that they would back up other units whenever they could, even though they didn't have to. Both officers felt the same and hoped other cops would do the same for them sometime.

They rounded the corner onto Ninetieth Street and headed east. The dark street made it impossible to see the numbers on the houses. Pete saw a movement to his left and looked over to see a small crowd of people in a yard. He yelled at Ron, but he just kept going east.

Shit, Pete thought, he'll see I'm gone and turn around. Pete made a U-turn and rolled up to the yard just in time to see two young black girls squaring off to fight. Pete got off his motorcycle.

"Okay, hold it!" Pete yelled. He stepped in between the two girls and held them apart. An arm came from behind and tightened around his neck. Pete knew then he was in deep shit. He was alone in the middle of a group of irate black people who obviously wanted his blood. As he started to go down, he thought to himself, If I've got to go, I'm taking this asshole with me! He wrenched his body around so that when he hit the ground, he landed on top of his attacker. He tried to move his arms to hit the man, but was unable to move. Then he realized other people had piled on top of him. He could feel the weight of the bodies on him.

He punched the man who had attacked him several times in the face but without much effect. No room to move, he thought as he struggled with his opponent.

Then Pete noticed the weight on top of him started to subside. Now he was able to get up on his knees. So did his attacker. They traded blows from their kneeling positions, none of which were effectual.

A large cop appeared behind the man in front of Pete. In his right hand, he held a heavy "beavertail" sap. It looked like a wide paddle. Pete's opponent saw it too and covered his head with his hands, knowing what was coming down on him. Pete reached over and grabbed the dude's hands and pulled them down below his shoulders.

Wham! The beavertail did its job, and the lights went out for the dude. Pete looked to his rear and saw Ron with baton in hand. He was laughing.

"What's so damned funny, asshole?" asked Pete. Ron tried to talk but still hadn't caught his breath yet.

"That's the funniest thing I've ever seen." He laughed. "I roll up, and all I can see is your boots sticking out from under this pile of dudes." He gasped and tried to get his breath again.

"I turn my back for one minute, and you get into trouble." Later, Ron told Pete how he ran up to the pile of people and started to whack heads. He would whack one and pull them off, then whack another, and pull him off. Finally getting down to Pete's level of the pile, he found a woman on top of Pete. He whacked her and threw her aside just as the other cops all came rolling in to save the day. It turned out to be a whole family that jumped Pete. All went to jail.

The next day, the local black community newspaper the *Sentinel* printed the story of how these two brutal Los Angeles cops rolled up to the "argument" and just started hitting innocent people on the head for no reason. It bothered Pete that probably all of the black community believed the lies.

It was early evening, and Pete sat in at an intersection in Hollywood Division and kicked back for a short rest. The sun was just starting down, and the air was cooling, like it does in California. He thought it would probably be cold tonight.

When he saw the old Chevy heading north on Western Avenue from Beverly, the signal for northbound traffic had just turned red seconds before the Chevy entered the intersection. It was close, but it was a violation.

Pete fired up and gave chase. He pulled along the left side of the Chevy and looked in the window. The driver was a young woman. Her red hair made her stand out. She looked over at Pete with a startled look that most people have when they see a traffic cop on their tail. Pete motioned for her to pull over.

As she stopped at the curb, Pete had decided not to write the woman a ticket. Just too chicken shit, he thought. Instead, he decided to have some fun with her and let her go. It was not the first time Pete had stopped someone and then jived and shucked them. When he did this, he always let the violator go without a citation. It broke the monotony of traffic enforcement.

"What did I do?" asked the redheaded woman, as Pete walked up to the car window.

"Well, ma'am, ya run at red light back at Lemon Grove Street. May ah see yer driver's license, please," said Pete, in his almost-authentic Southern accent. The woman started to rummage through her purse while the two kids in the backseat bounced around.

The kids were about seven and eight, respectively. Pete also noticed that the woman with the red hair was very attractive. He guessed she was about thirty to thirty-two years old. As she handed Pete her driver's license, she started to cry. Her name was Noel Smith.

"I knew this was going to be a bad day," she said, as she lowered her head into her hands. Pete looked at the name and address on the license.

By this time, Pete decided he had made a mistake in putting on his accent, and now it was not so funny. He backed off.

"Come on, Mrs. Smith, things can't be all that bad," he said, trying to console the sobbing woman. "It's only a minor violation," said Pete, trying to minimize the shock for her.

"I was just kidding around with that accent."

"Oh," she said, "it's not your fault. I just had a big fight with my mother, and I'm not doing too well, I guess." She wiped her eyes and smeared her mascara around. The kids jumped up and down in the backseat like nothing was new.

"Look," said Pete, "don't get all upset over this." She seemed so upset, and he was feeling like a dope for starting the whole thing.

Ordinarily, he would not have listened to her problems. Old-timers had warned him of women who cry when they are stopped for a ticket. Pete recalled the time he tested the theory on a couple of chicks in a T-Bird he and his partner had stopped.

The girls were apparently on a night out and had run a stoplight. Pete was up and stopped the car. Both girls were young and good-looking. The driver had no license with her. Pete had walked back to the motor and wrote the ticket. He walked back up to the window to present the citation for signature.

"You mean you wrote me a ticket?"

"I'm afraid so, miss."

"Wow! The cops in the cars just flirt with you and let you go," she complained.

"Well, miss, we're strictly business," said Pete, in a very straight voice. The girl signed the ticket, and Pete handed her the copy.

"Now that the business is over, would you care to go have coffee with me?" he asked, as he folded up his ticket book.

"Fuck you, pig," she yelled, as she stomped on the accelerator and sped away.

Hmm, I guess the old-timers were right, he thought and filed the experience away in his memory for future reference.

This one was different. He didn't know why, but she was. She seemed so sincere and helpless.

"Hey, look"—he took a chance—"forget about the ticket and just be more careful, okay?" he heard himself saying. "Just go home and relax. If you'd like to talk later, I'll be having coffee with my partner at Hollywood and Western at the drive-in at about eight."

He knew that these types of contacts could be trouble. One of the rules of the department was to never turn a police contact into a personal relationship. There were severe penalties. Many cops did it anyway. Some were sorry later. Evie crossed his mind for a fleeting moment. Pete weighed the chances and decided to go ahead.

"Well, I don't know," she said. "I'll see." Pete handed her back her license and said good-bye. As she drove off, he wondered what he was letting himself in for. He thought of Evie and the other women he had dated. So far, he had scored big zeros with his choices in women. Maybe he'd be lucky this time.

When he teamed up with Scott Hendrickson, his partner for the night, Pete told him about his possible "date" at eight. Scott was agreeable. Anyway, Pete admitted to his partner he was betting she wouldn't show up. He thought back to his experiment with the girls in the T-Bird. She won't show, he told himself.

Pete and Scott sat in the drive-in for about twenty minutes. He told himself he knew she wouldn't come.

"Green Chevy inbound," said Scott. Pete looked and saw her pulling into the driveway.

"I'll be damned," he whispered. Old-timers could be wrong, he hoped.

CHAPTER THIRTEEN

THE FARM AND BACK, 1965

It had been almost six years since Pete had been home to see his parents and his old cronies in Iowa. Since he had little seniority on the job, Pete's vacations had been usually early in the year. This year he'd resolved to go home and visit "the Farm," as he called his home state. Spring was a neat time to visit the Farm anyway.

Inside, he was proud of his origins in the Midwest, even though he didn't admit it to many of his friends on the job. There was a tendency for folks in California to think of people from Iowa as hayseeds. Pete thought this was strange since most of the people he had met in California were from Iowa or some other "hayseed" state.

He didn't let it bother him. He had noticed that the cops from California didn't have the education he had been given in his home state. The California schools had a bad reputation even in the late fifties and early 1960s. In many ways, he felt superior to his fellow officers when it came to education.

Pete looked forward to being back in a lifestyle that was devoid of the "hippie culture" he'd come to despise in California. He was sick and tired of the love-ins and the peaceniks and the Volkswagens that had psychedelic paint jobs and carried the bearded freaks that sought, in his opinion, to bring down all that was holy to his world. He saw the new direction in politics as a threat to motherhood and apple pie.

I can hardly wait to get back to Iowa where all this bullshit doesn't exist, and things are stable and dependable, thought Pete as the plane landed in Des Moines, the sanctuary of Americanism. He had called his parents, and they were there to meet him at the airport. Pete was feeling like a little kid as he got off the plane and was met by his parents and his old buddy Tim Knight.

It seemed like only yesterday that Tim and Pete had "borrowed" Tim's dad's car and drove around downtown Des Moines like real men. They had cruised the local "Foster Freeze" and impressed all the kids with the car. Little did they know Tim's dad had reported the car stolen. When the local cops had stopped them, they had almost shit their pants. Fortunately, one of the cops knew Tim and recognized the car, so the incident didn't amount to much. It had certainly made an impression on Pete. He never forgot the feeling of fear and helplessness as the officer snapped on the handcuffs. Later, Pete found out the cop, Officer Johansen, had put on the whole thing to scare the living daylights out of Pete and Tim. It had worked.

Pete thought of all the games he and Tim had played as kids. Their favorite game was "cops and robbers." Now it was not a game. All these thoughts and more rushed through Pete's mind as he got off the plane. It was good to see his mom and dad again and to be away from the fast life of Los Angeles for a while. Pete intended to enjoy it.

Iowa is not unlike most Midwestern states. Sports are a dominating influence there. If it's not basketball, it's football or track. The Hawkeyes rule in Iowa. Pete had always been one who was interested in sports but not quite. He couldn't see the point in most of the enthusiasm for football, and basketball left him cold.

"A bunch of black dudes running back and forth on a wood floor throwing a ball" was his definition of basketball. He realized he was alone in his feelings. Everyone else back here seemed to live for sports while the world went to hell.

The first thing he noticed was hippies in town. Hippies in Des Moines? No way! But there they were. Just like in LA. No! They looked worse here! What a bunch of scraggly-looking assholes, he thought. They had the same long braided hair and the leather vests and moccasins they wore in Los Angeles. How could this be? This was his "heaven." His sanctuary! Bullshit! It was as bad or worse than LA!

It seemed like all of Pete's dreams came tumbling down at one time. His old hometown girlfriend was married and had put on a lot of weight. His old buddies who he used to drink and act the fool with now spent their most exciting times bowling.

Bowling? Pete couldn't think of a more boring way to spend time. You throw the ball down the alley. Hit the wooden pins. The ball comes back. You throw it down again. Drink some beer and do it all over again. Shit! He had punched it out with bad guys on the streets of Los Angeles. He had watched people die. Bowling?

What has happened to me? he wondered. I'm different from how I was before when I lived here. He wondered if he liked his new self. Am I the asshole? he wondered. What happened to the farm boy who left Iowa a few years ago? He searched his mind for the answer to the questions that nagged his insides.

He came to the conclusion that nothing stays the same. It can't—and won't. He thought of all the experiences he'd had since he'd left home. The hunt for the head on the freeway. The other BCMCs and how they worked the streets. The injustices of life he'd experienced on both sides of the law.

"The world is fucked up," Pete told his buddy Tim as they got drunk that night. "You gotta take it as it comes and not like you think it should be."

"Right!" agreed Tim. But Pete knew Tim didn't understand. It wasn't his fault.

"Black people are mostly nice people," explained Pete to his partner Ben Vander Deven, also known as Captain Nemo to the guys because he served in the submarine service in the navy.

"It's just that white people don't really know how to take them." Pete had really tried to understand black folks and had some success. But, like most whites, he was hesitant to comment on what he had learned. Cops have a tendency toward realism in their thinking, and their opinions are usually based on what they see. What they see is not the whole picture for any group of people. It's usually only the bad side. That puts cops at a disadvantage. What is required is the ability to do the job without trying to pass judgment on all people for the actions of some.

Humor comes into play once again to help the cops do the job and keep their sanity.

"I stopped this dude the other day on Century Boulevard," said Ben, downing his last drink of coffee before he and Pete headed out to their Newton Division assignment.

"The guy was a well-dressed black dude driving a rental car back to the airport," Ben alluded. "He turns out to be some kind of engineer for Boeing Aircraft Company in town on business." Pete and Ben were walking toward the motor parking area as they talked.

"I tell the guy he's going fifty in a thirty-five-mile zone, and he says, in this very good diction, 'I can't understand, officer. I was watching my speed thermometer'."

"His 'speed thermometer'?" asked Pete, in disbelief.

"Can you believe it? This guy's an engineer that makes planes!" They put their ticket books and hot sheets in their saddlebags and headed out to the beat.

The night was passing with no real action and then—

"Thirteen A Twenty-Five, see the woman, a possible ADW in progress at 4725 Ascot. Thirteen A Twenty-Five, Code 2." Pete and his partner picked up an "all units" call and started heading in that direction.

As they rolled up to the address from the north, a black-and-white was stopping from the south. As the cops approached, they were met by two black females, one adult and a young girl about twelve.

"What's the problem, ma'am?" the patrol officer asked. Pete didn't recognize either of the patrol officers. The older of the two females pointed at a house on the corner and told her story.

"My daughter and I was in the house, and we had a argument with my boyfriend. He went and got his gun and said he was goin' to shoot us. I talked him out of it, and my daughter and I went into the bafroom. I locked the door, and we snuck out the bafroom window and called you'all." Her voice was excited, and the little girl was terrified.

"Does he still have the gun?" asked the officer.

"Yeah, he still got it. It's a pistol."

"Well," said Ben, "let's see if we can get this dude out of there. Pete, you and this officer cover the front, and we'll try the back door."

No one had a better idea, so they split up. Ben and the other officer moved quietly around the side of the darkened house on the corner. Pete could see a dim light inside that flickered like a television set. Pete and the remaining cop moved over to a car parked out in front of the house and crouched down behind it. Pete slid his gun out of the holster and started to think, What the hell am I doing here? He wished he was somewhere else—anywhere else. His heart started to race as the adrenaline shot through his system. His partner was out of his sight, doing something he couldn't see. The cop next to him looked as scared as Pete.

His mind raced, trying to plan what he should do if the guy came running out. What if Ben or the other officer got shot? Should he kick the front door? Do we really have enough for a felony complaint? Will this dizzy broad back us up if we kill "her man"?

Pete's thoughts were cut short by a muffled voice from inside the house. Then *bam, bam, bam, bam, bam!* There were gunshots inside the house. Who's shooting who? Pete wondered.

"Shit," Pete yelled out loud as he propelled himself toward the door of the house. He braced for the kick that would open it and reveal what he did not want to see. Brief flashes crossed his mind of Ben's body lying on the floor. He felt the panic of not knowing what would happen to him in the next two seconds. His pistol felt like a lead weight in his hand.

"Here I go!" he yelled to himself.

Suddenly, the door was opened. It was Ben.

"Come on in, you guys. It's all over." His voice was calm and cool. Pete's knees were like water as he entered the room. The room was dark and filled with gun smoke and its odor. A man was lying on the floor. It was not a cop. Pete started to relax. The officer who had accompanied Ben was sitting on the sofa, reloading his pistol. Pete grabbed the phone and called for an ambulance.

As the ambulance team lifted the injured suspect onto the stretcher, a bullet fell out of his back onto the floor. The ambulance carted the suspect away, and all the involved officers went to the station to make the appropriate reports. It was then that Pete learned what had happened.

"We found the back door open and slipped inside," Ben related later. "I peeked around the door jamb and saw the suspect sitting on the couch, watching TV in the dark. The patrol officer stepped into the room and identified us and told the dude to raise his hands and stand up slowly. The dude stood up and turned around. The light was dim, but we could see the pistol in the suspect's hand; and it was pointed in our direction."

By this time, a group of Newton cops had gathered around to hear the story. All cops like to hear the story of a shooting. Pete guessed it was because it could happen to any one of them, anytime. Ben continued his story.

"I ducked back behind the doorway as the dude started to fire. Funny how shots are so loud indoors and so quiet outdoors," recalled Ben. The cops all nodded, as if they also knew.

"The other officer fired all six rounds and then hit the floor. The suspect went down, but he still had the gun in his hand. It was waving around slowly, pointed up at the ceiling. I drew a bead on the dude's head, then thought better of it. So I walked in and kicked the gun out of his hand, and it was all over."

The total time lapsed from the first shot until Ben kicked the gun was probably fifteen seconds. During those fifteen seconds, Pete had been dying outside. They later learned the suspect was hit four times: once in the chest, once in the arm, and two more in the lower body. It was surprising that the guy lived. The cops made jokes about it, saying if it had been a cop that was shot, he would have no doubt died.

The lady that had called the cops was really pissed off because one of the shots that missed the gunman went through her stereo.

About a month later, the officers were in court at the preliminary hearing for the suspect. There he was, sitting in the jury box, looking as healthy as anyone in the room.

"We should have cut off his head and buried it a mile away, just to make sure," commented Ben in the courtroom. But Pete guessed that Ben was happy he had not shot the helpless man on the floor. Pete respected him for that decision. He also had his first experience at making decisions while in a panic situation. He had done what he had to do, even though it turned out different than he had anticipated.

It had been a different kind of fear. Different from the time a cowboy had pushed a gun in his gut in the backseat of a police car, after a beat cop had failed to properly shake him down. He had no choice there. It just happened. The shooting with Captain Nemo was forever burned in his memory as "the day I shit my pants."

CHAPTER FOURTEEN

THE LITTLE REDHAIRED GIRL, 1965

The red-haired woman sat across the table from Pete in the dim light of the Oriental restaurant. He couldn't help but notice her clothes. Her multicolored Oriental-style dress was split up the side, just enough to show a very nice portion of leg. Her hair was pulled up and rolled into a "French roll." The makeup was perfect and accented her fair skin.

Pete liked what he saw. This was the second time Pete had been out with Noel Smith since he had stopped her for the ticket on Western Avenue.

The first time he had called, she had invited Pete and his partner over for coffee and cookies. As he and Scotty walked into the small living room of her very modest apartment, he noticed how tall she was. About five feet six, Pete guessed.

He liked her red hair but wondered what her natural color might be. Pete was startled by her great shape and long legs. This was the first time he had seen her when she was not seated in a car.

She also had what most black people would have called a nigger butt. This term only takes on meaning when compared to what black people call a cracker ass. Many black people refer to white people as crackers, because they are white in color. Since most white girls have less buttocks than black girls, hence the term "cracker ass" was coined. The whole description would probably have been insulting and lost on Noel, but to Pete, it was a plus in her favor.

"Well, it looks like I'll be moving soon," she said, as they dug into the huge Oriental meal. The view from the window of the restaurant overlooked the lights of Hollywood. The night was very clear.

"When is this happening?" Pete asked. His first thoughts were negative because probably it would take her farther away from him. She told him of her job in Pasadena and the need for being closer to work and to try to get her two boys out of the Los Angeles school system and into a better, safer environment. Pete could understand that logic.

Noel had been living in a small house in a rather run-down court off Hollywood Boulevard for several years. Her divorce from her husband had caused her to move into low-cost housing near her work, which, at that time, was for the phone company. Now she had started a new career as a dental assistant.

Pete had been very impressed with Noel's daring and fortitude in obtaining the job as a dental assistant. She had never been to school to study dental work. She merely got books out of the library and studied them and faked her way into a job. Now she was sought after by several dentists because of her self-taught abilities as an assistant. Pete was awed by the guts and respected her for her ambitious efforts to better herself and to raise her two kids. On top of all that talent, she was a beautiful woman.

"I'll help you move your stuff, if you'll let me," Pete offered.

"That would be nice," she said. The night went uphill from then on, and when they returned to her house, they had a couple of glasses of wine. He took her in his arms and kissed her. His arms wound around her waist, and his hands slid down the silky material of the Oriental dress. As his hands came to rest on her buttocks, he couldn't believe how good they felt. He had never had his hands on such a well-rounded and shapely rear. The sentence that he could not freely express went through his mind, Wow, what a nice ass you have! As they went into the bedroom, Pete knew that this would be the most memorable night of his life. He was not disappointed.

The motorcycle repair shop was a popular place when you rode a Harley-Davidson. It seemed like there was always something going wrong or breaking off. Most of the cops didn't mind going to the shop, though. It gave them a chance to shoot the shit and get out of work.

The motor shop was located a block east of the PAB on Central Avenue. Once an old warehouse, its high-raftered ceiling had the paint coming off in big chunks. On night shift, there were usually two mechanics on duty to handle minor repairs. It was about 8:00 PM, and Pete had come into the shop because his rear chain was so loose it was about to fall off. There were several other cops in the shop. Pete recognized all of the guys in the shop.

Bud Fitzgerald was one of the clowns on the watch. It seemed he was always in trouble for something. The guys called him Gatemouth. One of the least-liked men on the shift was also in the shop. Glenn Ivans was shunned by most of the guys because he always appeared to be out for glory and fame.

He had special cards printed up to give people he had helped so they would write in commendations for him. Many people did too. He also thought he was "God's gift to all women." He had even made passes at some of the other cop's wives at the Christmas dance one year. When the word gets around, your reputation is made. In Glenn's case, it was a bad one. Bud Fitzgerald was not a fan of Ivans' at all either.

As Pete's motorcycle was being worked on, he, Bud and Ivans were standing near the large open door in the rear of the shop, which opened onto Alameda Street. The radio on Pete's bike was still on.

"All units in the vicinity, Thirteen T Twenty-Four is in pursuit of a GTA suspect northbound on Alameda Street from Olympic."

The cops listened intently as the pursuit headed right toward them up Alameda.

"Let's go outside and see if they come up this far," suggested Bud. As the three cops stepped out onto the loading dock that faced Alameda, they could see the red lights coming toward them.

"Man, I wish I was in this pursuit!" The two other cops looked at Ivans and shook their heads, knowing that no cop in his right mind wants to get in a pursuit.

As the fleeing T-Bird flashed by, Ivans whipped out his gun and fired off two shots at the suspect's car.

Pete and Gatemouth looked at each other, both thinking the same thing. This guy is out of his mind. Of course, Pete and Bud both knew LAPD policy stated you were not to shoot at moving vehicles unless your life was threatened.

Seconds later, there was the sound of a big bang from up the street, and they knew the car had crashed. Bud mounted his motor. "I'm going to run down there and see what happened," he said and roared off. Pete and Ivans stayed in the shop until Fitzgerald came back about ten minutes later.

"Wow," Fitzgerald said, "what a mess! The car hit a light pole and really got crunched. The driver was a fourteen-year-old black kid wanted only for speeding, and you hit him right between the horns, Ivans! Good shooting!" Gatemouth slapped Ivans on the shoulder.

Ivans' face went white as a sheet as the reality of what he had done was sinking in. "But . . . I . . . didn't think I'd hit him," he stammered.

"You nailed him good, Glenn Boy!" repeated Fitzgerald. Pete thought Ivans was going to pass out. Several other motor cops came into the shop from the street. They got off their motors and came over to the small group.

"Man, that pursuit ended the way all pursuits should. Splat!" said one of the newcomers. "All 211 suspects should get the same medicine."

"I thought it was a kid on a joy ride," said Ivans in a shaky voice.

"Hell no," said the cop, "those two guys were wanted for robbery."

Then it dawned on Ivans that Fitzgerald had played a joke on him. A cruel but well-earned joke. Fitzgerald laughed so hard he almost died. Pete laughed because he had been fooled also. Ivans never did learn his lesson and went on to become a legend in his own mind.

Pete's life seemed to change a lot after he met Noel. He thought about her a lot and wondered where the relationship would go. He was having a great time being a BCMC and had not contemplated marriage. Now he had a problem. Not only was he thinking about marriage, but he also had to think about Noel's two boys. A ready-made family, as he referred to them in his letter to his parents back in Des Moines.

Of course, parents all want their kids to marry and have kids. It's the only revenge parents get out of life, thought Pete. Watching their kids suffer the same fate as they did when they had *you*!

Pete's life went on, and his job still intrigued him. Every day he learned something new about people. He enjoyed working West Los Angeles once in a while, but he wouldn't like it for a steady assignment, he thought. Too many lawyers and rich assholes who think the laws don't apply to them because they have money.

The population of the West Hollywood area is what most people would call upper-middle class to what others refer to as the Gelt Belt. The "Gelt" was owned by mostly Jewish people who work in the film industry or own a business.

"I don't see why you like to work in this part of town." Pete was bitching as he and Ron walked out to their bikes after a lunch break.

"The difference between working in South Central Los Angeles and West Hollywood is like black-and-white," explained Ron to his dissatisfied partner.

"Black-and-white! Ha-ha. Real funny! At least, in Watts, you know where you stand and what to expect. So do the people who live there."

"Now you're starting to sound like old Sudinski again," Ron observed. They had been assigned to work this beat while the two regular men were on vacation. With the low seniority the two young cops had, it was the only time they could pull this beat.

"It seems like the more contact some people have with cops, the easier it is to get along with them," Pete continued to comment. "On this side of town, you run into the type of person who gets one or two tickets in his life. Not only that but, every other person you stop in West Hollywood seems to be from New York or New Jersey." Pete had always been amazed that every person he stopped from New Jersey gave him a bad time. They always argued over the violation or anything that they could think of to try to get out of the ticket.

"People over here are a pain in the ass," whined Pete.

"Well, at least, they won't shoot your ass."

"I'd still rather be in Watts."

"Yeah, eatin' them hot links and drinkin' Diet Pepsi," moaned Ron.

"Fuck you, you skin-headed, pencil-necked asshole," Pete continued to mumble as his engine fired up and drowned out the profanity.

As the car pulled over, Pete stopped about fifteen feet to the rear of it. An elderly man quickly got out and walked back to Pete's location before he could get his ticket book out of his saddlebags.

"Vat's da trouble, officer?" asked the old Jewish man. "Vat's did I do? I didn't do nuttin'," he asked and answered in the same breath. Ron snickered, as he stood on the sidewalk and observed.

"Well, sir," said Pete, "you pulled out right in front of that car coming north on Fairfax between Santa Monica and Fountain," explained Pete. The old man's hands were shaking, and he was breathing hard.

"I didn't see no car ven I pulled oudt," said the old man. "How could there be a car der ven I didn't see it?"

"I know you didn't see it, sir," said Pete. "I'm sure that if you had, you would have yielded to him and let him go by before you pulled out of that driveway. Didn't you hear him honk at you?"

The car door on the passenger's side opened and Mama got out. "Papa, vat's goink on? Vat's da matter?" she yelled in a loud voice.

"It's okay, Mama. The officer said I pulled oudt in front of anudder car. But I didn't do it!"

"Officer, you look like a nize boy. Vhy are you picking on Papa ven he didn't do nuttin'?" she pleaded, wringing her hands. Ron was having a hard time keeping a sober expression on his face.

Pete broke the news as gently as he could to the suffering couple. "Look, folks," he said, "I saw you pull out in front of the car, and now I have to give you a ticket."

"Mine Gott," screamed Mama, "he's goink to give you a ticket for nuttin'."

"Please, officer, don't give me a ticket," pleaded the old man. "I'm beggink you." The old man got down on his knees with his hands together in praying mode. Damn it, thought Pete, I'll bet this really looks good to the people driving by.

"Look, Pop," said Pete, as he started to lose his cool, "it's only a $15 ticket, not the end of the known world. Now please get up!" Pete was now the one begging.

Mama was now crying and walking around, wringing her hands. Papa was down on his knees, wailing. To hell with this. He started to write on the ticket book. Papa was up in an instant and grabbed Pete's writing arm.

"Please don't write da ticket," pleaded the old man. Pete started to write again. Again, Papa grabbed Pete's arm to stop him from writing. Pete was now mad. Ron was cracking up on the sidelines.

"I'm warning you right now," said Pete in his most sincere voice. "If you touch my arm one more time, I'll put you in jail for interfering with an officer!" The protests stopped, and Pete finished the ticket. The old man signed it, and as Pete handed him the copy, the old man took his parting shots at Pete.

"You got a vife? You got a kid? They love you?" questioned the old man. Not waiting for an answer, Papa and Mama got back into their new Chrysler Imperial and drove off up the street.

"I'd rather be shot at than go through this shit," yelled Pete as Ron, still laughing, slapped him on the back.

"Gestapo Schweine Hundt!" taunted Ron.

Pete was to see Mama and Papa again. This time, it was in traffic court; and they had their son, Irving the Lawyer, with them.

CHAPTER FIFTEEN

TROUBLE AND MORE TROUBLE, 1965

Watts was an old part of Los Angeles that had once been a station stop on the Pacific Electric Railway trolley back in the not-too-distant past. Now the PE lines were gone, and the Watts area was a predominantly black part of town. In fact, the name, Watts, had come to be the generic name for the black community in Los Angeles.

Pete was aware that many of the homes in Watts were old but well-kept. Many of the people who lived in Watts had lived there for decades and felt it was "their" community. The other half of Watts was made up of people who had come to believe they were the "real" Watts. These were transient blacks who worked little or not at all. Some by mishap, others by choice. Welfare was easily available here in the Golden West, and some people took good advantage of that fact.

The working men and women of Watts were doing all right, it seemed to Pete. He'd met black people who had always worked for a living. Several older men had bragged to Pete they had never been out of work. They said you just had to look for it and be willing to put in a good day's work for a day's pay, as they put it.

So Pete was not too sympathetic with those who said that the plight of the poor Negro in Watts was the reason for the crime that was rampant in that area. To Pete, and many of his fellow officers, the clamor and cries of the liberal press and political agitators for more jobs and welfare were not founded in truth but were politically motivated.

Pete saw the black people of Los Angeles as pawns in a game being played by those who would use the legitimate social complaints of many black people to promote socialism in the United States. Many cops on the job shared that belief. Whether they were right or wrong depended on which side of the local political scene you happened to be on.

The summer of 1965 had been a hot one so far, and Pete was training a new officer from the last motor class. "Big Frank" Clearidge was just that—big. He was about six feet three or four anyway. He was a fun guy to work with and a quick learner.

Frank had a loud laugh and used it often. Working in the Watts area was a first for him, since he had spent his first two years as a cop in the valley. Working in Watts was one laugh after another to Frank.

Pete was "up" as he and Frank rode south to their beat in Seventy-seventh Division that evening. As they approached an intersection, the light was red for the BCMCs, and they started to slow. A Chevy Corvair went flying through the intersection, going westbound. The Corvair had the green light, and Pete estimated it was going about forty-five miles an hour. Not quite fast enough to chase, he thought as he and Frank entered the intersection.

As they looked west in the direction the Corvair had gone, they saw the car sitting abandoned in the middle of the street with all four doors open. Pete wondered how that could have happened in the few seconds it took them to get to the intersection. Instantly, both cops knew the car was stolen and the suspects had bailed out. They both swung a U-turn and headed for the abandoned car.

After a brief stop, Pete and Frank split up and started to look for the suspects. They had no description whatsoever. As Pete and Frank came together after a quick circuit around the block in opposite directions, they saw a young black dude walking casually across the street at the corner about a block from the abandoned car. They pulled up and got off their motors.

"Hey, man," Pete called to the dude, "come here."

"What you want?" the young man asked. Pete grabbed the dude by the arm and put his hand over the young man's heart. It was thumping like Gene Krupa playing "Sing, Sing, Sing" at Carnegie Hall.

"Been running, huh?" asked Pete. The young dude knew the cops had nothing on him but a faint suspicion. Pete and Frank knew that too. The officers called a patrol car and dumped the dude on them for a follow-up investigation on the stolen Corvair.

The two motor cops had a good laugh speculating on the sight of the dudes in the Corvair, seeing the approaching cops, slamming on the brakes, and bailing out of the car. If they had just kept going, Pete and Frank would not have chased them anyway. It was a good laugh, though.

The next night was uneventful until about 10:30 PM; then all hell seemed to break loose. The radio started to broadcast "officer needs help" calls all over the southern part of Seventy-seventh Division. Pete and Frank were working the north end and listened to the calls with growing trepidation.

"I'll bet the shit hits the fan tonight," speculated Frank. "It's a hot August and the natives are restless."

Pete laughed, but it wasn't quite as funny as it might have been a few years ago. Too many cities across the country had suffered riots. It was getting close to home, thought Pete. We've been lucky up to now, he thought. I hope our luck holds out. It didn't.

The number of calls involving unruly crowds on the streets increased by the hour. Crowds throwing rocks at cars at Imperial Highway and Wilmington. Crowds looting stores in the Watts area. Then things seemed to calm down a bit, and the department relaxed.

According to the news media, the local black community leaders were trying to talk to the people in the streets and calm them. The TV and radio announced that the incident that had sparked the disturbances had been an arrest for drunk driving made by the California Highway Patrol that had escalated into a near-riot scene. Rumors went wild in the black community about white officers kicking a pregnant black woman during the CHP arrest.

To make matters worse for the Chief of the Los Angeles Police Department, the legendary William H. Parker, the Mayor of Los Angeles, Samuel Yorty, was out of town; and Governor Pat Brown was vacationing in Greece. Those left in command seemed to be reluctant to do anything that could turn out to be wrong. The news media seemed to love to crucify people on Monday morning after the game. So they did nothing.

The so-called leaders in the black community did little or nothing to quell the rioting that had started.

Things quieted down for a while. Then the next night near End of Watch, Pete and his partner heard the call, "All night watch motor units, stand by in the field until further notice. This is an emergency."

This was the second night of trouble in south Los Angeles. Everyone was uptight. Now the proverbial "shit" had hit the fan. Looting had broken out again in various parts of Los Angeles's black community. Pete and Frank listened and looked at each other in disbelief as they heard the radio just cancel their end of watch.

A few moments later, the radio ordered, "All night watch units, report to your watch commander's office immediately." Well, here we go, thought Pete as they headed into downtown Los Angeles toward the police building where the TED offices were located. As Pete and Frank pulled in, they saw about eight or ten other motor officers arriving. Once in the roll call assembly room, the lieutenant gave out the orders.

"I want all of you, guys, to report to the command post that is set up at 111th and Avalon. Do not go down Central Avenue. There is rioting there. Any questions?"

Of course, there were a million, but nobody asked them. Pete went to his motor with a group of about six or eight officers. They headed out onto the Harbor Freeway toward the riot area. Pete's mind raced, and the adrenaline was pumping. It seemed like they were riding into a dream. More like a nightmare, he thought.

As they had previously agreed, the group of BCMCs turned off the Harbor Freeway at Century Boulevard and rode east toward Avalon. Pete found himself in the lead of the group. How did that happen? he wondered to himself. As the group rounded the corner off Century to go south on Avalon, the sight that met Pete's eyes was unbelievable. Shops were on fire. There was a Yellow Cab sitting on its top, slowly burning. But what made Pete's blood run cold was the crowd of people on both sides of the street that appeared to be "waiting" for them.

Both sides of Avalon Boulevard appeared to be lined three or four deep with black people. Each one had something in his hand to throw at Pete as he rounded the corner. He knew if he were knocked down now, it would be the end of his ass. His only escape now was to screw the throttle on and duck.

The big Harley jumped forward and Pete hung on. As he accelerated down the street, he saw a man carrying what looked like a large chunk of concrete. He lugged the chunk over to the curb and, as Pete accelerated by, lobbed the huge chunk of concrete at him. Pete knew that if it hit him, he would be down and probably out. It was too late to swerve, and there was no place to go.

Bang! The chunk of cement hit the headlight nacelle of Pete's bike. The impact sent a shudder through the bike, but he stayed upright. A little farther down the street and—*pop! Pop!* Pete knew that sound well: the sound of gunfire. Out of the corner of his eye on his right, he saw a man shooting at him with a pistol. Pete tried to pull in his head like a turtle but couldn't. *Pop! Pop!* More shots behind him. At him? Pete didn't know. He only knew he was still up and running.

Crack! A different sound. An impact near his left side. Don't stop now! Pete yelled at himself inside his head. Go! Go! He thought of the field of tumbleweeds at the motor school in Griffith Park. Go!

Ahead, he saw the lights of police vehicles and cops standing around them. "The command post," he yelled out loud (or did he?). The friendly faces of cops were all around him now. The other cops with him came rolling in. By some miracle, none of them had been hit by the gunfire, although many had been hit with other projectiles. Pete got off his motor to look at the front.

"Wow," said one of the cops standing in front of Pete's motor. "Look at that," pointing to the smashed-in area of Pete's motorcycle that used to be a headlight. It was gone, and in its place was a very large dent about four inches into the metal. There was also a large dent in his rear fender near the back of his seat. Pete now realized his baton was missing from its clamp under the seat. He guessed that whatever had hit the rear fender had knocked his baton off. Later, he borrowed a baton from a deputy sheriff to replace his.

Pete was really upset at the route the supervisors had chosen to send them to the command post. Didn't they know what the area was like? We were nearly killed! He looked at his broken motorcycle and cussed up a storm. He noticed one of the ranking officers standing within hearing range, but he cared less and ranted all the louder.

After Pete arrived at the command post, a sweep of the street on foot was organized to go north on Avalon to where the looting of stores was taking place. The men were positioned in a V-shaped "squad wedge" formation with Pete and Frank on the right.

They started up the street. Pete's thoughts were racing now. Is this what war is all about? He was sure none of the men there ever dreamed they would be in this situation. Not in our town, they thought. Not in America!

As the formation moved forward, Pete could see the light from the fires burning ahead. Shadows of people running back and forth in the firelight gave an eerie feeling to the men as they walked slowly toward the riot area.

Pop! Not again, he thought. Over to his right about a half a block away, a man jumped out from behind an apartment building and fired at them.

"Shit," yelled Pete, wondering where bullets go in the dark. He looked vainly around for cover, but there was none. He dropped down flat in the gutter and tried to hide behind the curb that was about eight inches high. This is stupid, he thought, but eight inches is eight inches.

Some cops started to shoot back at the attacker. Pete looked up as the shooting man grabbed his stomach and turned and ran back behind the building.

The officers regrouped and started off down the street again. As they made their way up the street, they yelled at people to go home and to get off the street. Many of the people on the street challenged the cops and tried to get them to separate from the group and chase them down into the dark streets. The cops were not falling for that.

Pete noticed a TV news crew had attached itself behind the squad and was filming as they went up the street. The bright lights of the cameras illuminated the cops, making great targets of them. We've already been shot at a couple of times, and these jerks want to put spotlights on us? he thought. Most of the cops mistrusted the newsmen anyway. It seemed that they were there to try to catch the cops doing something wrong to the "poor rioters."

"Put those fucking lights out," someone yelled at the news crew. They ignored the order and continued to film with the bright lights on the advancing cops. Then a couple of officers separated from the squad and broke out the lights with their batons. The newsmen were irate and cursed the cops. A little while later, they were scampering back to hide behind the rotten cops when "they" were attacked by rioters. Typical, thought Pete. The slimy pricks are real brave when they are behind us! Most of the news crews changed their antipolice attitude as the riot progressed, and relations with them got better.

After the wedge-shaped squad of men had gone another half-block up Avalon, a car came rushing toward them from the riot area. As they watched the car speed directly at them, they assumed it was trying to ram the group. Shades of kamikazes, thought Pete. Closer and closer sped the car. As it got about one hundred feet from the group, the squad formation parted in the middle, as if on command. The car raced between the two groups of cops, which were now lined up on both sides of the street.

Pop, pop! Poppity pop, pop! Shots flew everywhere. Pete shot at the car, and so did everyone else on the street. That means we are shooting at each other, he thought as he stopped firing.

The car was riddled with holes, but not one shot hit the driver. That was good because he turned out to be some poor whipdick Mexican that got caught in the riot and was trying to get to the cops for "safety." Two officers were hit by the gunfire. One slug went into the spare ammunition pouch on the belt of a guy named Olson, where it embedded itself harmlessly. The other round apparently ricocheted off something and hit a CHP officer in the heel of his boot, knocking him off his feet. He was also unhurt.

What a bunch of dumb bastards we are, Pete thought. Then he wondered if either of the hits were his bullets. He went over to each officer who had been hit and asked, "Which side of the street were you standing on?" To Pete's relief, both cops were on his side of the street. Then he thought, Hell, they might have hit me! Riot or no riot, Pete resolved to be very careful from now on where and when he shot.

The newcomers to the command post were transferred to a local school yard, where they left their motorcycles and got on a school bus. Pete was relieved not to have to ride a motorcycle through any more riot-filled streets of Los Angeles. The bus transported the conglomeration of officers, which now included Los Angeles County sheriffs and highway patrol officers, north to the area of Washington Boulevard and Central Avenue. The officers got off the bus and started to take control of the streets, moving crowds out of the street and chasing looters out of stores.

Several officers yelled that there were some looters in the back of a liquor store. Pete and a couple of officers ran over to assist. While the others went into the building, Pete stayed outside, using a parked car as a shield, and covered the rear for the officers. Unruly crowds milled around in the street, threatening to overwhelm the cops, who were outnumbered about a hundred to one.

Pete leaned on the hood of a parked car with his pistol in his hand, watching for any sign of trouble. There was a scuffle and yelling voices inside the store. A black man came running out of the store with Officer Jim Roth hot on his tail.

"Stop, or I'll shoot," yelled Roth. The dude didn't stop or even slow down. They must not think we will shoot, thought Pete. *Pow!* Roth fired a shot at the fleeing burglary suspect.

"No shooting!" yelled Sergeant Willis as he grabbed Roth's arm.

"What do you mean 'no shooting'?" shouted Roth angrily. "That asshole was looting that store and was setting it on fire, and you say, 'No shooting'! That's crazy!" Pete thought so too and recalled he had already been shot at twice in just a few hours.

"That's an order!" barked Willis. Pete remembered Willis from when Pete had been a rookie on motors. Willis was then a motor cop about to make sergeant. Some of the guys who knew Willis said they thought he would be a good supervisor. Now his actions as a new supervisor were a little suspect. Willis proved to be a real "company man" in later years. Now he was a threat to the security of the troops, thought Pete. He wanted to get away from the jerk as soon as possible.

The cops moved down the street a few blocks to another liquor store being looted. Billy Woodworth, a black BCMC, got there first. He took off his police helmet and stuck his head around the corner of the doorway and yelled, "Here come the po-lice!" Then, as the looters ran out of the store, Woodworth smacked them with his baton. After dusting off three of them, he turned to the other cops, who were watching in amazement. "These niggers are lawless!" he said, shaking his head.

The cops were returned to the school command post and then relieved of duty until the next day. Pete went home and watched the action on TV. It was unbelievable. The whole city was burning down around their ears. It was plain that the police were unable to handle the situation anymore. Had they acted sooner with force, maybe, but they hadn't, and things were out of control. Rumors circulated that roving bands of rioters might invade the suburbs. People were arming themselves.

The police department soon discovered it had too few shotguns and even fewer rifles for the officers in the field. Pete had only fired a shotgun on two occasions while in the academy. He hadn't handled one since. It was painfully clear that the cops were outgunned in the streets. Snipers were reported in several locations, shooting high-powered rifles against the cops' puny .38 revolvers. Pete got out his .45 automatic and cleaned and oiled it. He would take it with him tomorrow as a second gun.

CHAPTER SIXTEEN

THE SECOND DAY IN HELL, WATTS, 1965

The next night, Pete and Frank were assigned to what were called Brush Fire patrols. These were plain cars driven by officers in uniform who were to respond to all emergency calls for help or assistance. The officers now carried a variety of firearms. The department had relaxed its ban on "nonuniform" weapons. The shortage of weapons had prompted some of the local gun stores to loan out rifles and shotguns to the cops. Big Frank had received a 12-gauge, single-shot shotgun from one of the gun shops. Pete was allowed to wear his .45 in a cross-draw holster he'd put on the left side of his Sam Browne belt.

The fire department had been unable to put out some of the big fires set by rioters and had been shot at for their efforts. From the air, the city looked like it was burning to the ground. Brush Fire units rolled to protect the firemen. Pete and Frank were in one car with three other motor cops from their watch. A second car cruised with them, containing four or five other BCMCs.

Their first call was to assist the fire department at Jefferson and Wadsworth. Snipers had reportedly shot at the firemen when they rolled up. One fireman had been hit in the ear. Nothing serious. They pulled up and talked to the fire captain in charge.

"The shot came from that building there," he said, pointing to an old two-story brick apartment house. "We couldn't tell if it was a gun or a pellet gun," said the captain. It really didn't matter anyway. It was a felony either way.

Pete and his companions went into the building and started to kick down doors that would not open on command. The second door that Pete kicked twisted his ankle, but the pain was not bad. Pete and the other cops searched the building for the shooter. They didn't find the gun or the shooter, which did not surprise Pete. They left the scene with nothing else to do there.

"Any unit in the vicinity, a shooting, man down at Jefferson and Denker," the radio advised. They rolled on the call. A small group of black men were standing around a man lying on his back on the sidewalk. A man was sitting on top of the victim and pushing down on his chest periodically, as though trying to revive him. The cops got out of the cars and walked to the scene. It was bizarre. The victim had a large bullet hole right between his eyes. From the size of it, Pete guessed, .45 caliber. The dude sitting on the victim's chest kept pumping in and out on the dead man's chest, which caused blood and other stuff to come out of the hole. The others just stood there and watched.

"Hey, man," yelled Frank, "stop doin' that! Can't you see you're just pumping the seeds out of his gourd?" The man on top stopped and slid off. No one laughed until later when it was necessary. They never found the killer or the reason why the "Man with the Gourd" was shot.

"Looters at the intersection of Fifty-first and Broadway. Any unit in the vicinity, handle." Frank rogered the call and Brush Fire 1 and 2 rolled. At the intersection, the street was covered with running people. They were carrying everything and anything that wasn't bolted to the floor. Store windows were all broken out by now, and wholesale looting was the business at hand.

Pete and the guys got out and started chasing looters in all directions. There were few arrests during the riot. It's too much trouble, and the cases would probably never get to court anyway. The next best thing is to punish looters when they are caught in the act. It seemed fair to Pete.

Pete saw two black guys carrying a large TV set between them. A cop with a shotgun blasted the TV set to pieces out of the looters' hands as they walked with it. "If I can't have it, neither can they," the mad cop yelled. Oddly, that seemed to make sense to Pete.

An elderly black woman approached Pete and said, "Officer, not all of us are like that," she motioned to the looting going on in front of the officer's eyes.

"I know that, ma'am," said Pete. He saw the hurt and despair in her dark eyes and understood how she must feel. He thought briefly of how these things get started. Once they do, everything changes. It then becomes a survival game with very few rules to play by. He watched her walk sadly away.

Just then, a bottle crashed to the ground a few feet away from him. It almost had his name on it. He spun around in the direction from where the bottle had come. About a block away, he saw a man winding up to throw a second bottle. This one came closer, but Pete sidestepped out of its path.

Why are black people better athletes than us whites? he wondered. I couldn't throw a bottle that far on a bet, he thought as he raised his Smith & Wesson and took careful aim at the guy who was trying to brain him.

Pop! The .38 sounded weak in the open air of the night. No reaction from the thrower. He was winding up for another throw. *Pop!* Pete's second shot must have been too close for the thrower because he went away.

A large piece of concrete came by Pete's ear with a swish. He spun around and faced three black men, one of whom had just tried to kill him. Pete hadn't seen which one had thrown the rock. His first thought was to shoot one of the men, and that would be the guilty one. But that would make me just as bad as they are, he thought.

"Get the fuck out of here before I kill you, motherfuckers," he shouted. They left.

"Any unit in the vicinity, assist the officers with looters at Forty-seventh and Wadsworth," the radio blasted. They rolled. When they arrived at the location, they saw two officers covering the front door of a small "mom and pop" market on the corner. The Brush Fire units deployed and went in and dragged out the looters.

There were five men looting the store. Pete stood guard while the suspects were being searched. All at once, a suspect knocked one of the cops down and ran. Pete brought his pistol up and fired one shot at the fleeing burglar. His left arm flipped a little as the bullet hit it, but the dude didn't miss a stride. Pete decided not to shoot again. We'll nail the prick when he comes to get treatment at a hospital later, he thought.

Boom! A shotgun went off right next to Pete's ear. Pete saw the flame shoot two feet out of the barrel. The running dude pitched over forward on his belly and fell dead. The cop who had been knocked down had put an end to that criminal's career. Pete really couldn't feel sorry for the guy. It was stupid to run. He wondered why he did that.

The two plain-colored police cars cruised up Vermont Avenue and across Vernon. As the Brush Fire units passed Vernon, they saw two men in front of a jewelry store. One man was down on his hands and knees, trying to squeeze under a metal security fence that covered the front of the store. The fence had been bent up, and the man was just about in. The other dude was the lookout. He stood in front at the curb, shifting his head back and forth. The lookout obviously wasn't doing too well at his job because he failed to identify the approaching police cars full of uniformed cops.

As Pete and the other cops piled out of the two cars, they yelled, "Hold it! Don't move!" as seven loaded pistols were pointed at the pair. The lookout dude froze in his spot, but the other fool ran. He ran south on Vermont and was obviously trying to make it around the corner at Vernon and get away. He ran behind his lookout buddy, who was still frozen to his spot. At least a dozen shots were fired at the fleeing man. Pete did not shoot. He felt there were too many shooting as it was.

The running man slipped to one knee for an instant, then was up and around the corner, apparently unharmed by all the shooting. The lookout, however, had taken a round in his ass. A quick look showed a superficial wound, so the cops all piled back into the cars and went north.

"Make a right at the next street and come down the alley," Pete said. "Maybe we'll catch him doubling back." The car leaped ahead and the driver followed Pete's suggestion. As they turned into the dark alley behind the jewelry store and drove quietly south, they saw a shadowy figure near the rear of the jewelry store. The figure moved into the shadows as the cars approached him slowly. Since the night before, a curfew of 8:00 PM had been declared in an attempt to keep people off the streets. Anyone out on the streets after that time was subject to misdemeanor arrest. Whether this was the dude who got away or not, he was still committing a crime just by being there, since it was now about 2:00 AM.

As the car came abreast of the dark figure, Pete opened his door and stepped out of the car. He swung his baton and caught the man across the nose. The guy went down like a sack of potatoes. Pete shined his flashlight on the unconscious man.

"Wrong dude," he said. "Wonder what building he was breaking into?" Two of the cops helped Pete drag the man over to the side of the alley and laid him on a pile of trash.

"That guy will have to use two handkerchiefs just to blow his nose from now on." Frank laughed. Pete didn't feel sorry for him at all. Fuck him! If he were a law-abiding citizen, he would have been in his house, thought Pete. They piled back into the cars and drove around the corner to see a black-and-white stopped and two officers holding a man at gunpoint.

The man was seated on the sidewalk, leaning against the building. The cops stopped and got out.

"What you got?" asked Frank. They noticed the dude leaning on the wall was bleeding from several wounds and was, in fact, the man who had rabbited from the jewelry store around the corner.

"We heard shooting, and then this dude comes running around the corner like the cavalry is after him," said one officer. The dude looked up and wailed.

"The police shot me. They shot me here and here and here," he cried, as he pointed to his wounds, none of which looked to be life threatening.

"You, guys, know anything about this?" asked the cop holding the shotgun on the dude.

The Brush Fire guys looked at each other and in unison said, "We don't know anything about it."

Frank looked at the dude and waved his hand over him, saying, "Aw, he refused medical treatment anyway." So they all got back in their cars and left.

Pete thought about it as they drove away. He recounted in his mind the event that had just happened so he could understand his own feelings. Let's see, he thought. These two dudes are just getting ready to break into a jewelry store and steal the fucking place bare. We come along and catch them in the act. A felony. Burglary. One dude refuses to heed the warning to stop and runs away. He gets shot. Then he wants us to call an ambulance for him. As he recalled the incident, he felt better. He felt no sorrow for criminals who got what they asked for.

"Any unit in the vicinity, sniper shooting at vehicles on Washington Boulevard near Alameda Street." The Brush Fire units answered the call and headed for the location. Pete recalled the area was nothing but warehouses. What would a sniper be doing there? They rolled up and parked on the south side of Washington just west of Alameda. Pete and the other cops got out and stood listening to the silence of the night. It was about three in the morning. Damp quietness then *ping!* The sound of a bullet ricocheting off something. Pete and the other cops ducked behind their police car with their guns drawn.

"Where's it coming from?" asked Frank. "Sounded like a small caliber, probably a .22." There was a long silence. Time for the men to think. Pete's thoughts were probably similar to what all were thinking. Where was the shooter? What was he shooting at? Was he shooting at them? Did the shooter even know they were there? What do we do next? About five minutes passed.

Ping! Damn it, thought Pete. If we only knew where the asshole was, we could do something. "Anyone get a line on where the shots are coming from?" Pete asked.

One of the cops said, "They sound like they're coming from the west and north of us." His guess was as good as any, thought Pete. The hair on the back of Pete's neck went up as the realization dawned on him that he might be the target of a hidden sniper. Right now, the guy might have his ass in his sights and was squeezing the trigger. What a shitty, helpless feeling, he thought.

The officers decided to use the lead car as a shield and drive slowly down the alley near where the shots sounded like they were coming from. Pete recalled seeing soldiers in news reels doing the same things behind tanks during World War II. It worked for them, he thought.

Pete drove the car over to the entrance of the alley, and the other guys got out and walked behind the car as Pete drove it down the alley. He drove with one hand on the wheel while crouching down in the driver's seat, letting the idle of the engine move the car. About halfway down the alley, they stopped and listened.

Ping! Another shot! At them? They couldn't tell. There was a streetlight overhead in the alley about fifty feet away. Too much light. Pete raised his pistol to shoot the light out. His third shot hit the light. Why isn't it like in the movies? he wondered. His .38 now sounded loud in the alley. They waited and listened. Silence. Five minutes. Ten. Nothing. What do they do now? they thought. They waited another ten minutes. No more shots.

"Maybe the sound of you shooting out the streetlight scared them off?" offered Denton.

"Maybe," said Pete. They left a few minutes later and never found out who was shooting at whom.

Cruising down Avalon near Ninety-fifth Street, the cops spotted a small group of black men standing in a parking lot behind a closed filling station. It was well after curfew, and they had no business there. The officers drove into the lot and questioned the men.

"Man, we ain't doin' nothin'," said the smart-ass dude wearing a wig with a high pompadour. His attitude was lacking in understanding of the current situation. Frank and Fred Dourgherty decided to change that. Frank snapped the muzzle of the 12 gauge up under the chin of the smart ass and cocked the hammer. Pete didn't like that. What if the dude jumped and the gun went off? The dude's attitude was changing rapidly, however. Fred grabbed the man's wig off his head.

"Hey, man, dat wig cos' me $125," cried the smart-ass.

"No shit," said Fred. Then he threw the wig in the ground and stomped it a few times.

"Let's get out of here," said Pete. "You, assholes, get off the street, or we'll throw your asses in jail for curfew. Do you understand?" Pete said with his face up close to the dude's.

"Yas, sir," said the smart-ass, who had now seen the light. "We be gone!" The dude picked up his trampled wig, and the group left.

A tow truck driver was waving wildly at the approaching police cars. Pete's crew stopped. "There are two guys in that Hudson's store there. They are stealing clothes, and we think they set it on fire," came the breathless explanation of the man behind the wheel of the tow truck. As the two police cars and the tow truck drove toward the Corvair parked outside the department store, two men were seen running out and putting items of clothing into the backseat of the Corvair.

The cops, in full uniform, rolled up and jumped out. "Okay, motherfuckers, you're under arrest." Pete wondered who yelled that. The two men dropped the clothing they were carrying and ran south on the sidewalk. "Don't do that, you dumb assholes!" yelled Pete in his head. A volley of shots rang out, and one of the men fell to the ground. The other ran behind a building. The fallen man started to get up. Pete had not fired his revolver—yet. Stay down, you dumb shit, Pete thought. *Pop! Pop!* Several more shots, and the guy stayed down. He was dead when the ambulance arrived.

In the meantime, the store *was* on fire. Several of the guys went in and alerted residents who lived on the second floor. They were saved. The store went up in flames, no doubt set by the two suspects. The big windows in front of the store crashed out onto the sidewalk. Soon the whole store was a vacant lot of the future.

The dawn was coming up. Pete and the Brush Fire unit were beat. The night had flown by fast but had taken its toll on the stamina of the troops, who had been on twelve-hour shifts for the second day. Rumor had it the National Guard would soon come into Los Angeles, the City of the Angels. Hurry up, thought Pete. He found a phone that worked and called Noel to let her know he was safe.

Just hearing her voice brought him back to reality. Back to the world he wanted to return to. This world was going the wrong way. Black people acting crazy. White people acting crazy because black people were acting crazy. Where will this end?

He had not shot at people when he didn't feel right about it. He had knocked some heads, but this was looting and riot. This city didn't deserve this! This city wasn't the cause of the black people's problems. It was more like the answer, thought Pete. How dare anyone—black or white or any color, for that matter—screw up his city? There was a lot of good in the city. A lot of good people here. They look to us, the police, to protect them. Most of them can't protect themselves or don't have the guts. Someone had to do it. Hasn't it always been the cops? Don't we always clean up the mess that society makes? The poor, dumb bastards hate us most of the time, but when there's dirty work, call a cop! We'll do the dirty work because it's for ourselves we do it, as well as for you, assholes. Pete thought of all the times he had saved people's asses and got nothing from it but the self-satisfaction of doing something good.

Hell, one time he had pulled several people out of a burning hotel on First Street on his way to work. Flames weren't licking his ass, but the smoke was just as dangerous. He got them out. The fact that there was no press or news media there didn't matter to him.

Then there was the time when he and two other cops saved an old man from a robber. They had just happened along in time to see the dude jump on the old man and take him down like a lion making a kill. The asshole went to jail. Nobody cared but the asshole, the old man, and the cops who made the bust. No fanfare. No TV or radio. Just doing the job.

Pete knew that most cops operated that way. They don't look for any reward or notoriety. They don't give a shit about that anyway. He thought about all the times cops had pulled the public's collective ass out of the fire. Where would this country be if it didn't have independent police departments? The "thin blue line," they called it. The line between life and death. The line between tyranny and freedom. Between sanity and chaos. Only those who have lived in a foreign country know the feeling. There, the state controls the police. Here in the United States, the police are locally controlled by cities and counties, not countries. Local control of police is the essence of freedom. We have it, and most people don't even know it!

All these thoughts and thoughts of Noel ran through his mind as he dropped off the edge of sleep. Tomorrow loomed as a challenge he didn't want to face. Fuck it! He fell asleep.

CHAPTER SEVENTEEN

THE END AND AFTERMATH, WATTS, 1965

On the third day of the riot, the National Guard moved in. As they rolled in with jeeps and trucks, some of which had .30-caliber machine guns mounted on them, Pete started to relax and think positive about the outcome of what had been happening the last few days. The Guard consisted of many veterans of the Korean War and even World War II. Some of them were also police officers in civilian life. Pete ran into one of his friends from night watch who had been activated into the Guard.

"You know those crazy people in Sacramento were going to send the Guard in here with empty rifles and no ammo," said Bill Haymes, who had been called up as a soldier. That made him no longer a BCMC but now a second lieutenant in the Fortieth Division, California Army National Guard. "I told them I just came out of the riot zone after two days, and if they didn't send the men in with loaded weapons, they might as well not send them at all!"

"Don't they know what's been happening here? Don't they watch TV?" Pete asked. It seemed as though those in elected offices were more concerned how they would look after the fact and didn't have the balls to act assertively now. Someone should send their asses out there, and maybe that will change their minds.

"Well, fortunately," said Haymes, "the second in command of the National Guard is an LA cop, or we'd all be in deep shit." Pete now recalled that he had heard about the cop who was high in the Guard.

"Boy, did we luck out there," Frank said as they all shook their heads in agreement.

The rioting was quickly put under control by setting up roadblocks and a show of force by the National Guard. The rioters soon found out that the military way of controlling riots is much more direct and efficient than the civilian police.

For Pete, the riot from this point on was merely a cleanup action. He pulled guard duty on the PAB one night. The fourth night, he and a bunch of other cops were assigned to protect the main jail in Lincoln Heights. There was a rumor that an attack would be mounted to break the prisoners out of jail. Though it sounded very far-fetched, the city was taking no chances. Pete and a squad of motor officers were assigned to stand guard duty in the front of the jail at Avenue Nineteen. At the jail's rear was the Los Angeles River bed. That was easily covered. The street in front was blocked off at each end of the block, and no one but police or sheriffs were allowed into the perimeter. Inside the jail was a zoo.

"Listen to those mothers howl," said one of the troops in front of the jail with Pete. Frank was there; so was John Sudinski and Ron Byron. "Someone said there are over three thousand assholes in there from riot arrests," advised John Sudinski. "I wonder how many of them will ever serve time behind this?" he questioned.

Ron answered with the opinion that everyone agreed with, "I bet not one of the whipdicks ever serves a day. The only punishment they'll probably get was the ass kickin' they got in the street!" Everyone laughed and nodded agreement. The howling inside the jail went on all night. It sounded like feeding time at the zoo. The "attack" never materialized, and the boys went home tired and cold as the dawn came up.

After the Guard secured the streets and the fires were put out, the cops had a chance to really see the damage that had been wrought by the riot. It was mind-boggling. Whole city blocks had been leveled by fire. The business district that used to be 103rd Street looked like a war zone after the bombers had dropped their loads. Stores had been completely stripped clean. Dudes on the street were sporting new clothes. The joke around the police station was "How do you like my new riot jacket?"

The BCMCs wondered what had been accomplished by all of the destruction and crime during the riot. What was the point? To protest? Protest what? Slavery in the 1850s? The way people live in Mississippi? Los Angeles was nothing like that. Never had been. It shocked the police department to the very foundations.

LAPD found out they were not prepared or trained for anything like the Watts Riot. They hadn't nearly enough shotguns to meet the need. The cops were not trained in how to handle snipers on rooftops. They didn't know anything about Molotov cocktails. Crowd control training was a joke. Baton training was badly needed. "In other words, we almost lost the city," one of the old-timers stated in a debriefing after the riot. He was right.

Information from inside sources revealed that the National Guard fired over thirty-five thousand rounds of ammunition in putting down the riot. The official count of the injured in the riot was 1,032. The number who died as a direct result of the riot was officially reported to be thirty-four. All the cops knew better. They had seen and heard too much to believe that. They had seen a number of Crispy Critters burn with the buildings in which they had been caught looting. They had found several bodies that had been unceremoniously buried in backyards and under houses to escape notice. Hundreds came in for medical treatment for "accidental" gunshot wounds in the days after the riot. The men in Brush Fire 1 and 2 learned a little about their experiences from the newspapers. Of the 3,952 people arrested during the riot, more than three-fourths had previous police records. More than six hundred buildings were damaged during the riot and over two hundred were totally destroyed, mostly by fire.

The man who Pete had shot in the arm and who was later killed by the cop with the shotgun—he had been wanted for jumping bail on a rape charge. No wonder he didn't want to go to jail. The man with the seeds leaking out of his gourd—no one ever found out who shot him or why. The two dudes who burned the Hudson's store and ran—ballistics showed the man who died was killed by a bullet from Fred Dourgherty's pistol. A coroner's inquest was pending.

The officers who were subpoenaed to the coroner's inquest couldn't understand why until they got there. The attorney representing the deceased's family was a local black dude who was rumored to be a Communist with the ACLU. All the officers had been warned that this was serious business and not to show any emotion during the hearing.

Coroner's inquests may be held any time there is a dispute as to how a human being died. In most cases, the procedure is routine. An auto accident, a heart attack, and an accidental drowning are all handled in a routine manner because the cause of death is plainly seen. In cases of murder or suicide or some disputed cause of death, the coroner calls an inquest to hear evidence, under oath, as to the facts of the death, and then a coroner's jury will determine the legal cause of death. These causes may range from accidental to homicide to justifiable homicide and several others types of rulings. In this case, the family of the deceased was accusing the police department of murder.

Murder? thought Pete. How could anyone stretch the imagination so far to think that the dude Fred shot was murdered? The Brush Fire cops sat quietly in court while the attorney for the family put on his case. As the case unfolded, Pete could not believe his ears. They had witnesses who testified that Pete and his fellow officers rolled up on these "poor, innocent boys, who were just trying to save their clothes from the fire, and shot them down like dogs!" One witness testified that she was in a phone booth, "callin' her mama in Loosiana," when she saw these cops drive up and get out of their cars and shoot the man down in cold blood.

The second witness was in the upstairs apartment across the street from the store and "saw the whole thing." He told the same story as the woman who was calling her mother at four in the morning. For the first time, Pete felt a chill go up his spine. His mind started to realize that if the jury believed these witnesses, their asses were in bad trouble. Pete knew how juries could swing from one extreme to the other. He also knew that the press would have a field day on this if it went bad for them. Pete's guts started to go cold. His mind raced with doubt. What really happened that night? Were those guys just trying to save their belongings from the fire? Did we shoot at innocent men?

He reeled back the memories of that night and reviewed them in his mind. Then it dawned on him. Wait a minute, he told himself. Remember when you pulled up there, the witnesses told you the dudes were stealing from the store? They had watched them do it! You and the guys saw them come out and put stuff in the Corvair. After the shooting, you saw the clothes, and they still had the store tags on them! You dumb shit! These assholes are playing with your mind!

Then the detectives testified that the clothing was stolen and still had the price tags on them. They had arrested the other dude, who got away, later when he came to the hospital for treatment for gunshot wounds. It was a clear-cut case, and the jury deemed the shooting to be justifiable homicide. The BCMCs went home very relieved and a lot wiser.

Things started to get back to "normal" for Pete and the rest of the motor cops. Back to the routine traffic stops. But now there were different feelings in the street. Black people were waiting to see what whites would do and whites waiting to see what blacks would do. They both did the same things: got into traffic court. In court it was business as usual.

Traffic court is a place about which many books could be written. Some of them humorous and others serious. Of course, to a BCMC, traffic was serious business. Yet the humor was always there. Stories went around the department about some of the humorous happenings in court. Pete recalled one story that

G. L. Wilson told in the coffee room one evening as the cops prepared for roll call. Wilson was one of the funniest storytellers on the watch.

"The court is in session," related Wilson, "and the judge was calling the cases for the calendar. He told everyone in the court to stand when he called their name and tell him if they wanted a court trial or a jury trial or if they wanted to change their plea to guilty. The judge started to call the names, and when he got to J. Willy Gumbutt, the dude stood up. 'What do you want to do with your case, Mr. Gumbutt?' the judge asked. 'I wants a coat trial, Yo Honor.' 'If you want a court trial, Mr. Gumbutt, you must waive your right to a trial by jury. Do you waive your right to a trial by jury?' J. Willy Gumbutt looked at his friend Leroy for advice, and he say, 'Waive your right!' So J. Willy waved his right hand in the air at the judge, and the whole courtroom came apart laughing!" The coffee room erupted in laughter. "That's no shit, man," said Wilson, as he waved his right hand in the air. "I swear!"

Other courtroom incidents were not so fun. One patrol officer was being harassed by a judge during a trial. Contrary to popular belief, all judges were not friendly toward police. Many judges were hostile toward police and would give the defendant every break possible. This particular judge was very hostile. Sometimes they just didn't like the manner in which officers testified or just flat didn't like cops. This judge ridiculed the testimony of the arresting officers and was giving them a hard time.

"Officer, your testimony here today has been a disgrace to the police department," said the judge with his lip curled up in hate.

"Well, Judge," said the officer, "if you'd get off your dead ass and get out and see what's going on in the streets, maybe you'd change your mind!"

"Don't speak to me like that, or I'll hold you in contempt of court," yelled the judge.

"I have nothing but contempt for this court," said the officer. The judge then had his bailiff take the officer into custody and put him in jail for three days. The cops on the street thought of the officer as a hero. Not to mention the fact that the sheriff's department gave the officer a private cell with all the comforts of home during his three-day "vacation."

Pete saw court as an important part of his job and tried to do the best job he could in his testimony. He found that sometimes it's not what you said, but it's how you said it that impressed judges and juries. Many officers looked too stiff and military when they appeared in court. They reminded him of the comic character Dudley Do-right on TV. Pete always tried to be relaxed and natural when testifying. Another trick of the trade Pete discovered was to always testify in an assertive manner, whether you knew the answer to the question being asked or not. If he didn't know the answer, he'd simply say, "I don't know" and not try to fake his way through. When he was asked of his opinion about the sobriety of a defendant, Pete would always answer with a definite answer. "In my opinion, the defendant was under the influence of an alcoholic beverage at the time of arrest." Very straightforward and with no doubt in mind. After all, that's what the defense was looking for: reasonable doubt. Many officers answered questions with "I believe so" or "I think so." These types of answers were not positive enough in Pete's estimation. "What the hell did you arrest the guy for if you only 'believed' he was drunk?" Pete would argue with his partners when they would testify like that. "If you are not sure of the guy's sobriety, then you shouldn't book him" was Pete's philosophy. After a few years of experience, Pete got very good at playing the court game with clever attorneys. It's similar to mental chess, Pete thought. He enjoyed it. He liked to make defense attorneys squirm when they couldn't get the answers they wanted from him on the stand.

CHAPTER EIGHTEEN

THE LONE RANGER RIDES AGAIN

When officers went end of watch on motors, they were required to take their motorcycles home and garage them before they went anywhere else. Sometimes that rule got in the way. Pete had been spending a lot of time in court and working hard on night watch, and his love life was suffering. He had been invited to come over to Noel's new house in Altadena after work. What a pain in the ass, thought Pete, to ride all the way home and then come all the way back to Noel's. He decided to go to her house right from work when he got off at 11:30 PM. Pete rang off in Highland Park and stopped by a liquor store for a bottle of scotch. He put the bottle in his saddlebags and headed for Noel's. He parked the motor behind her house, out of sight of inquisitive eyes. Pete and Noel had a nice evening snack and some drinks and sex. A lot of drinks for Pete. When he left Noel's, he was pretty loaded. He told her he would be very careful while riding home and not to worry.

Pete looked at his watch. It was after 3:00 AM. The streets should be quiet by now, and he could make it safely home with no trouble. As he rode south on Allen Street to the stoplight at Washington, he heard sirens to his left. He looked east on Washington and saw a dark car driving without headlights swerve around a corner about a block away. A few seconds later, a Los Angeles County Sheriff's unit came around the corner in hot pursuit. This was too much for Pete. He made a left turn and headed in the direction of the pursuit. The fleeing car and Pete approached each other head-on. Then the dark car made a right turn and went north with the sheriff's car right on his tail. Pete turned in behind the sheriff, thinking to back him up, if necessary.

Suddenly the suspect's car slammed on its brakes and skidded to a stop. The left door flew open, and the suspect was out on foot. By the time the two sheriffs reacted, the suspect was by then running in the direction from which they had come. He ran straight at Pete's motorcycle. When he saw Pete, he swerved into a service station lot. Pete turned left and yelled, "Stop, asshole!" Pete's bike hit the curb and bounced up and over onto the sidewalk. Oh shit, thought Pete, I'm going to fall down. But, by some miracle, he didn't fall down. Pete rode around the filling station to the left to head the suspect off. On the other side of the station, Pete pulled up and got off his motor at the same time the suspect came running around the other side. He saw Pete and skidded to a stop, trying to reverse his direction. When he turned around, he ran right into the arms of one of the deputies who had been chasing him. They both went down in a pile of arms and legs. As the deputy and the suspect struggled on the ground, Pete walked over and waited for the right opportunity. When the suspect rolled over on top of the deputy, Pete saw his chance. He kicked the suspect in the head. *Clunk!* The suspect went out like a light. Surprised, the deputy looked up at his, until now, unnoticed helper. While the deputies were handcuffing the suspect, other sheriff's cars were rolling in on the location. Pete mounted his motorcycle and was about to get the hell out of there. He didn't want to be questioned as to why he was the only person there wearing a blue uniform in a sea of khakis, nor his sobriety while riding a police motorcycle. As he started to leave, a sheriff's deputy ran over and asked, "Hey, who are you?" Without even thinking, Pete's hand went down to his spare ammo pouch, and he took out a rather dirty bullet. He handed it to the deputy and crammed the bike in gear. "Hi-yo Silver, away!" Pete yelled as he sped off into the night. He got home safely and vowed not to do that ever again. He also decided not to tell anyone what had happened. Sure enough, the next day the watch commander was looking for "The Lone Ranger" who had been reported by the Altadena sheriffs the night before. Pete waited a whole year before telling anyone about the incident, until the one-year statute of limitations for misdemeanors had expired.

"Hey, did you hear about Dwight Davidson?" asked Ron Byron as they met in the hall outside of the roll call room. Pete hadn't heard the news that was on everyone's lips that day.

"No," said Pete, "what's going on?"

"Davidson shot his wife and then killed himself," said Ron. The reality of the news hit Pete hard. Police suicides were nothing new. Being a cop was a tough job for keeping positive and out of depression. Pete knew Dwight Davidson and had worked with him several times at Central and also since Dwight had come on motors. Dwight had been a quiet sort of guy. He was friendly but not what you would call gregarious. Several guys, including Pete and Ron, knew Dwight was having a tough time at home. He had separated from his wife and had been drinking heavily lately.

At roll call, the sergeant made the announcement about the death and funeral arrangements. Not much else was discussed about the circumstances except for some comments by Lieutenant Cabbage Head, who always seemed to say the wrong thing at the wrong time. He seemed to think this was a good opportunity to impose his warnings to the troops about the evils of liquor and loose women.

"Men," said Cabbage Head, "the easiest way to get yourself in trouble on this job is to mess around with other women. We all know they are out there. I've turned down many offers that I knew would get me in trouble. Anyway, I've got more than I can handle at home."

"Well, let's all go over to your house, Lieutenant," came a voice from the back of the room. The laughter seemed to break the tension, and the guys relaxed a little. Cabbage Head could see he was fighting a losing battle and shut up. After roll call, Ron and Pete went to their coffee spot prior to going to the beat.

"What happened?" Pete asked Ron as they sat down at the table.

"I heard that Davidson was trying to get back together with his wife, and she wasn't going for it. She had found out about the other woman and was pissed, I guess. I got it from a friend in Homicide that he had dumped the other broad and was really trying to get things straight. He had quit drinking and was getting his act back together. The problem was the two women had been arguing back and forth, and Davidson was in the middle. He was so fucked up that he blew his cool and went to his house, wanting to talk to his wife. They drove somewhere, and when the talking broke down, I guess he pulled his two inch and let her have it, then himself," explained Ron.

Pete thought of the times he and Dwight had worked together. How could a guy get so screwed up as to do a thing like this? There had been times when he had been really down himself but never contemplated suicide. He thought about Evie and her murder and how strange it seemed to think about a person being a living, moving thing one day and the next day—dead. Cops thought about death on many occasions but only for brief periods of time. They realized how quickly death can come. Not just to the other guy but to you or a friend. Pete and Ron sat and discussed other guys they had known who were gone.

"Remember Rick Monahan who got nailed by the drunk on the Golden State Freeway?" asked Ron. Pete remembered. The poor asshole was standing alongside a car on the shoulder of the freeway, and a deuce hit him.

"What about Lee Sweet?" reminded Pete. Lee had crashed while in pursuit of a violator earlier that year. Big cop funeral. Police always did a good job of burying their own.

"It's one thing to get done in by a job-related incident," Pete noted, "but I can't think of any reason I would blow my own brains out."

"That is, assuming you had any," said Ron.

"Fuck you, you bald-headed asshole!"

"*Officer* Bald-headed Asshole, please!" Ron corrected. That ended the conversation about death.

Pete and Noel were hitting it off pretty well over the last few months. Noel had asked Pete to move in with her. Pete had to be careful because the department frowned on couples living together without benefit of marriage. But, to Pete, it seemed like the thing to do. Noel's ex-husband had been giving her a bad time. He didn't pay his child support regularly, and Noel didn't make enough to live on and support two growing boys too. Pete had a real dislike for people who failed to follow the orders of the court. Pete told Noel that unless she did something about the situation, he would. She explained it to her ex-husband and got some action. The child support payments resumed promptly. It's amazing what a man can do when he finds out he no longer has someone buffaloed and scared.

After Pete moved in with Noel, life seemed to smooth out for both of them. At first, Pete had trouble getting used to the kids. After all, dropping into the "ready made" family can be traumatic. The boys were only boys, and Pete understood that, having come from a family of all boys himself. Noel's career in dentistry was doing well. She was in charge of a dental clinic that served the Pasadena area's poor and welfare recipients. Noel's job brought her in contact with some of the same humorous incidents Pete had been telling her about from his job.

"You'll never believe what a woman said today when she called in for an appointment for the VD clinic next door to mine," Noel related to Pete at lunch. "My friend Aggie was working the switchboard when this call came in. Aggie asked her what seemed to be the trouble, and the lady replied, 'I's havin' trouble with my Virginia'!" They laughed as they compared stories about funny happenings on their respective jobs. Pete had an equally funny story.

"I stopped this guy one time for a violation and asked for his driver's license. When he handed it to me, it was torn in four pieces! I told him I had to cite him for having a 'mutilated license.' He said, 'That can't be, officer. My license don't mutilate 'til 1969.'" They both had a good laugh over that one.

Pete hated to shop while on duty, although the activity seemed to be one that many cops enjoyed. Not that he was above doing it. Pete just hated to shop for anything—period. His partner Bill Haymes was always building something or repairing something that required a part. Bill and Pete had been partners long enough to know each other pretty well. When Bill wanted to stop off at the local hardware store at the beginning of the shift, Pete rebelled.

"Bullshit," said Pete, "if you want to go rummaging through piles of nuts and bolts, go ahead. Call me when you get through." Pete and Bill knew that splitting up with your partner was not permitted, once you were teamed up. The purpose of the two-man team was to provide security for each other. Sometimes officers violated the rule.

"Okay," said Bill, "I'll call you on the air to meet me. Stay out of trouble!" Bill went off down Washington Boulevard. Pete rode south on Figueroa Street from Washington. He had only gone a couple of blocks when he saw a Chevy ahead of him swerve over the double center line. Pete flipped on the red lights and got behind the Chevy.

As the Chevy continued south on Figueroa, Pete checked the speedometer. Thirty-five right on the button. The Chevy didn't slow down, so Pete honked his horn at the violator's car. No results. What the hell is wrong with this dude? he wondered. At Twenty-third Street, Pete hit the siren. The Chevy made a left turn and then another left on Flower Street, but didn't slow or pull over. With siren wailing, Pete followed the Chevy for about two more blocks. Great, thought Pete, here I am split up from my partner, and I can't go in pursuit! In order to "go in pursuit," Pete would have to go on the radio and announce to the operator at Communications Division that he was in pursuit of a vehicle that would not stop for a violation. Communications would then shut down all frequencies so they could devote all efforts to the apprehension of the pursued vehicle. Then everyone would find out that Pete and his partner were split up. If there were an accident or other injury, the team would be criticized for splitting up during patrol hours. Pete was in a dilemma. He wanted to stop that car but didn't want to go in "official" pursuit.

The car was now northbound on Flower Street, approaching the overpass of the Santa Monica Freeway. The Chevy was not trying to get away; he just wasn't stopping. The vehicle continued at thirty-five miles an hour under the bridge. Pete's mind raced for an answer to his problem. Something was definitely wrong with the dude driving the Chevy, and Pete wanted to know what it was. As Pete was about to go under the bridge, he remembered a trick that one of the old-timers had told him about. The older Harley-Davidson motorcycles had a hand grip on the left handlebar that you twisted to retard the spark to the engine and make it easier to start when the kick starter was operated. Pete remembered that when you retarded the spark, then shut off the ignition switch, the engine would backfire when the ignition switch was turned on again. He gave it a try. *Pow!* The engine backfired as Pete rode under the bridge, giving the sound even more volume. The Chevy swerved right and then left and pulled over to the right curb and bumped to a stop. As Pete pulled up to the car, he drew his pistol. The young black kid who had just stolen the car from a used car lot jumped out and started to run.

"The next shot goes through you, asshole," yelled Pete, as he leveled his pistol at the dude. The youth stopped and raised his hands in the air. Pete approached the youth from behind. Putting away his gun, he grabbed the young man and slammed him to the sidewalk. As he cuffed the dude's hands behind his back, he noticed several people watching his actions. He wondered how they would react to his arrest method. Things were still sensitive since the riots.

"Good work, officer," said a man standing nearby. "I put in a call for help for you."

"You did what?" asked Pete.

"I heard you shooting at that guy, so I put in a call for help for you," said the man, proud of his good citizenship. Pete was thankful that some people would still help a cop in these days; but now, damn it, every cop in the vicinity would be headed his way to 'help' him, and he was trying to be cool because he was split up from his partner. He quickly went to his radio and put out a "Code 4" on any assistance and advised that there had been no "shooting." Haymes rolled up about that time, his eyes rolling around in his head.

"I leave you alone for a few minutes, and you get in a shooting," he complained. Pete explained what had happened, and Bill felt better. Just then, a man who said he was a reporter for a local radio station came up in response to the "all units" call that the Good Samaritan had put out. Pete explained that there had been no shooting and how he had fooled the dude by backfiring his engine under the bridge. The newsman was fascinated by the incident and insisted that Pete do an interview on tape. At first, Pete declined. If the boss heard it, Pete could get in trouble. On the other hand, Pete's ego was at stake. He did the interview. Fortunately, it played in the early morning hours of the next day, and only a few of the guys heard it. Pete got away unscathed. He also got a commendation letter from the Good Samaritan who called for help. Pete appreciated that, in spite of the scare it caused him.

Off-duty cops sometimes work jobs with the movie studios. Pete had several friends who did. As Pete was cruising east on Hollywood Boulevard, his beat for the night, he saw a movie crew working on a set in front of a building on Hollywood Boulevard. The off-duty cops direct traffic around the movie set locations. In California, only regular sworn police officers can legally direct traffic, so movie studios have several on each location. Pete recognized an old-timer named Blackberg as one of the off-duty cops working the set. Pete pulled over to say hello.

"Hi, Blackie," hailed Pete. "How's it going?"

"Hey, Pete! Not bad. Just rakin' in a few extra bucks for my retirement," said the wrinkled old BCMC.

"What movie are they shooting?" asked Pete, hoping to see some important, famous people today.

"It's a movie about our favorite subject . . . cops and robbers." Blackie smiled. Pete hated cop movies. The moviemakers always portrayed cops in a manner that was, in Pete's opinion, irresponsible. They made cops do things in the movies that would get a real-life cop fired instantly. It made people think that cops really did those kinds of things and gave people a wrong impression. If a real cop skidded around the streets in a car like they did in the movies, he wouldn't last a minute. He'd either be dead or fired. Cops don't skid cars around, except in very rare pursuits. Damaging a city vehicle is a big no-no on the department. Cops never say, "Freeze" either. Movie cops all say it. Pete had never heard any cop say that. They said, "Stop" or "Hold it" or "Don't move" but never "Freeze."

Movies cops always hold their pistols with two hands. The only time a real cop would do that was if he actually had time to take aim to fire. Most cops involved in shootings say that things happened so fast the officer never had time to aim anyway. Movie cops even run holding their gun with both hands. "Did you ever try to run clasping your hands together?" Pete had asked a friend who was not a cop. "It's hard to run that way."

"Another thing that makes me sick about movies is when a cop has to shoot someone in self-defense or in the commission of a crime. The movie cop always agonizes over having to shoot another human being to save his own ass. That's bullshit! None of the cops I ever knew who had to kill someone in the line of duty ever lost any sleep over it because of guilt. In most cases, it was him or them! As long as the cop was right, that's all that mattered to him."

"Do you mean cops are that cold?" asked the friend.

"It's not a matter of cold or warm. It's a matter of self-preservation and logic. No cop wants to kill anyone, unless he has to. It puts their whole future and their family's future on the line. The reports are horrendous, and the news media will eat you alive, if they can. What I'm saying is that, if it was necessary and righteous, cops don't dwell on it like the movies and TV make it sound. That's all."

"Well, I think they are cold," said the man in defense of his position and feelings.

"I'm sorry, pal," said Pete, "do you know what people have told me when a cop gets shot and killed?"

"What?"

"That's what he gets paid for!" they say. That's what he gets paid for? To die? In fact, they pay truck drivers and plumbers more than they do cops! Should they die too for their jobs? Shit no!" Pete heard himself starting to get loud. He thought of the time when John Sudinski got on his soapbox at the station. Now Pete understood how it happened.

As Pete stood talking to Blackie on Hollywood Boulevard, the director of the movie walked over and greeted Pete.

"How about a part in your movie?" asked Pete in a kidding way.

"Have you had experience in films before?" asked the director with his nose up in the air.

"No, but I have a lot of Polaroid time," said Pete. The director looked at him strangely and walked away, shaking his head.

Hollywood Boulevard is a strange place to work in 1968, thought Pete. He thought of all the interesting things he'd learned about people since he became a BCMC. People will believe almost anything a cop tells them, if the cop can keep a straight face. Pete was working Hollywood Boulevard one evening when he had an idea for an experiment in psychology. He saw this "extremely graceful" man walking down the Boulevard and pulled alongside of him as he walked down the sidewalk.

"Pull over to the wall," ordered Pete, as he motioned with his gloved hand. The man moved over and stopped close to the wall of a building. Pete got off his motorcycle and took a little extra time taking off his gloves, pulling the fingers out one by one, and then tossing the gloves onto his motorcycle seat with a graceful gesture.

"What did I do, officer?" asked the man with the unmistakable lisp to his voice.

"You were taking ten steps in a five-step zone," said Pete in his most serious "cop" voice.

"You mean there's a speed limit for walking now?" asked the man with a wide-eyed expression of disbelief. Pete stifled his smile and remained serious in the interest of science.

"Yes, sir," he explained. "You see, people were starting to walk too fast on Hollywood Boulevard, and there have been accidents caused by it; so the city has passed a new law about walking too fast." The guy was close but not quite buying Pete's story.

"You see those lines on the sidewalk?" asked Pete, pointing to the expansion cracks in the cement.

"Yes," answered the man.

"Well, we hired an expert in walking safety, and he has advised us that a person should not take more than five steps in one of those squares. Do you understand?" asked Pete, looking directly into the eyes of the man. The guy fell apart under Pete's gaze.

"Well, I certainly didn't know about it, officer."

"I won't cite you this time, but please tell all your friends about the new law, okay?"

"Yes, sir! Thank you for not giving me a ticket."

"That's all right," said Pete as he put his gloves back on and mounted his motorcycle. About two blocks down the street, Pete cracked up laughing. His experiment was a success. Most of the time, people will believe anything a cop tells them.

On another occasion, Pete was working 77th Division with Bill Haymes on "Imperialist Highway." Pete and Bill had been involved in a couple of contacts with the local citizens who had been rather bizarre. When Pete had told Noel about it, she didn't believe people would do those things. Bill's wife had said basically the same thing, so Pete and Bill decided to offer proof in the form of tape recordings.

Bill got hold of a small tape recorder and a microphone with a long wire. Pete put the recorder in his saddlebag and the microphone wire up the sleeve of his motorcycle jacket so he could hold it in his hand while talking, and they waited for an opportunity to record some good stuff.

The car went speeding east on Imperial Highway, and Pete and Bill went after it. When they pulled the car over, Pete plugged in the microphone and went up to the driver's window. There were two middle-aged black men in the car. Both had been drinking and were borderline candidates for the slammer.

"What I do, office?" asked the driver with a very nervous voice.

"Well, sir," said Pete in his "official" voice, "you went through the cataforce back there by that moorat. You could have had a sudigat fender and cravitzed real bad," explained Pete as he held the hidden microphone up close to the driver.

"Say what?" asked the old man behind the wheel. He turned to his passenger and asked, "Did you understand what da man said?"

"Man," he answered, "I doan' unstan' white folks no way."

"What I did, office?" asked the driver again. Pete repeated the phrase verbatim for the man.

"Please, office, if you let me slide this time, I swear I'll never do it again," pleaded the old man.

"Do what?" asked Pete as he looked the man in the eye.

The old man was stuck for an answer, but after a brief hesitation, he answered.

"What you said I did!" That was good enough for Pete and Bill, and they let the dudes go with a warning. The tape came out great except no one would believe it hadn't been staged.

CHAPTER NINETEEN

CODE B

Rainy days are a pain in the ass, thought Pete. Motor cops are more or less "grounded" in foul weather. The LAPD motor squad does not ride in the rain. The safety of the officers is the main reason. So little rain falls on the City of Angeles that the rubber from tires and oil from engines collects on the street's surface and becomes very slick when rain finally does come to Los Angeles. When the weatherman predicts rain, the motor cops go on alert for communications to advise them whether or not to ride in to work or to drive their cars. They listen to the police radio on the motorcycle or telephone Communications Division for the code. "Code A" meant ride the motorcycle. "Code B" meant drive your car.

On Code B days, officers are assigned to work Accident Investigation (AI), or they may be assigned to serve warrants. Serving warrants is the easier of the jobs because the officers can goof off and make a few stops looking for people for whom warrants have been issued for various misdemeanor violations, such as unpaid tickets and other failures to appear in court. When you work AI, you usually end up working pretty hard because the Los Angeles drivers seem to go insane when it rains. Even though most of the people who live in Los Angeles come from somewhere else, amnesia sets in, and they forget how they used to drive when it rains in Southern California.

It was Code B today, and Pete was assigned to work AI with an AI officer named Joe Adama. Joe had been working AI for several years, so Pete could relax and depend on Joe to help him do the accident reports properly. Accident reports must be done according to specific rules and procedures that require special training for officers. Motor cops do not get that training—to a great degree. Their job was to enforce traffic laws. The job of accident investigation was mainly the responsibility of Accident Investigation Division.

Pete checked out the car while Joe got his gear together. They had been assigned to work 77th Division on day watch. The first call was a minor accident involving a vehicle that ran into a fence around a school. Pete and Joe arrived and determined that there were no injuries, but since the school fence had been damaged, a report was necessary because city property was involved. The lady driving the car was elderly and black.

"What happened, Mrs. Johnson?" asked Joe as he prepared to take down the party's statement.

"Well, I was pullin' out my driveway an' I went to mash on the brakes, an' I mashed on the foot feed instead," said the old woman.

"You mashed on the what?" asked Joe.

"The foot feed," repeated the woman.

"Hey, Joe, don't you know what the foot feed is?" taunted Pete. "You'll have to excuse him, Ma'am. He hasn't been in this country very long," chided Pete. "The foot feed is connected to the carvarator, and when you mash on it, the car goes faster," explained Pete.

"Das right," agreed the lady. Joe went along with the program, and the tow truck arrived to pull the woman's car out of the school fence. After they left the accident scene and cleared, Pete explained the language barrier to Joe.

"Joe, I thought you'd been around long enough to translate the language," said Pete as they cruised down Avalon Boulevard. "To be a good cop in LA, you gotta speak three languages: English, Spanish, and Dude. I know you speak Spanish. Your English is a little suspect, though," kidded Pete. He knew Joe had been working in the Valley for most of his career and had just transferred into metro LA a few months ago. He was still in the learning process in the black community.

"If you're gonna make it here, Jose, you gotta learn the language. Let me give you a free lesson. You already know what the 'foot feed' and the 'carvarator' are. When you stop someone, you always ask for the vehicle 'restoration.' They usually keep it in the 'glove department.' Also, be sure to check their 'reviewing mirrors' and make sure the 'speed thermometer' is in good working order. See that they aren't driving on 'bald-headed' tires. And don't forget the 'fog advise,'" cautioned Pete.

"The 'fog advise.' What the hell is that?" asked Joe.

"The smog device, you Pendejo." Pete laughed. Then they both laughed.

The radio broke the laughter. "Any unit in the vicinity, a 415 man with a gun. Southwest corner of 88th and Avalon. Any unit, Code 2," said the hot-shot.

"That's just down the street a couple of blocks," said Pete.

"Twelve T Seventy-nine, we'll take the call at 88th and Avalon," Joe rogered the call.

As they drove the three blocks to the scene, Pete knew they would be the first unit on the scene. His mind went through the usual routine thoughts that cops have as they go into a potentially dangerous situation. Why me? Be cool and don't do anything foolish. Don't take any chances. Watch out for your partner. Adrenaline started to pump as they approached the intersection of 88th and Avalon and saw the small crowd on the corner.

Pete pulled the car up and stopped with the front wheels touching the curb at right angle to the west curb of Avalon. The crowd was mostly facing the other direction, and Pete wanted to take every advantage he had. As the two officers got out of the car, they both took positions behind their respective doors. Their guns were out and ready.

The man with the gun had his back to them. The man with the pool cue was facing the man with the gun. Several other people were just watching. Pete thought, If he turns around with the gun in his hand, I'm gonna nail him. Pete yelled out to the crowd who had not noticed the cops as yet.

"The man with the gun, drop it right now! The rest of you all, step back!" The small group froze in their places. Pete and Joe had their guns pointed at the gunman, as they were leaning on the door for steadiness. Pete's mind raced ahead. If he turns with the gun, he's dead, he thought. His finger tightened on the trigger.

The man with the gun moved his arms as though he were trying to hide the gun in his waistband. His back was still toward the officers. The other guy with the pool cue dropped it to the ground. Pete yelled again.

"I said drop the gun or you're dead, asshole!" Pete watched the man as he started to turn toward them. His mind went into slow-motion mode as time came almost to a standstill. As the man was turning, Pete's finger was tightening on the trigger. The hammer on his pistol started backward as the pistol readied to fire. The man's hand slowly came out of his waistband with the pistol. Pete's mind heard a voice from his memory, saying, "Always wait a second or two before you act. Things may not be what they seem," said the voice of Bubba Iglesia, the old beat cop who had broken Pete in on the job. Pete held the trigger at half-pull and waited. The dude slowly bent over and placed the gun on the ground, then stepped back. Pete and Joe relaxed and moved in to see what the beef was about.

As it turned out, the "bad guy" was the guy holding the pool cue. The guy with the gun was really defending himself, although he was illegally carrying a concealed weapon. They handled the call, and nobody went to jail; but Pete had some serious thoughts afterward. He wondered what would have happened if he had fired as the guy turned. The shooting would probably have been justified, under the circumstances; but the news media and the black community would have freaked out, Pete was sure. He gave himself a pat on the back for being in control and blessed Bubba's name for teaching him well. It rained all day.

Pete understood how people could drive while under the influence. He'd done it himself, but some people just couldn't handle their liquor. That's the key to the whole thing. Everyone was different. Pete hated the ones who were just intoxicated enough to be driving illegally because they were usually obnoxious. In California, at that time, the maximum level of blood alcohol was .10 percent.

Pete was breaking in a new officer on motors one night in Highland Park. Bill Salansky was long and lanky and was really trying hard to learn the ropes of the motor squad. They had arrested a deuce, and he had been transported to the main jail for booking. Pete and Bill had met the patrol car there and were walking the suspect into the jail through the back door. The arrestee had been nothing but a pain in the ass ever since he was stopped. He had the knack of getting the goat of officers. Some people have that knack. This guy was a pro. As they walked through the jail's back hallway, the guy kept it up.

"You cops are all alike. If you take away the badge and gun, you're nothing," he proclaimed. "You're all a bunch of cowards hiding behind those guns," he sneered. Pete had had enough.

"Okay, asshole," Pete said, "you want a shot at me? Come on in here." Pete pushed the guy into one of the abandoned holding tanks that lined the hall leading into the jail. The place was deserted. Pete took off his badge and gun belt and handed them to his partner. "If this guy kicks my ass, he goes free. Agreed?" Salansky looked at Pete in disbelief but agreed.

The smart-ass thought it was a good idea too. He was a good-sized man, and Pete guessed he was the bully type who was probably used to kicking people's asses. The two squared off in the holding tank with the rubber floor and went at it. As it turned out, the bully was all talk and little talent. Pete jabbed him with a couple of lefts and then nailed the guy with a good right. The guy went down and stayed down, although still conscious.

The guy reached up and wiggled his two front teeth with his fingers as if checking to see if they were still there.

"If my teeth come out, I'm going to sue your ass," whined the guy.

"Fuck you," said Pete. "Now get up and go to jail." The guy went quietly and did not go to court or sue. His teeth must have stayed in.

In the early 1960s, the primitive, old "balloon test" for drunk drivers was replaced by more modern breath analyzing machines. The balloon test consisted of blowing into the mouthpiece attached to a balloon. When the balloon was full, the breath sample was released in to a tube filled with a chemical that changed color if alcohol existed in the breath sample. The time it took for the chemical to change color indicated how much alcohol was present. Primitive but useful. The word about the new test method was slow in getting to the public, and people were still used to the balloon tests.

Pete was frequently asked by arrestees for the balloon test, so as a joke, he started to carry little balloons in his pocket. One night a middle-aged black man was stopped as a drunk driving suspect. He wasn't too bad, and Pete and his partner were contemplating letting the dude go anyway, when the guy started demanding the balloon test. Pete obliged him. He took out one of the penny balloons and explained the rules.

"Okay, I'll give you the balloon test," said Pete as he stretched the balloon to limber it up a little. "I'll blow up the balloon, and when I let it go, you catch it," Pete explained.

"Wait a minute," said the old dude, "I'm s'posed to catch dat?"

"You said you wanted the balloon test, didn't you? So get ready," said Pete, holding the balloon by the valve stem. The dude was hunched over and ready to spring when Pete let the balloon go. *Thhhrrooopp!* The balloon went swishing through the air in a zigzag path. The old man grabbed for it in vain.

"Hey, man, give me another shot at it, please," pleaded the man. Pete couldn't see any harm in that, since no one had ever caught the balloon and never would.

"Okay," said Pete, and he blew up another balloon and held it ready. The old man got into his crouch again. "One, two, three, *Thhhrrooopp!* The balloon shot up into the air. The man's hand reached out for it. Then it happened. The balloon flew right into the old man's hand. His hand closed around it, and victory showed on his face. Pete couldn't believe his eyes.

"I gots it," yelled the man. Pete and his partner looked at each other.

"You sure did," admitted Pete. "You passed the balloon test!" So they let the guy go, and Pete said, "We gotta revise the test to make it more difficult."

CHAPTER TWENTY

BEING THERE

"Okay, listen up, you clowns," said Sergeant Cory. "The President of the United States will be in town next week, and there will be a special detail for security. The following personnel are to be assigned to the detail." He began to read off the names of the twelve officers assigned.

The personal security of VIPs when visiting the City of Angels is the responsibility of the Los Angeles Police Department. Even though the Secret Service is there, the main responsibility falls on the BCMCs. It's a special job for traffic control, as well as the personal security of the dignitary, as they are called. Only experienced officers and those trusted by the management are chosen to perform these special details. When Pete's name was called for his first "escort detail," he was excited. He got on the phone to tell his partner about his assignment.

"Hey, Ron, I'm on the Nixon escort detail!"

"Well, that will teach Nixon to come to LA," said Byron in his usual dry manner. Pete was too excited to even hear the smart remarks. He could hardly wait until next week when he would be on the escort for President Nixon.

The men usually chosen for these details were the cream of the crop on motors. They were usually the older guys who had been around for a while, which made Pete feel even more privileged. After roll call, some of the men talked about past escorts they had been involved with. Pete was all ears, trying to pick up bits of information he could use when he was on the detail.

The rest of the week went by slowly until the day of the escort arrived. The men were to report to the south parking lot of Dodger Stadium, where the president's helicopter was to land. The arrival time was to be in the evening. Pete and the other men assigned reported to the command post at the designated location for briefing.

"Here's the information on the escort," said Sergeant Cory. "When the president arrives, we escort him to the Music Center at First and Grand. The president and his wife will attend the concert and return here for takeoff in the helicopter." Pete was somewhat disappointed that the escort was not going farther than downtown. The total distance was only a couple of miles.

"This may sound like a routine trip," said the sergeant, "but we have complications." Pete's interest was again peaked. Even though the detail offered an opportunity to meet the President of the United States, the event had been sounding boring so far. How wrong he was.

"Here's the problem," explained Cory. "The concert will be picketed by anti-Nixon, peace-loving, antiwar, hippie assholes. The Secret Service thinks the protesters might try to enter the Music Center and endanger the president." Pete now wished he were not on the detail. His thoughts went back to the Watts Riot experience with uncontrolled crowds of people. The sergeant continued his briefing.

"Our job is to keep the protesters from getting into the Music Center, if they try to gain access. The Secret Service will be inside with the president. They are armed with Uzi machine guns. We can't have anyone shot for storming the concert. The results would be a major disaster for the city." The information and its import sank into the officers as they imagined the results of such a happening. Pete imagined the news headlines the day after: Protesters gunned down by LAPD as they try to see the president." Naturally, the shooters would all be Los Angeles cops. The Feds take care of their own in cases like this. The escort cops knew their asses were on the line.

The evening was cool and crisp as the cops stood waiting for the president's helicopter to arrive. There was a little small talk, but most of the men were thinking of what could happen on this detail. The Secret Serviceman in charge waved to the sergeant, and the sound of an approaching chopper was heard in the distance. The cops mounted their motors and lined up for the start of the motorcade. Pete's heart pounded.

The method used by the escort was standard procedure. The officers rode ahead of the motorcade and blocked off intersections and held up traffic until the motorcade passed. Then they jumped back on their motorcycles and rode like hell to catch up to the motorcade. They passed up all the vehicles and made their way up to the front, leapfrogging the cops ahead, and blocked off the next intersection. The procedure was always dangerous. This one would be especially so because it went right through heavily congested city streets. The operation takes at least ten or twelve officers, each leapfrogging the other until they reach the destination of the dignitary.

The leader of the escort was Sergeant Cory on his motorcycle. Next was a Secret Service car, a station wagon, loaded with men. Pete had seen the weapons in their car. Each man had a 9-mm automatic pistol. The machine guns were not visible on the floor of the vehicle. Pete was about fourth or fifth in line, as they got ready to leave. He looked over his shoulder to see Mr. Nixon and his wife walking from the helicopter to the limo in which they were to ride. Visions of the Kennedy assassination flashed through his memory and out as his radio sounded.

"Okay, let's move out," came the voice of the sergeant. The cops all turned on their red lights and flashers. The lead officer sped out to the first intersection. He entered on the green light and parked his motor in the middle of the intersection. He got off and blew his whistle and raised his hands to stop traffic. Traffic was light, and there was no problem stopping anyone. Once he had the traffic stopped, he held them as the officers who were headed for the next intersection sped past.

As Pete roared down the street, following the officer ahead, he was thinking fast. He saw the more experienced officers pulling traffic over on the street ahead and telling them to remain stopped until the motorcade had passed. These were cars that were traveling on the same street with the motorcade. These vehicles offer only a minor threat since the motorcade gathers speed as it travels and usually passes these stopped vehicles at about forty or fifty miles an hour.

Looks like I've got the next intersection, Pete thought as he roared ahead. He approached the intersection and pumped his brakes hard to a near stop. Then he rolled slowly into the intersection, watching for approaching cars. There were none close, so he dismounted in the middle of the intersection. He stopped the traffic in all directions and waited. In the distance, about three blocks away, Pete saw the flashing red lights of the oncoming motorcade. He thought to himself, I'm doing fine.

As the motorcade went through "his" intersection, he caught a glimpse of the occupants of the limo. They appeared to be humans. Funny how we think of people in high places as not being human, thought Pete as he mounted up to chase the motorcade down. He went flying down the street, riding the double centerline as he had seen the older cops do ahead of him. Fortunately, traffic was light in this part of town. By this time, the motorcade had covered the entire distance to the Music Center. It's a fast trip when there's no traffic to make you stop.

The limo and escorting cars stopped at the Grand Street entrance to the Music Center. The motor cop escort team arrived one by one as they completed their traffic control duties and parked together with the rear tires backed into the curb. They dismounted and took up predetermined positions on the sidewalk in front of the entrance. Barricades had been set up on the other side of the street, and patrol cops from Central Division were already controlling the crowds on the west side of Grand. It appeared to Pete that there were about a thousand people in the crowd. They seemed fairly tame.

As the president and his entourage got out of their cars and headed for the entrance, the crowd came to life. They started to chant and yell antiwar slogans as they surged forward against the barricades. The patrol cops held them back as best they could. Pete and the rest of the escort cops were the second line of defense between the crowd and the president. The impact of the scenario started to sink in. Here they were, facing a crowd who outnumbers them by about a hundred to one. If they want to go through the "thin blue line," they could very easily do it. Inside the Music Center was the last line of defense, with automatic weapons that can "never be used." If the crowd decides to go in, they will be used to protect the president. Machine guns against American citizens? What a standoff this is, thought Pete. He wished he were somewhere else.

The time seemed to drag by while the president was in the building. It was about two hours actually. The crowds had calmed down since the president went in, and some had gone home. Great! Go home! The alert was given to the officers that the president was returning to his car. Speed is essential in these escort activities. Get the dignitary into the car and away from the crowd and moving. A moving target is harder to hit. The crowd began to make noise again as the president reappeared. He was quickly hustled into his car, and the escort started off for the return trip to Dodger Stadium. By now, it was about nine o'clock in the evening. The night was getting cold, but it was clear. The return trip to the helicopter was uneventful. Traffic in the downtown area is generally light after business hours.

The motorcade swung back into the parking area where it had begun. It had been a success. No one had been hurt. No motor officers had gone down. The crowd had satisfied their needs to protest. Protocol after these types of escorts dictates that dignitaries thank the members of the escort for their services. The troops line up at attention, and the VIP shakes hands with each one and personally extends thanks.

As the BCMCs lined up, Pete felt excited at the prospect of shaking hands with the President of the United States. Pete had voted for him once but lately had not been too happy with his actions. Anytime Frank Sinatra switched his political support from the Democrat to the Republican, Pete knew there was something wrong. But he was still the president. Pete could not think of anyone in his family who had met a president of this country.

The president moved from one officer to the next in the line, and Pete thought of how lucky he was to be where he was, doing the things he was. Just being there was a thrill. That's one of the biggest thrills about being a cop.

Being there when things are happening. Sometimes you don't like it when it's happening, but after it's over and you survived to tell about it, it's great.

"Thank you very much, Officer Felix," said Richard Nixon, as he read Pete's nameplate on his right breast. He was about the same height as Pete's. He should be taller than me, thought Pete. Nixon's hand clasped Pete's in a medium soft grip. Pete noticed Nixon's hand was small and soft in his grip. As Pete mumbled something about "You're welcome," he felt disappointed that the most powerful man in the world was a kind of a wimp that couldn't even go to a concert by himself. Pete could probably kick his ass. He thought he'd rather be a motor cop right now than President of the United States. The world was different now for Pete. As he rode toward home with another of the escort cops, Pete was in deep thought about his experience on the detail.

Wally Smith rode ahead of him on Wilshire Boulevard as the two BCMCs headed for home. A light rain had started to fall, and the streets were getting wet. Wally lived in the same part of town as Pete's, so they rode together. They had decided to take the surface streets back to the freeway. The night was still warm enough, and the rain wasn't heavy enough to get the cops very wet. When Wally and Pete approached Bixel Street, they decided to enter the freeway at 8th Street from Bixel and catch the Santa Monica Freeway east.

Wally rounded the corner and started down the steep hill at Bixel Street down to 8th. Pete hesitated when he saw Wally start to slide and lose traction on the wet pavement. As Pete eased to a stop, Wally's bike slid out from under him and went down. Fortunately, his speed was slow, and the motorcycle only slid a few feet. Wally bounced back up onto his feet instantly. He was unhurt, but his pride was somewhat bruised.

It was near midnight, and the traffic was very light; so Pete wasn't too concerned about the traffic behind. It seemed, as if they were alone on the street. Pete parked his motor at the top of the hill and went to help Wally pick up his bike.

"Slicker'n snot out here," complained Wally, while he looked his uniform over for damage.

"You did that pirouette very gracefully."

Pete felt smug that he had not fallen. He knew the streets were very slippery, but he felt Wally should have slowed down more when he turned. The streets were not *that* slick, he thought. He was still laughing as he walked out into the street to help Wally. The motor lay on its side about halfway down the hill. Pete walked out to the fallen motorcycle to help his friend put the bike back up on its wheels. Suddenly, his feet started to slip on the slimy pavement. Before Pete knew it, he was sliding downhill like a skier.

"Whoa!" yelled Pete, as he picked up speed sliding down the hill. Flailing his arms to keep upright, Pete slid all the way to the bottom without falling.

Pete could hear the loud laughter of his partner as he skied the down slope. When he finally came to a stop, he turned around and saw how far he had slid; he wondered how he could have made it without falling.

Pete meekly walked back up the hill (on the sidewalk) to where his partner was doubled over with laughter. Pete had to join in the laugh when he visualized how he must have looked "skiing" down the hill. The tensions from the escort melted away, and Pete came back to reality. It was great just to be here, he thought.

CHAPTER TWENTY-ONE

YEE HAW!

Many people think that it's always warm in Los Angeles. BCMCs that work night watch know better. Pete and Bill Haymes worked together on Vermont Avenue. It was one of the coldest nights of the year.

Tonight they had on every item of clothing they could get on under their uniforms. Granted, it wasn't freezing, but the temperature was down in the low forties; and that's cold for motorcycle riding. Pete actually liked the cold weather better than riding in the heat. Maybe it was his Midwestern upbringing; he didn't know.

Most of the cops wore thermal underwear in cold weather. It made the uniform fit tight, but it kept you warm. Heavy gloves and a wool scarf helped keep the warmth inside the black leather jacket Pete wore. As the night wore on, the temperature got lower still.

"Jesus, it's cold!"

"Hell, Bill, you should be used to this kind of weather being from Boston." Pete had met Bill while they trained for the motor squad in 1961. They had teamed up several times as partners. Bill was tall and dark with a slight eastern accent. The two motor cops usually got along well, but Pete's sense of humor sometimes irritated the more sober officer.

"I never did like cold. Let's hit the coffee shop and thaw out."

It was Saturday night, and Vermont was hopping. The beat they were working went from Venice Boulevard south to 54th Street. The area was a predominantly black business district.

It was approaching midnight and freezing. The motor squad ordinarily goes end of watch at 11:30 PM, except on Friday and Saturday nights when they ride until 2:30 in the morning. The idea is to catch the drunk drivers after the bars close at 2:00 AM.

Pete and Bill rode the beat as much as they could, with frequent stops to warm up. As they headed for the coffee shop, they rode north on Vermont. Near Adams Boulevard, they both saw the car ahead swerve over the double centerline of the street. Suspecting a possible deuce, they hit the red lights and pulled the car over.

The driver decided to pull into a closed service station to stop. Bill and Pete pulled up behind and kicked down the side stands on their Harleys. Bill was up and approached the driver.

"Let's see your driver's license." The driver got out and searched his wallet. He looked as if he were pretty sober. Bill asked the young white man if he'd been drinking.

"I ain't gonna lie to ya, officer," he confessed. "I had two beers. But I ain't drunk."

Pete guessed he was probably telling the truth. He noticed there were two women in the car and another man in the backseat. A double date perhaps. The man in the backseat got out of the car and started to walk around. He *was* drunk. Pete decided the drunk man might become a problem.

"Look, pal," Pete said to the man, "you'd better get back in the car before you fall down." He spoke in a friendly tone and smiled.

"You'd better tell your friend to get back in the car," Bill advised the driver.

"Damn it, Leroy, git back in the car."

Leroy was a tall, lanky young white boy about 22 or 23. He and his buddy were both from some Southern state, judging from their accent. Leroy got back into the backseat of the car. Two minutes later, Leroy got out again and started to stagger around the service station lot.

"If you don't get back in the car, we'll have to arrest you for being drunk in public."

Leroy looked at the cops and smiled. He did not make a move to get in the car. Pete and Bill looked at each other.

"Okay, pal," said Bill, "you're under arrest." Pete moved to the right of the tall man, and Bill started to move to left to get on either side of Leroy. All of a sudden, Leroy spread his arms out wide and gave out with a rebel yell.

"Yeeeee haaaww!"

Bill and Pete moved in on either side of the man. They reached out, and each grabbed an arm. Leroy gave another yell and started to swing the two cops around in a circle.

Pete thought, What the hell are we doing? After a couple of revolutions, the three men spun to the side and fell over the hood of the car. Pete saw his chance and let go of Leroy's arm. Pete punched Leroy in the eye, and he went down to the ground with Bill on top of him. The fight was gone out of him. Pete spun around to face the other man, thinking he would probably try to help his buddy. Pete grabbed the other guy by the coat and pulled him down on the hood of the car. As Pete drew back to punch the second guy, the man put up his hands and yelled.

"I ain't fightin'. I give up." Pete relaxed and let the guy go.

They booked Leroy for "plain drunk," after taking him to the hospital to have his huge black eye treated. His buddy was kicked loose with the ticket.

The boys forgot the incident until a couple of weeks later when they got a radio call to meet the detectives. When cops get these kinds of calls, they usually mean trouble is brewing. Pete and Bill wondered what they had done now.

"You guys remember this dude?" asked the detective, holding up the mug shot of a man. They looked at the picture of the guy with the huge black eye.

"Yeah," said Pete, "we busted him a couple of weeks ago for 41.27[a]. He put up a fight, and I punched him in the eye." Pete didn't feel the need to try to hide anything since the whole thing was related to a lawful arrest.

"Well, we were able to make this guy on a robbery because of the black eye you gave him," said the detective, smiling. "Thanks," he said.

"You're welcome," said Pete, feeling a little relieved anyway. After the detective left, Bill and Pete had to laugh about the whole affair.

"Did you see the see the eye on that dude? Fucking Leroy!" Bill chuckled.

"Yeeeee haaaww!" yelled Pete.

Pete liked working the Hollywood beats except for one thing: the idiots who hang around and live there. There seemed to be more weirdos per square inch in Hollywood than in any place else in the world. But maybe that's what made it interesting. Hollywood had gone a long way down the tube since the glamorous thirties and forties of yesteryear. Now Hollywood seemed to be destroying itself with homosexuality, dope, and an overabundance of scumbags and prostitutes.

Working traffic there was not as bad as working patrol, though. Traffic is generally the same everywhere in Los Angeles: bad. Pete was working Sunset Boulevard between Hollywood Boulevard on the east and Highland Avenue on the west. That takes in almost all of the Hollywood area.

Cruising east on the Boulevard, Pete saw a motorcycle riding ahead of him in the right lane. The light for eastbound traffic changed to green, and the motorcycle sped off ahead of the rest of the traffic. Pete accelerated after him and got a reading on his speedometer of 52 miles per hour during the time he was pacing the motorcyclist.

The BCMC

Motorcycle cops use their speedometers to "clock" violators for speed violations. The method was very simple. You positioned yourself in a location of good observation of the vehicle you're clocking and paced him at the same speed. You looked at your speedometer and "clocked" the speed either mentally or by stopping the speedometer needle by pushing a button on the handlebar. Police motorcycles' speedometers must be calibrated every 90 days, and the officer must be able to produce the calibration card certificate in court. Officers can use estimated speeds, but those are harder to prove in court.

Pete thought his clock of the motorcycle he was following was good. He had followed the violator for about three blocks, during which he had passed every car on the street. Pete pulled in behind the motorcycle and hit his reds and beeped his horn. The man pulled over and stopped. Pete pulled up behind and parked. Pete walked up to the man and saw that he was a rather short, stocky person about his own age. He wore scruffy-looking clothes and a two—or three-day growth of beard.

"What seems to be the trouble, officer?"

Why do they always ask that? wondered Pete to himself.

"Well, sir, I clocked you at 52 in a 35-mile zone, and you were passing all of the other traffic. May I see your driver's license, please?" The man seemed disturbed, but who isn't when they know they're about to get a ticket?

"Hey, man," protested the rider, "this is bullshit! I wasn't going no 52. I was going 35."

"That's not what my speedometer said," advised Pete, "and mine's calibrated. Is yours?"

"I don't need no calibrated speedometer to know you're just looking for another ticket to fill your quota."

Pete walked back to his motor to get his ticket book and started the ticket without comment. Traffic officers were taught to understand that people will sometimes react very negatively to getting a ticket, and cops will put up with most of the crap that people will throw at them while writing a ticket. Sometimes they ran into people who are just too obnoxious to stand. This dude turned out to be one of the worst Pete had ever met.

"You fucking cops are all a bunch of assholes that oppress people and make money for the state," ranted The Rider. Pete continued to write but kept the dude in his peripheral vision at all times. Rider went on raving about the so-called quota that all traffic cops are supposed to have, but really don't, and tried to cast doubts on Pete's ancestry. None of these really bothered Pete. He'd heard it all before.

"I'm gonna find out where you live and come over to your house when you are at work and rape your wife and kill your kids," threatened Rider.

Now, since Pete had neither a wife nor kids, the threat was foolish, but this type of asshole might just do that to some other officer. Pete decided he'd had enough from this guy.

"Look, asshole. If I ever see you around my home, I'll blow your fucking brains into the gutter and kick them down the sewer. Do you understand?" Pete was standing about two feet from the man, face-to-face. The Rider smiled as Pete handed him the ticket to sign. The Rider signed, and Pete took the ticket out and handed it to Rider. As Rider reached for the piece of paper, Pete let it fall to the ground in the gutter. Rider bent over to pick up the ticket.

"Now you look normal down there in the gutter," commented Pete with a smile on his face. The Rider's face got red, and Pete knew he'd scored at last on The Rider.

Pete walked back to his motor and fired up. He pulled away and rode east on Sunset. He looked in his rearview mirror and saw The Rider start up and pull in behind Pete. He slowed as The Rider pulled alongside on Pete's right.

"You ever been knocked off that motorcycle?" asked Rider, as he rode alongside Pete.

A threat had been made, aimed at a police officer, on duty. He took it seriously coming from this jerk. He started to formulate plans for his defense if this idiot tried to assault him. Pete decided that any attempt to knock Pete off his motorcycle would be an "assault with a deadly weapon"—or ADW, as the cops call it—which is a felony. That entitled Pete to use any means necessary to defend himself, including deadly force. He needed to be careful here. Any time deadly force is used, there will be many who review the case to determine if the officer was justified in his actions.

"You'd better stay away from me," yelled Pete. "I'm warning you!" The Rider laughed and rode in a position to Pete's rear and to Pete's right so as to be in Pete's blind spot. Pete sped up. Rider sped up. Pete slowed down, Rider slowed down. Pete yelled again.

"I'm warning you for the last time! Stay away from me!"

"You can't do anything to me," yelled Rider. "I'm just driving down the street."

Pete pondered his next move. He couldn't really do anything to the guy because he hadn't done anything to follow up his threat. But as long as the guy was behind him, Pete was fair game for the Rider, and he couldn't let that continue. It was an ongoing threat in itself.

He decided to force the issue. He slowed and let the Rider come up on his right. As the other motorcycle came alongside, Pete pulled his baton from the holder and swung it at the Rider.

"I told you to stay away from me, asshole." The baton missed the guy by about three feet. Pete knew he would not connect but did it only to warn The

Rider off. It didn't work. Rider kept following him in his blind spot. Deciding on another action, Pete slowed his motorcycle down and watched his mirrors. The Rider slowed also. There was no traffic behind them. Pete came to a stop. Rider stopped next to a car parked at the curb.

"Okay, man," yelled Pete, "pull over there and park." Rider pulled over.

"Now I'm going to give you a ticket for double parking," said Pete. This ought to get the message across to the asshole, he thought. He didn't mind going to court on this one just to hear the dude's story of how he got the ticket. If it was thrown out, Pete wouldn't care. He just wanted the asshole off his back.

Pete got out his ticket book and wrote the ticket and handed it to Rider. After Rider signed it, he started to hand it back. Pete caught the look in The Rider's eye and knew he was going to drop the ticket book as Pete had dropped the Rider's ticket before. Pete quickly reached out and took the book before he could drop it. Pete smiled at The Rider and handed him his copy of the ticket. Rider grabbed it fast.

"Now," said Pete, "I'm going to go west, and if you follow me again, I'll arrest you for assault!" Just then, Pete saw a two-man patrol car coming west on Sunset. He waved them down, and they pulled over to meet him.

Pete briefly explained what had happened and advised the Rider once more. "I'm telling you in front of these two officers, as witnesses, that if you follow me again, you will be arrested. Do you understand?" The message finally sank into the dull brain of The Rider, and Pete rode away unmolested. Pete soon forgot about The Rider. Several weeks went by.

"Thirteen Mary Twenty-four clear," said Pete into the microphone as he pulled out of the gas pumps behind PAB and headed south on San Pedro Street. He had only gone a block or two when the radio came on with, "Thirteen T Three. An ambulance traffic at 9th and San Pedro Street." A traffic accident with injuries had occurred on the path of Pete's ride to his beat. Pete decided to stop and see if he could help the accident investigation officer at the scene.

As Pete rolled up, he saw the AI officer standing, talking to what appeared to be a victim in the accident. Parked at the curb was a motorcycle with the front forks bent all to hell. The man talking to the officer had a very large bump on his forehead. Pete got closer.

Then he recognized the rider. It was The Rider! Rider glanced at Pete and then did a double take, then kept on talking to the officer. He was pretending not to see Pete, but Pete knew Rider had recognized him. Pete walked over to the wrecked motorcycle and pretended to examine it closely. Then he started to chuckle under his breath. Then he started to laugh out loud. The officer and Rider both looked at Pete. The AI officer had a queer look on his face. Pete played it straight. He looked at the large bump on The Rider's head and laughed louder, pointing to the bump.

"What's so funny?"

"You!" Pete laughed. "Your motorcycle is totaled, and look at that bump!" Now Pete was laughing hysterically. Of course, it was all an act, but only Pete knew that. He was on a roll now, and revenge was sweet. Pete noticed a man standing by who seemed to have some involvement in the situation. Pete walked over to him.

"Are you involved in the accident?" Pete questioned.

"Well, no," answered the man. "I was a witness driving behind him when the accident happened. I was following him to the traffic court to help him pay a ticket. I loaned him the money, you see."

"Does this guy work for you?" asked Pete.

"Yes, he does," replied the man. Rider was glaring at him, and Pete was loving every minute of it. Pete put on his most serious face and spoke to the boss.

"Well, if you don't mind a friendly word of advice, I'd be very careful with this guy. He's a psycho, and we've had a lot of trouble with him in the past. Rape, assault, things like that. I'd be very careful if I were you. Of course, this is off the record, you understand?" As Pete talked, he was leaning close to the boss so that The Rider couldn't hear.

"Gosh," said the boss, "thanks for the advice, officer."

"You're welcome, sir," said Pete, walking away. He walked by the spot where the AI officer was still talking to The Rider and wondering what that crazy motor cop was doing. Pete thought it better not to tell him. As he walked to his motor, Pete knew Rider's eyes were glued on him. Pete rode away laughing, as he passed by The Rider, whose face was smoking red by now. The bump in his head seemed to pulsate and throb. Pete rode to his beat with a warm feeling, knowing that the tickets The Rider was going to court on were the ones Pete had issued. He never got a subpoena on either of them, and Pete's faith was reaffirmed that there was a god.

CHAPTER TWENTY-TWO

MARRIED LIFE AND DEATH

Pete had thought a lot about marriage lately. Many cops have a hard time with marriage. It's one thing to get married before you come on the job, but he felt that any woman foolish enough to marry a cop after he's on the job had no one to blame but herself if it didn't work out. A substantial number of police marriages don't. Many factors are usually to blame. Job stress, alcohol, other women, and failure to communicate are among the most common reasons for marriage failures. When you look at the differences between police and "humans," the reasons for marriage failures are basically the same. Pete was contemplating all of these things as he thought about his relationship with Noel.

Two years had gone by since they had met. They had been living together for about a year now, and he was satisfied with the program; but there were always doubts. The doubts were mostly based on the experiences of other cops and their problems. Some of the cops didn't mind sharing their problems in the coffee room. Pete recalled the day when Bud "Gatemouth" Fitzgerald told the guys in the coffee room how he had returned to his house one night to find all the furniture and family gone. His wife had moved out and taken everything they owned while he was at work. According to Gatemouth, he had no idea this was about to happen. Pete wondered at the time how that could be true, but it still left an impression on him. Then he thought about Dwight Davison and the tragedy of his marriage that had ended in murder and suicide. He wondered if marriage was for him.

Pete had gotten used to the kids and was settled into the groove with Noel. They were living in the little house in a court of three other houses in Altadena. The foothills of the San Gabriel Mountains loomed up about a mile from their house. On a clear day, you could see the TV and radio towers on top of Mount Wilson. The neighborhood was old, and so were most of the neighbors.

Pete and Noel looked for a house to rent so the kids could have more room and they could live like normal people. They found a small two-bedroom house about four blocks from the court where they lived and moved in.

The house was old but cozy. Built in the early 1920s, it was the original home of one of the large property owners of old Altadena. The man had built the house himself, and it had been well-made. It had a large garage and a utility room in the rear, which the kids used as a playroom. Pete liked the atmosphere of the neighborhood, and its older inhabitants were quiet and reserved. Pete and Noel settled into the new home, and all was well.

The subject of marriage was still an unspoken topic in both their minds. Finally, it came to a head one night when he and Noel sat watching TV and having a few drinks. When the subject came up, Pete was not in the mood for it and complained. An argument ensued, and Noel stood up and poured her drink out on top of Pete's head, as he sat on the floor next to the couch. Not to be outdone, Pete reciprocated by pouring his drink on her head. Then the fun started,

"You asshole!" she screamed at Pete as the fluid dripped off of her nose.

"*Officer* Asshole to you," corrected Pete, laughing at the whole situation.

"I don't think it's funny! You're so full of shit," Noel screamed, frustrated at Pete's seemingly lackadaisical attitude. She couldn't stand it and started to scratch and hit him on the arms and chest. Pete fended off most of the blows but took a few. He decided to end the little misunderstanding because he could see it was getting out of hand. He reached up and slapped Noel on the cheek. He made sure it was not a hard blow but hard enough to hurt. *Smack!* Noel stepped back with a shocked look on her face.

"You hit me," she cried in amazement, holding her hands to her face.

"Did it hurt?"

"Why did you hit me?"

"Because you hit me first," he said simply.

Noel turned and ran into the bathroom, and Pete heard the door lock. Pete went into the kitchen and poured himself another drink. He hadn't hit a woman since the time a female had slammed her purse into his balls during an arrest. Then he had reacted so quickly that she was down from his retaliatory punch before he knew what had happened. He was not inclined to strike women. His conservative Midwestern upbringing had taught him to always respect women as the "weaker sex" and to treat them with courtesy. In his experiences on the job, he had learned that women can be very dangerous and are usually a pain in the ass for cops to deal with.

Nonetheless, he was sorry he had hit Noel and decided that the argument was as much his fault as it was hers. He knew he loved her and that his failure to make a commitment of marriage to her was the underlying cause of the tension that had erupted in the violent incident. Pete resolved to straighten things out once and for all. After about ten minutes, Noel came out of the bathroom. She was holding a wet cloth over her eye.

"How am I going to explain this eye to the girls at work?" she moaned.

"Why not tell them I hit you in the eye?" suggested Pete. He waited for an answer that didn't come back. That is what Noel did, however. She told the truth, and Pete respected her for that. Later, they talked about it.

"I know why you hit me, really," said Noel.

"Why?"

"You wouldn't have hit me if you didn't love me."

Pete thought for a moment. "You're right," he said. "Let's get married and make it legal for you to hit me back." They were married in a wedding chapel not far from their house. Bill Haymes was best man, and a few of their family and friends attended.

The evening was cool. Pete sat in the living room watching TV and sipping a glass of Bushmills. He had taken off his shoes and his shirt and was about to hit the sack. Noel and the kids had already gone to bed. The sound of voices came through the open front door, and Pete got up to see what was happening. It was about eleven o'clock in the evening, and the old neighborhood was usually quiet. Pete saw some movement in the street and in the yard of the house across the street from his. He moved out onto the front porch to investigate.

Pete softly moved out onto the sidewalk in front of his house. He felt the effects of the whiskey he had been drinking, and little warning bells went off in his cop brain. "Be careful," said the bells. The damp night air smelled fresh and cool.

The three young men had gotten out of their car and were starting to throw toilet paper around the yard of the house across from Pete's. As he watched unnoticed by the trio, he wondered to himself why they would want to paper this house. As far as Pete knew, the occupants had no kids. Usually, this type of activity is performed on houses of young people who know each other. Pete reviewed the legal aspects of their actions in his mind. Technically, papering a house is classified as malicious mischief and/or trespassing by the police. Most of the time, it isn't even reported. Just good clean fun, right?

Pete had moved quietly to the end of his sidewalk and was standing, watching the trio at work. Then one of the young men noticed him.

"Why don't you guys just wipe your ass with that paper and leave that house alone?" asked Pete.

"Fuck you," yelled one of the young men. They started to move toward their car parked in the middle of the street. Pete didn't like their attitude and started to move toward them.

"Come on. Let's get out of here," said one of the smart-asses.

"I think that's a good idea," said Pete.

"What? Are you a tough guy or something?" yelled the biggest of the trio. "Fuck you, asshole!" yelled the big guy. By this time, the other two guys were in the car and ready to go, but the big guy wasn't ready yet.

The big guy stood in the street facing Pete, challenging him to do something. Pete ran full speed at the guy and leaped into the air with his right leg extended. The sidekick hit the guy in the neck, making him stagger backward. Deciding he'd had enough, the big guy ran for the car that was starting to move slowly away. Pete ran after the car, wanting more of the smart-ass.

Pete caught up to him as he attempted to get into the right side of the car. Pete landed a glancing right to the side of the guy's head, and he fell into the backseat. The car started to move away.

"Don't forget to close the door," yelled Pete, as he slammed the door on the leg that was still hanging out of the door. The car sped away into the night. They didn't come back.

Pete knew the department frowned on officers becoming involved in off-duty altercations, so he decided not to report the incident to the Altadena authorities and risk criticism for getting personally involved. It was hard not to get involved when things were happening to other people or their property. Too much of a cop, he thought. I'll never change.

"You working the Rose Parade this year, Pete?" asked Ron Byron after roll call. "I don't know. I probably will. I need the bread." Although the city of Pasadena had the responsibility for the Rose Parade each year, they also hired officers from other departments to assist with the huge crowds of spectators. Other departments, including LAPD and the Los Angeles Sheriff's Department, were given the opportunity to make extra money working the parade.

"It's a pain in the ass trying to ride herd on a million people up there," whined Pete, thinking of the past years he had worked the event. Most of the jobs on riding motors during the event went to cops with seniority. Pete usually ended up directing traffic in the middle of an intersection.

"To hell with it. I'm not going to work it this year," decided Pete.

"Well, I need the money more than the peace and quiet," said Ron. Pete knew he would have to work New Year's Day on the streets of Los Angeles since many cops would be up in Pasadena at the parade. That's okay, he thought.

The first day of the new year was cold and bright as Pete wheeled his Harley-Davidson north toward the beat he'd been assigned. San Fernando

Road between North Figueroa and Eagle Rock Boulevard is a speed beat in Highland Park Division. Pete had always liked Highland Park, but this area was not one of his favorites. The neighborhoods were full of Latino dopers and gang members.

San Fernando Road ran in a northwest/southeast direction and had railroad yards on one side and a residential district on the other. The absence of through streets made it a speed beat. Although the street was posted thirty-five, the traffic usually ran at more like forty-five normally. It was still early in the morning as Pete pulled into Arvia Street to sit in on traffic. He felt the ache in his head from the booze he had drunk at the party the night before. Bobby Wheeler had thrown a great party, and Pete had gotten only about four hours' sleep. Pete thought he'd just sit there a while and let those aspirin he'd taken soak in.

The first car going north caught Pete's attention. After working traffic for a few years, BCMCs learn to scan the roadways for speeds that attract their attention. Many people think that bright-colored cars or certain styles, like sports cars, attract cops. That's not true. It's the actions or speed of the vehicles that catches the eye of the BCMC.

This car was moving out. Pete kicked the Harley into action and moved toward the intersection to give chase. Before he could cover the thirty feet or so to get there, another car went screaming north after the first. Pete turned right onto San Fernando Road and twisted the Harley's throttle wide open through the gears. The roar of the bike's engine drowned out all other sounds. Pete was starting to gain on the two cars, which were now side by side in an apparent race. Pete decided not to turn on his red lights or siren until he was closer, so the speeders would not have a chance to run.

These assholes are mine, thought Pete as he came within a block of the two speeding cars. Suddenly, and without any reason, the first car, an Oldsmobile, swerved to its left over the double yellow centerline of the street right into the path of a southbound Corvair. There was no time for the southbound car to react. The two cars met head-on at a closing speed of what must have been at least a hundred miles an hour.

The scene in front of Pete's motor went into soundless slow motion. The impact was too far away for Pete to hear over the roar of his motorcycle. The cars, locked together at the grilles like two animals biting each other at the mouth in life-and-death combat, rose in the air about five or six feet and spun around 180 degrees, coming to rest in the middle of the street. Another car southbound crashed into the first two. The second racing car kept going without even slowing down. Pete started to slow his motor and grabbed for his radio at the same time.

"Ah. . . . ah . . . Eleven-Mary-Thirty-three . . . ah . . . requesting . . . an ambulance . . . ah . . . no . . . two . . . ambulances! Ah . . . ambulance traffic . . .

ah . . . ah . . . San Fernando Road and Frederick Street. Ah . . . this unit is not involved." Pete's voice broke as he stuttered to put out the appropriate information on the accident. He almost forgot to put the side stand down on his motor as he pulled up to the smoking wreckage of what used to be two cars and three humans.

"Oh shit! Damn! Son of a bitch!" Pete heard himself saying out loud. As he peered into the window of the Olds, he knew what he was about to see. The two men—in their thirties, Pete guessed—were still and very dead. From the second car came moaning noises. Pete moved around the Corvair to see inside. The driver was a man about forty or so. His legs were stuffed under the dashboard, and there was a large hole in his forehead. The noises he was making told Pete the man was probably near death.

Pete decided there was nothing he could do right then for any of the occupants of the two cars and turned to the third vehicle. The Mexican family had been driving about thirty-five when the two other cars crashed in front of them, leaving them nowhere to go. Pete helped them get the injured out of the car and over to the side of the road. The little girl had a broken arm, and the rest of the family all had lesser injuries. They were lucky.

Ambulances arrived, along with the fire department, to try to get the men out of the twisted wrecks. It was far too late for the two men in the first car and probably too late for the second party. A TV mobile unit showed up on the scene, wanting an interview with Pete. He didn't want to, but there was really no choice. It was Pete's responsibility.

As the camera rolled, Pete stammered out the story for the media and wished all the time he had chosen to work the Rose Parade. The tow trucks hauled away the last of the wreckage, and Pete headed for the station to complete his part of the reports. As he rode through the cool morning air of the first day of 1967, he couldn't stop the thoughts that inundated his mind. Thoughts that all cops have after an experience like he'd just had. People were dead and injured. The two cars racing north on San Fernando had caused it. The poor son of a bitch in the Corvair didn't have a chance. Pete visualized what the man might have thought as he saw the Olds swerve toward him. No time to think. Just takes a second to die! What did that poor bastard do to deserve that? Who knows? Does anybody care? Only a few. Was drunk driving the cause? Probably. I hope it never happens to me, thought Pete, knowing very well it could. Anytime.

"Next time I'll work the fucking Rose Parade," he mumbled as he parked his motor and went into Highland Park Station.

CHAPTER TWENTY-THREE

THE LITTLE NIPPER

"Let's take the kids up to the canyon tomorrow on your day off," said Noel. "We can take a picnic lunch." Pete was not the one of your outdoors-type people, and the idea of camping made Pete sweat. To him camping should be done at the Holiday Inn. But he knew he was overdue for an outing with the kids, and they loved the canyon in the San Bernardino Mountains. They had been there several times and enjoyed the stream that flowed through the canyon.

"Sure, honey," said Pete as he put on his uniform to go to work. They had been living in the little house in Altadena for two years now. Things had been going fairly smoothly for them. Pete had been a BCMC for six years now, and he was starting to have some seniority on the job. Other cops on motors knew him and respected him, which was very important to Pete. He wanted to be one of the squad, to be thought of by the rest of the cops on the job as "one of those crazy motor cops." He liked the feeling of being a member of an elite group of men whose job was like no other in the police field. Sure, he did the usual things all cop's duties require, but motor cops were a different breed. A special group within a special group. It was a dangerous job, he knew. He'd been down several times since he started riding the big Hogs. The first time was a very minor accident in which he had slipped in some gasoline spill while making a turn. It all happened so fast that it was over before Pete knew what had happened. His helmet had hit the pavement and probably saved him from serious injury. There was a saying among the BCMCs: "There are two kinds of motor cops: those who have been down and those who are going down." Pete took it for granted that he would go down again someday, but still, he tried not to bring it on himself by being careless.

Pete lazily cruised north on North Figueroa past the park that separates Figueroa Street and the Pasadena Freeway. His thoughts were on the plans for tomorrow's trip to the canyon. As he passed the intersection of Avenue Fifty, he was in the left lane at about thirty-five miles per hour. He noticed a stake bed truck ahead of him going a little slower than he. There were no cars ahead of Pete in the right lane. Pete decided to change lanes to the right and go around the truck. As he checked his right mirror for clearance, he saw a movement out of the corner of his eye. The truck had changed lanes at the same time Pete had. Pete saw another car that had been ahead of the truck in the left lane.

In the next fraction of a second, Pete saw the brake lights come on from the back of the truck, and its tires started to skid. It all happened so fast that Pete had not had time to react to the quick lane change of the truck nor the truck's emergency stopping action. There was not enough distance for Pete to stop and nowhere for him to go. The reason big Harleys were called Hogs was they were big and cumbersome to handle. Trying to maneuver nearly a thousand pounds of motorcycle and man in an emergency situation is very difficult, even with police training.

The only place Pete could see open was the space between the truck and car ahead of him. Pete aimed the front of the big bike for the hole. His rear tire started screeching, Pete's motor dove in between the truck and the car, slowing as he went. The space was only about three to four feet wide, and as Pete went in, his left rear saddlebag hit the car's fender, throwing the bike to the right. Pete's right shoulder struck the side of the truck's bed and slammed him back to the left. By this time, most of Pete's momentum had gone, and he fell over onto the right side of the motorcycle with his right leg pinned underneath. All the vehicles were stopped. To Pete's horror, he saw that he was trapped on the ground just in front of the huge double wheels of the truck. His leg was pinned tightly to the pavement, and he couldn't move. If the truck decided to move forward, he would be crushed under the wheels.

"Hey!" Pete screamed desperately. "Don't move the truck! Hold it!" The thought crossed Pete's mind that the driver may not speak English. Terror made Pete yell even louder. The left door of the truck opened, and, to Pete's joy, the driver got out. The driver and several other people helped to pull Pete out from under the truck. It was then that Pete realized he had somehow banged his testicles on the gas tank of his motorcycle. The pain caused Pete to double over as he staggered to the curb to sit down.

The cause of the whole incident now became clear. Just as the truck had changed lanes, an elderly woman had stepped off the curb in a crosswalk. The truck driver was aware of Pete's presence behind him and, as many people do, overreacted when he saw the cop. The old lady was also wrong by stepping out in front of oncoming traffic too abruptly.

"Are you all right, officer?" asked the sweet little old lady. Pete's balls ached and pained.

"I'm okay, ma'am."

"Where are you hurt?" she asked in a sincere, innocent tone. Pete would have laughed if he could.

"Never mind," he said. "Just wait here until the car comes to take the report."

Pete knew the fun was now about to start. The department had a fleet safety program that reviewed all accidents involving officers on duty. A panel of officers and a sergeant would review the accident and determine if it was a "preventable" or "nonpreventable" accident.

A preventable accident usually got the officer involved a day or two off without pay, depending on his accident record. Pete thought about the manner in which his accident had happened and felt confident he could convince the panel his accident was nonpreventable.

The sergeant came out of the office to notify Pete it was his turn "in the barrel" for his review. Right away, Pete got the feeling he was up against a stacked deck. Pete came in and sat down in front of the panel. There were three motor cops and a sergeant reviewing cases. Pete saw they had drawn diagram of his accident on the blackboard.

"We've reviewed the facts of your T/A, Felix. Now we'd like to hear your story," said the old sergeant. Sergeant Moore was an old-timer who was the captain's adjutant. He'd been around since dirt was invented and should have retired years ago. He also had a reputation for being an ass kisser to the supervisors of TED. All this made Pete real insecure in his position on his accident.

"Well, I think my accident was not preventable because the truck changed lanes in front of me, and before I had time to adjust my distance, he crammed on the brakes to avoid the old lady in the crosswalk. That left me with nowhere to go but where I went," explained Pete. As he listened to his own version of the accident, he thought it sounded too simple and clear-cut. It was more complicated than that, he thought as he went on talking.

"All of the circumstances happening the way they did left me no alternatives to avoid the accident."

"Why were you following the truck so closely?" asked Officer Hamilton. Pete didn't know Hamilton because he worked the valley and never came downtown. Hamilton was a wrinkled-up, old fart.

"I wasn't following too close until he pulled in front of me," Pete explained with a pleading tone that he didn't like to use but just came out on its own. "Then after he pulled into my lane, he slammed on his brakes."

"But if you had been at a safe distance from the truck, you could have stopped, right?"

"I wasn't even behind the truck until he pulled in front of me," pleaded Pete again, hating his tone. "If I had had the few seconds to readjust my distance from the truck, I would have done it, but the asshole didn't give me the chance because of the old lady in the crosswalk," Pete repeated. Now he was getting mad. These guys weren't listening. They had apparently made up their minds already, or someone had made it up for them.

"Do you have anything else to add?" asked Moore. Pete thought for a moment.

"Yeah. What do kangaroos drink, and I'll send you guys a bottle of it."

"Thank you, Officer Felix. We'll notify you of our finding on your accident."

About a week later, Pete got the notice that he had "relinquished two regular days off" for his "preventable" accident. Pete smoldered inside on how the department treated the men sometimes. Pete and Bill Haymes discussed it over coffee at the Cooper's Donut Shop on their beat.

"You can't beat the system. You're just a number to those guys," philosophized Bill.

"It isn't right, Bill. We go out and work traffic in conditions that are bound to cause us to get into accidents. We expose ourselves to high risk to enforce traffic and reduce accidents, and we get penalized for the inevitable that happens to us," Pete protested. "Why should a cop put himself in that position?"

"Remember when we came on motors? We wondered why some of the motor cops would never chase speeders. Remember the guys you worked with who only took the easy tickets. The jaywalkers and chickenshit violations? They used to tell us not to bust our asses for the speed tickets and take the easy ones. Now you know why. It isn't worth it!"

"That's bullshit!" said Pete. "Writing a good ticket is one of the few gratifying jobs on the department to me," said Pete. "Think of all the times you've seen some asshole driving like an idiot, and there was no cop around. Then you catch one of them doing what you hate and get to sign him up. I love it!"

"I've got the answer to the problem. I'm going to make sergeant and join 'em because you can't whip 'em," proclaimed Bill. "That's the only answer."

"No, it isn't," said Pete. "Not for me, it isn't. I work for me, not for them anyway."

"You'll learn."

"I guess I'm just too fucking dumb, sweets."

Pete strolled into the coffee room before roll call a few days later. As he got a cup from the machine, he overheard the Beach Ball saying, "Well, today the Little Nipper comes down and makes the Safe Riding Awards at roll call." Those in the room knew that the awards were given to officers who had gone a period of time without a preventable accident. The award was in the form of a tie bar with the number of years of "safe" riding on it.

What a farce, thought Pete. Most of the guys that get the award are the ones who don't do the job as it should be done. They're the ones who don't chase speeders and just write the little old ladies jaywalking. The others probably lied and covered up some of their accidents. Officers had been known to fail to report minor accidents they had just, so they could keep their safe riding record. Pete could feel the anger growing in his gut. His recent confrontation with the kangaroo court had dashed any hopes for a safe riding tie bar for him. The captain, fondly referred to as the Little Nipper, liked to make a big deal out of the awards. Most of the men thought it was bullshit. Then Pete had an idea. He remembered that Frank Schultzer was currently pulling light duty in the office since his accident on the freeway. Frank had gone down and slid on his knees and butt for a long distance and was still recuperating. Pete ran upstairs to the office.

"Frank, is your torn-up uniform still in your locker?"

"Yeah, Pete, why?"

"I need to borrow it for a while," said Pete as he got the key to Frank's locker.

As the roll call began, the Little Nipper took his place at the head of the room and started to do his bit on safe riding and the "prestige" of "his" award. He was into his speech only a minute when the back door of the roll call room opened. All eyes turned to see who the latecomer was.

Pete walked slowly into the room and took a seat on the aisle about the center of the room. He crossed his legs and calmly stared at the Little Nipper. Pete's knees protruded through the torn holes of the tattered garment. Small bits of flesh still clung to the shredded material of the uniform. The men started to laugh when they realized the whole thing was a joke. Pete remained straight-faced as the laughter built around the room. The Little Nipper's face flushed, and he started to sweat. Pete knew the captain was in a tough spot. If he disciplined Pete, he would look bad, so he decided to go along with the joke.

"Well, maybe we can get Officer Felix to come up and make the award presentation," said the captain. Pete knew the Nipper wanted to make him look bad, but that's just what Pete wanted him to do. Pete got up and walked slowly to the front of the room. The shreds of cloth from the seat of Pete's breeches hung down a few inches and exposed part of his ass as he strolled slowly up to the front of the room. The volume of laughter increased to a high pitch. The guys were eating it up. Sergeant Moore sat motionless behind the desk on the stage, his face red with anger.

"The first award goes to John Rogers for ten years of safe riding," read Pete from the paper the captain had handed him. "John has survived a number of *low-speed* wobbles through the years and has rarely exceeded the fifty-five-mile speed limit, except in his car to and from the old folks home in Seizure World," said Pete as he handed the tie bar to the old cop.

"Hubba Hubba Burke," called Pete. Hubba Hubba was one of the guys who Pete knew had been involved in several accidents that he had not reported and had saved his safety record. "Officer Burke has not only passed all lie detector tests but has shown great initiative by carrying a generous supply of spare parts, such as footboards, red lights, and clutch levers in his saddlebags! Congratulations, Officer Burke!" Hubba Hubba mumbled some threats under his breath as he took his tie bar from Pete.

"And last, but not least, Ron Byron, my partner! Ron is the only guy I know who can have a hard-on and run into the wall and break his nose!" More laughter from the troops. Ron was laughing too as he came up to get his five-year award.

"Fuck you, asshole," mumbled Ron as he took his tie bar.

"Sorry you'll have to get in line. There are others who outrank you waiting." Pete smiled.

The roll call was over, and the guys went out laughing, except the Nipper and his staff. Pete knew they would be on his ass for his actions at the award ceremony. They wouldn't do anything now, but later, they would get him somehow. It was worth it to Pete. He felt better inside. He had made the guys laugh at the supervisors and at themselves. They needed that laugh once in a while.

CHAPTER TWENTY-FOUR

SOME FUN AND SOME NOT

Pete was not real happy to be back on night watch, but at least, he had a good area to work. Highland Park had always been his favorite division to work. It brought back many happy and sad memories working there. As he and his partner Fred Doby rode up North Figueroa Street toward York Boulevard, Pete thought of Evie Barone and wondered whatever became of her daughter. They turned west on York and cruised through the small business district of Highland Park. The area had changed a lot since the early sixties when Pete had first worked the division. Mostly for the worse.

"Let's stop at the bowling alley for coffee," yelled Fred over the rumble of the motors. Pete nodded, and they made a right onto Eagle Rock Boulevard. The bowling alley hadn't changed too much since Pete used to come in to see Evie when she worked there. As the two BCMCs walked in, Pete recognized that one of the waitresses who had worked there years ago was still working at the restaurant.

"Well, there's a familiar face I haven't seen for a while," said the tall, slender woman behind the counter. "Hi, Beverly," said Pete. "It has been a couple of years, hasn't it?"

"More like five," she corrected. "You heard about Evie?"

"Yeah," said Pete. "The asshole that killed her is probably out by now." The officers sat down and had coffee and planned the rest of the evening.

The night was warm, and traffic was heavy. As the two BCMCs patrolled, the radio got their attention. "Any Highland Park unit in the vicinity, an ambulance injury to the rear of 5224 York Boulevard." Pete and Fred were approaching the 5200 block on York at that moment. As they rolled up, they noticed the small house in the rear between two stores. They parked in the street and went "Code 6." The ambulance arrived with siren blasting as the officers walked into the house.

The small boy looked to be about seven or eight years old. He lay motionless on the mattress on the floor. Pete touched his arm. It was cool. He was not breathing. Pete noticed a red rash on the neck of the little boy. He hated when kids die. He'd seen many men and women die, but he never got used to kids dying. Fred and Pete listened as the other kids in the house told the officers in charge that their mother was at work. The boy had been sick and had a fever, but no one knew he was that sick.

"Where does your mother work?" asked the officer.

"At the bowling alley on Eagle Rock," said the kid. A sharp jolt went through Pete's body as he instantly wanted to be somewhere else. "What's her name?" asked the diligent cop. Pete knew what it was already.

"Beverly Suarez," said the kid. Shit! Pete knew what had to be done.

"We know her, guys. We'll go and break the news. Send a car over to pick her up and bring her here in about fifteen minutes, okay?" Pete and Fred headed to the bowling alley. Pete's mind numbed itself for the scene to come. As they entered the door, they met Beverly's eyes.

"Back again, huh?"

"Beverly, we've got bad news. An ambulance is at your house right now. It's about your son. It's pretty bad." Pete's eye told the story. The woman's mouth dropped open as she tried to speak. "Let's go outside," said Pete. They went outside, and they told her straight out. It's the only way it can be done. The officers were surprised and relieved at the mother's composure. The radio car arrived to take her to her house, and the BCMCs cleared and went back to work.

A few days later, Fred and Pete got a call to go to the station. The watch commander told them to report to Central Receiving Hospital. What the hell is going on? they wondered.

"I'm Dr. Goldberg," said the skinny man dressed in white. "You both have been exposed to spinal meningitis and must take medication to eliminate the chances of getting the disease," explained the doctor.

"Spinal meningitis?" asked Fred. "From where?"

"You both responded to a call in Highland Park a few days ago where a young boy died of it. Did either of you touch the body?" Oh shit, thought Pete.

"Yeah, I did," answered Pete. "Am I gonna get it?"

"Probably not," said the doctor. Pete's mind immediately recalled all the times he had been in danger and had survived. Now, the thought of getting some God-knows-what disease and shriveling up and dying made Pete's stomach turn over.

"What do we have to do?" asked Fred.

"Take these pills as directed and come back next week for a checkup, or if you feel sick, come in."

"Thanks, Doc," said Pete as he took the bottle of pills from him. "Hey, Doc, does your dick fall off with this disease?" The nurse standing nearby frowned at Pete, but he didn't care. The doctor just shook his head and turned away to more important things.

The BCMCs did not get sick, but the experience hung in their memories for a long time; and neither touched any dead bodies again.

Bobby Wheeler was a tall dark-haired Southern boy who Pete had worked with a few times before. Pete enjoyed working with Bobby because he always learned some new Southern slang from his partner. Slang that would always come in handy like: "It was slicker than deer guts on a doorknob," or "shiny as a dime in a goat's ass." Although Bobby never let his personal prejudices against blacks interfere with his job, he did have some quirks. When working the Pasadena Freeway, Bobby showed Pete where he would sit in at the on-ramp to the southbound Pasadena Freeway to "catch the hooks driving from Pasadena back to Watts." "Hooks" were black people to Bobby. Pete never asked where the name came from. He really didn't want to know. The population of Pasadena had a large percentage of blacks, which apparently Bobby resented.

Pete was assigned to work with Bobby on a night watch beat in Newton Street Division. After roll call, they met and walked out to the motors. "What you been up to, Pete?" asked Bobby. It had been nearly a year since they had worked the Pasadena Freeway together.

"Just hangin' in there, Reb. How about you?"

"Aw, the department's gettin' so chickenshit it ain't no fun no more. You can't even call 'em hooks anymore!" he exclaimed with a barely discernible twinkle in his eye.

"Yeah, and I got news for ya," said Pete. "The South ain't gonna rise again either."

"I ain't givin' up, though," Bobby chuckled as they fired up their motors and headed south into Hookland."

The evening had passed uneventfully so far, and it was Code 7 time. "Let's go over to Mary's for some Chinese food," suggested Pete. His mouth had already started to water just thinking about the pork fried rice and egg foo yung that had made Mary's Chop Suey House on Central Avenue near Olympic. One of the most popular places to eat in the whole downtown Los Angeles area, the place was run by Mary and sister, Mitzi. They had always been friendly with the cops on the street. Pete had frequented the place for many years. Mitzi had the knack of remembering names and always remembered Pete. Mary's husband was the cook.

The history of Mary and her family was similar to many Japanese-Americans who lived in Los Angeles when World War II broke out. They, along with thousands of loyal Americans of Japanese descent, lost all their property and were forced into "relocation camps" until the war was over. Mary's parents had owned a restaurant, and after the war, they started over again. Mary's father named the new restaurant after his daughter, and she and her family continued to operate it for many years. The cops loved the place, even though there were no police discounts.

"Hi, Pete," said Mitzi as Pete and Bobby walked into the restaurant. "We haven't seen you for a while." Mitzi and her older sister were cut from the same mold. Both short and somewhat heavily built. All business, with a sweet smile.

"I'm all over the streets of LA like horse pucky after a parade, kid," said Pete. Mitzi laughed and smiled the sweet smile. Her sister, Mary, was always nice but a little more businesslike. "How about some of that great pork fried rice and some egg foo yung, to go?"

"Comin' up."

The place was always full of people, no matter what time of day or night. Mary's hours of business were varied. You had to check to see when they were open. They kept strange hours, but they worked hard and, it was their business, Pete thought.

The cops picked up the food and headed for the firehouse to eat. Many cops went into the firehouses to eat. Firemen and policemen in Los Angeles shared a common "protective league" at that time. Camaraderie was close between the two departments. It had to be to give better service to the public. Pete discovered long ago that firemen were crazier than cops. He figured it was because firemen sit around too much and have time to think of crazy things to do. Like pulling practical jokes on cops.

The two BCMCs parked their motors in the hose tower of the engine house on Central Avenue near Santa Barbara Boulevard. They had parked there many times before. The hose tower was where the fire hoses were hung up to dry. It was about sixty feet high. The officers remembered to put rags under their Harleys to keep the oil off the clean floor.

"Hey, Pete! Where have you been?" greeted one of the firemen Pete had come to know. "You guys want to join the mess?" he asked. Pete had joined the firemen's dinner mess on many occasions. All they asked was the cost of the food. They cooked it. It was usually very good.

"Why should I want to do that when Mary's is just up the street?" he answered honestly. The cops sat down and ate their chow and watched TV. After they had finished, one of the firemen came over and said, "Come on up on the roof. We want to show you our invention." Bobby and Pete were curious. They followed the fireman up to the roof of the two-story building. From the roof, one could see over most of the surrounding buildings and several blocks in either direction on Central Avenue. It was Saturday night, and the "Avenue" was jumping.

"We invented a new game," informed the fireman. He unveiled the invention. It was a giant slingshot. Made from metal tubing and rubber inner tubes from cars, the instrument looked menacing. The fireman continued. "From here, we can hit anything almost a block away with a balloon filled with water," he boasted. "See that bahr-be-que stand down on Central?" asked the man, purposely putting an accent on the words. "See that dude in front dancin' around like a fucking idiot? Watch."

The fireman picked up a water balloon about four inches in diameter and hefted it in his hand. Apparently finding it satisfactory, he motioned to two other firemen on the roof with them. One man pulled the rubber tubing back while the other man steadied the slingshot. After the balloon was in place, the contrivance was aimed with the painstaking preciseness of an artillery piece. *Sprang!* The water balloon launched into the air and arched out over the buildings. Pete and Bobby watched as if hypnotized. The balloon splashed down right in the middle of a crowd of three or four black dudes in front of the stand. When it hit, the dude doing the dance jumped about three feet in the air. The firemen laughed and slapped one another on the shoulders in congratulation. Pete and Bobby laughed too. The dudes on the corner a block away were looking all around for the culprit who had dowsed them but to no avail.

"We've been hittin' these jitterbugs every Saturday for weeks now. I think they are convinced that God is droppin' water balloons on 'em," the fireman said, trying to get his breath from laughing so hard. Pete turned to Bobby.

"And people think *we're* crazy," said Pete. They walked back down to get their motors since their forty-five-minute Code 7 had long since expired.

"Where's my motor?" gasped Pete as he walked into the hose tower. His mind raced for an answer. Was it stolen? Those fucking firemen! "Okay, you guys, where's my motorcycle?" Just then, a drop of dark-colored oil hit the floor from above. Pete looked up into the tower to see his motorcycle swinging slowly back and forth, suspended from the rear wheel like some giant pendulum filled with oil, with a small leak. "You assholes! Get my motor down from there! Fucking idiots," he mumbled as he paced while the firemen all had their laugh. "You, guys, need more fires to keep your criminal minds occupied," Pete complained. Inside, he loved those guys almost as much as he did the guys he worked with. Once his bike was down on the floor again, the firemen helped Pete wipe off the oil and gasoline that had leaked out of the various tanks and holes of the motorcycle, and he and Bobby were back on the beat.

The night was nearing end of watch and had been one of those routine nights that comprise most of a policeman's shifts. The radio broke the boredom as the two motor cops rode along. "Thirteen A Twenty-nine, Thirteen A Twenty-nine. A 211 in progress at 5497 South Central. Use caution. Shots fired."

Pete and Bobby looked at each other. They were about one minute away from the location of the call and headed that direction. They both knew they would be the first units on the scene. Not the most desirable position to be in, unless you were in the movies, thought Pete. This ain't the movies, he reminded himself as they twisted the throttles and headed for the call. About a half a block away from the address, Pete grabbed his microphone and went Code 6 at the location as they were starting to slow down. The place was a liquor store. Since it was Saturday night about ten o'clock, the store was still open. As Pete slowed and prepared to stop just short of the liquor store, Bobby was a little ahead of him. Before they could come to a stop, a black man came running out of the liquor store with a pistol in his hand. "Shit," yelled Pete. "He's got a gun, Bobby." Bobby's bike skidded the rear wheel and started to slide sideways. Pete could see Bobby's hand groping for his gun even as the bike was going down. Pete was sliding too, but his attention was on the man with the gun. The man with the gun stood frozen for a moment in time as the two motor cops came sliding toward him. Then he ran toward the officers with the gun pointed in their direction. The warnings of old Bubba, the beat cop, flashed before Pete's mind. The word "wait" screamed in Pete's head. Bobby's gun was out and coming into position as his bike fell on its left side. But the first shot from Bobby's pistol had just gone off. The second and third shots followed shortly. The running man fell, and the gun went spinning across the sidewalk. Pete knew what had happened before the echoes of the last shot had stopped bouncing off the walls of the buildings. The man with the gun turned out to be the owner of the store running out after the robbers. Bobby had shot the wrong man.

Later, when robbery and homicide got through with their part of the investigation and internal affairs was about to start theirs, there was time to think. Pete's thoughts were for Bobby, but he thought mostly of himself. He thought about the terror he had felt when the cowboy had the gun in his side, and he knew he was going to die. What if he had been ahead of Bobby? Would he have done the same thing? He didn't know. Maybe. Bobby was his friend, but Pete was glad it was him and not Pete who had fired the shots. Under the circumstances, the shooting was justified by the law. It had been a mistake. The radio call had primed the officers' defense mechanisms with the "shots fired" information. The adrenaline was pumping, and survival was the goal. Survival. Pete wondered if he would survive. Would he make it to the retirement they were all working toward?

The liquor storeowner survived the gunshot wounds and received, I'm sure, a large settlement from the city. Bobby shrugged the incident off as part of the game. What choice did he have to do anything else? Pete understood.

Hollywood was a pit, but it was fun to work there. There was always something happening. As Pete and Bill Haymes, his partner, patrolled east on Santa Monica Boulevard, the sun had gone down; and it was cooling off for the night. One thing about California, thought Pete, it usually cooled off at night. Not like Iowa, he thought, remembering the humid, hot evenings he had spent sleeping in the front yard, trying to cool off from the merciless Iowa summer days. California had its faults, but one of them was not the weather.

As the two partners rode east, they passed through the intersection of Gower Street. Pete was on the left, and he instinctively looked both ways as he entered the intersection. On the south-bound side of Gower, he and Bill saw the two cars take off side by side down Gower. It was obviously a race. As if by mental telepathy, both cops switched off their headlights and made a right after the speeding cars.

The cars looked like a pair of Corvettes to Pete, an idea that would be dismissed anywhere else but in Hollywood, thought Pete, as he and Bill accelerated after the two racing vehicles. As the two cops got closer to the speeding cars, they turned on their headlights and hit the reds and sirens at the same time. The surprise was effective and the two cars slowed and started to pull over. Pete took the one that pulled over to the curb. The other car pulled into a driveway and stopped across the sidewalk due to a chain blocking the entrance to a parking lot.

The cars turned out to be Ferraris instead of Corvettes. That idea was a little less likely in Hollywood but still believable. As Pete walked up to his violator, he saw Bill walking toward a young woman who was getting out of the left side of the other Ferrari.

"Sorry, officer," said the young man as he got out of the car. "I guess we got carried away."

"I guess you did," answered Pete. "You know Gower is a twenty-five-mile residential zone, don't you?"

"You're right. We were wrong," said the young man. Pete now recognized the man as a movie personality who had been a popular star in some of the B movies the last few years. He's also been on a number of TV shows. He seemed to be a nice sort of guy and very apologetic. Pete started to write the ticket. He heard Bill lecturing the girl from the other car as he also wrote her a ticket. Because both parties were cooperative and sorry for their actions, Pete and Bill didn't write the section in the code for racing on the street but only a violation of the basic speed law for fifty in a twenty-five-mile zone.

Pete didn't give the incident much more thought until the next day when he walked into the coffee room.

"Hey, Pete," yelled Robertson, "I hear you and your partner fucked up last night."

"I don't know what you're talking about, man," answered Pete with a quizzical look on his face.

"You know! The right-hand-drive Ferrari your whipdick partner signed up!" The rest of the guys in the room all laughed.

"Would someone please let me in on the big joke?" pleaded Pete. Robertson then laid out the story that he had overheard in the watch commander's office just a short while ago. A man had called in to confess that he had been racing with another car on Gower Street last night and had gotten pulled over. He was about to be inducted into the armed forces in a few days and was afraid that a ticket would screw him up, so he made his girlfriend get out and take the ticket while he stayed in the car and hunched over to hide the steering wheel on the right side of the car.

A right-hand-drive car! thought Pete. That asshole. Then he started to see the humor in the situation and the opportunity to hassle his partner who was "always right." He joined in the chuckles as they waited to hit Pete's partner with the news. Bill took the news with his usual "Oh, no shit?" exclamation. Then he started making plans to rectify the situation. The suspect had left a phone number for Haymes to call. When he and Pete got out to the beat, Bill called the number.

"I want you to meet me at Olympic and Vermont at the drive-in restaurant at eight o'clock tonight and bring that ticket I wrote to your girlfriend with you," ordered Bill in a serious voice.

"What are you going to do?" asked Pete after Bill hung up on the guy.

"I'm gonna write him another ticket and cancel the other one."

"You can't do that," said Pete.

"He doesn't know that does he?"

The guy showed up with the bad ticket, and Bill wrote a new one for him to sign, while the guy kept apologizing all over himself. Bill and Pete made the whole thing seem very serious, and the guy went away happy and relieved. So did Bill and Pete, but Pete never let Bill forget the episode of the "right-hand-drive Ferrari."

CHAPTER TWENTY-FIVE

EARTHQUAKE!

Pete rode in to work, taking his usual route on the Santa Ana Freeway. It was February, 1971, and still dark at 6 am. The air was very cool. As he was about to enter the transition road to downtown L. A., he noticed sparks lighting up the dark sky off to his right. He wondered who would be welding at this time of the morning. Then he saw bricks in the street that had apparently fallen from an old building on First Street on his way to Parker Center. He again asked himself, "What the hell is happening?" When he arrived at roll call he found out. An earthquake had just hit and all of the BCMCs were being mobilized to do various jobs in the stricken area in the San Fernando Valley. He realized that the sparks were coming from a broken power transformer.

Funny, he thought, that he did not feel the jolt of the quake while riding. He decided that his motorcycle suspension had absorbed the movement of the earth and when riding a motorcycle, one is always moving left and right and may not notice the quaking of the ground.

The cops were sent to the Command Post at a school near Balboa Boulevard and were assembled and given instructions.

"The area beneath the Van Norman Dam has been evacuated," advised the Captain in charge. Pete did not recognize him since the Valley was like a different city to the motor cops who worked in the metropolitan LA area.

"No one is allowed to go into the evacuated area. We have assigned teams of motor officers to protect the property in the evacuated area. There is a possibility that the Van Norman Dam might break and inundate that area with a ten foot wall of water."

Uh Oh. Pete's mind went into overdrive. If the dam happens to break, what will happen to the cops in the danger area? Pete was getting a bad feeling.

Ron and Pete received an assignment to an intersection in the "danger area" about a quarter of a mile from the dam. "Well, here's another fine mess you've gotten me into, Stanley!" said Pete, trying to imitate a Laurel and Hardy saying.

"Excuse me but, what do we do if the dam does break, Partner?" asked Ron.

"I guess we could tie ourselves to a tree," joked Pete. Then he thought that might not be too far from the truth! Pete's imagination saw the solid wall of water rushing toward him and he wished he were somewhere else!

Several cars with residents arrived over the next hour and had to be turned away. Some were very angry at not being able to go to their homes. They were advised that, to do so would result in their arrest. A couple of the people tried to get past the barricades by driving around the service station on the corner where Ron and Pete were assigned. They were caught and warned and released. To eliminate the possibility of people getting in around the barricades, Ron rode down to the next intersection inside the restricted area to prevent anyone getting in who had managed to get around Pete.

An SUV with two men in it drove up to the barricade where Pete was stationed and demanded entrance to the evacuated area.

"I've gotta get in to my house!" he yelled. Pete advised him that it was against the law to go into the area and that he was subject to arrest if he did.

"By God, no one is gonna stop me!" The man jumped back into his vehicle and swerved around the barricade. Ron saw him coming and waved him down. It happened that both Ron and Pete had received training in the new baton techniques that had recently been developed for the LAPD. Ron and Pete were given the job of training the officers on their watch and had trained the BCMCs over the last few weeks.

Pete could see that the man and Ron were engaged in a nose to nose argument now and Pete was about to ride to his aid as backup. Then Pete saw Ron's baton whip out and the man was the recipient of a few well-placed jabs with the baton. The man went down. The man's companion stayed in the car and out of trouble. Pete called for a sergeant as Ron handcuffed the downed man.

"I warned the guy to back off and he refused to comply and pushed me away so . . . ."

"Looks to me like a case of self defense, Your Honor," said Pete. The sergeant arrived and turned out to be Paul Harvey, not one of the favorite supervisors. The sergeant talked to the arrested man and then told Ron to let the man go.

"Sarge, I just lumped this guy for assault on a police officer and failing to obey a lawful command and you want me to turn him loose? What if he decides to sue my ass or the City?"

They turned the man loose and made a mental check mark on this supervisor's conduct "Chart" in the bad column.

Fortunately, the dam held and the area was soon cleared for re-entry. The San Fernando Valley Earthquake killed 57 people and injured 653 others. One fatality was an unsuspecting BCMC who was responding to the quake and didn't see that the freeway had collapsed and he rode his motorcycle off of the broken bridge to his death!

When Pete and Ron got back to the Command Post, they related their story to some of the men standing around. "Ron really put some lumps on that guy," as he told the story, expecting to get some interest from the men.

"Big deal!" interjected Beach Ball. "You guys missed the naked lady who put on a show for us last night from her balcony across the street in those apartments!"

When faced with the possibility of being drowned and getting into an altercation with an irate citizen, Pete had to agree. Big deal!

To Pete and the other BCMCs it was another incident where the motorcycle squad was used as the disaster response team. Pete liked the thought of being a part of the first ones in on an important event and helping to protect property and lives.

CHAPTER TWENTY-SIX

NEW BIKES

Rumors were going around on the department that Harley-Davidson Motor Company was about to lose the contract to provide police motorcycles for the LAPD.

"None too soon for me," expressed C. K. Williamson to Pete when he told C. K. about the rumor. "You know, every year the bidding process for the motorcycle contract comes up for renewal, and Harley always gets it."

"One reason is because it has been a policy of the city not to buy anything not made in the USA for city use," said Ron Byron. Ron had been involved in testing some of the motorcycles offered for city purchase in the past. "First the bidders have to pass the specifications; then we test 'em. Of course, Harley always gets a little bit better shot than some of the competitors."

"Why do we always end up with Harleys?" asked C.K.

"Because," answered Ron, "that's the way it is."

Pete was tired of hearing that phrase on the job. It seemed to be the stock answer for questions that involved politics.

"Well, it looks like 'the way it is' might be the way it was," said Pete. The men walked to their motorcycles, trading horror stories about bad motors they had ridden. Most of the stories revolved around the poor braking and handling characteristics the men attributed to the Harleys. Still, many of the old-timers swore by them and scorned all other motorcycles.

A few weeks later, Pete and Ron received invitations to attend a meeting about the new motorcycles the city was planning to test.

The Moto Guzzi Company had been making motorcycles since 1921 and was a well-known name on the international market. They had produced a model that seemed to fit the needs of the LAPD and was to be tested in the field by the BCMCs.

The room was buzzing with comments as the officers waited for the meeting to begin. There were about ten motor officers who had been chosen to do the testing. Most of them Pete and Ron knew. The Moto Guzzi Company had sent several representatives, including technical people, to the meeting. The program was explained to the officers.

The testing would be done over a year period during which the selected officers would be assigned a motorcycle. He would ride the bike in the same manner he would have during his usual assignment. Pete could hardly wait. Although the bikes looked sleek and well-equipped and the black gas tanks with white pin stripping and white fenders looked like a police bike, there were a few strange-looking differences from the police bike folks were used to seeing.

The engine was a V-twin, like the Harley, but the engine was mounted with the cylinders protruding from the sides under the gas tank in front of the rider's legs instead of from front to rear, as on the Harley. The red lights on the front were larger than the ones on Harleys. The size of the lights was mandated by the California Highway Patrol. Pete wondered why those same specifications were not enforced on Harley-Davidson. That's the way it is, again, he thought.

Pete felt privileged to be among the test group and that he would be a part of a new program that he thought would improve the motor squad's capabilities. The men picked up their new shiny bikes at the motor shop and headed out for their beats. As Pete rode along, the first thing he noticed was the ease of handling of the motorcycle. The balance seemed good, and the Pirelli tires seemed to corner well. The brakes seemed a little weak, but Pete loved the bike. An article appeared in the local newspaper about the new Italian police bikes, so the public was aware of the testing. Many questions were asked about the new machine, but not all of the people got the word.

"Is dat one of them new police bikes?" asked one black dude Pete was writing up.

"Yes, sir, it is."

"Motto Guzzi," read the dude, mispronouncing the words.

"Tha's Japanese, ain' it?" asked the dude.

"That's right," said Pete because he was tired by this time answering all the dumb questions he'd been asked.

Pete pulled the guy over on the freeway and told him he was going to issue a ticket for speeding. The guy was not too happy about it and got out of the car to try and change Pete's mind, which didn't happen often. As they stood on the side of the freeway, Pete took his usual position, facing the violator, while he filled out the ticket. Pete practiced what he had been taught when he became a BCMC: never let a person get too close to your gun or get behind you while you're writing a ticket. This guy had decided he wanted to look over Pete's shoulder while he wrote.

"Sir, I'll be happy to let you read the ticket after I fill it out, but let me finish it first," pleaded Pete, as he moved away from the man who seemed determined to stand right up close to Pete's right side. His "gun side." The man moved right back to his close-up position.

"I want to see what you are writing about me. I have a right," he said.

"You have a right to see the ticket *after* I write it but not during. Would you please let me finish it?" said Pete firmly, and he again moved away from the obnoxious man. The man was persistent, and Pete was losing his patience. Pete searched his mind for a way to discourage the man from following him in his every move. The more Pete asked the man not to interfere, the more obnoxious the violator became. Pete realized this was getting to be a dangerous situation. Then he had an idea. As the man again moved up to Pete's gun side, Pete let him stand there for a few seconds, and then Pete sneezed. Well, really, he pretended to sneeze. He turned his head in the direction of the man and made sure to blow spit in the guy's face. *Achoo!*

The guy jumped back, wiping his face with his hand. "You did that on purpose," he yelled. Pete put on an innocent look and shrugged his shoulders.

"Gee, I'm really sorry, sir," he whined. "I've got a bad cold. I told you to get away from me. I just couldn't help it." Pete knew the guy could never prove otherwise, and it did solve the problem.

CHAPTER TWENTY-SEVEN

MOTOR SCHOOL AND PAIN

Pete had now been on motors for nearly ten years and had gained a reputation for being a good worker, but had a hard time keeping his mouth shut. It seemed like he just couldn't pass up the opportunity to get a laugh at the expense of the police supervisors. Even so, the motors supervisors liked Pete, with a couple of exceptions. Most of the supervisors were pretty nice guys, having come up through the ranks. But some had short memories of when they were out in the field. "Elf Ears" was one of those kind. When he came to motors as a lieutenant, he brought along a chip on his shoulder. Pete and Elf Ears clashed immediately.

Lieutenant Morind had ears that kind of stuck out and were pointed like an elf. He had been a cop for more than twenty years, most of which he'd spent on motors. When he made sergeant, he had left the squad and done his time as a field supervisor. During that time, he had not endeared himself to the troops. He was very self-centered and was a strict disciplinarian. Both traits were wasted on BCMCs.

The first couple of roll calls with Elf Ears in command had gone without incident, but that didn't last. The men were sitting in the roll call room, filling out their daily field activity logs for the day before. Some of the guys were talking, and there was the usual daily loud fart from Fred Dougherty as the lieutenant and the sergeant entered the room. Elf Ears was in a bad mood from the beginning. "Okay, you men," barked the lieutenant, "listen up to announcements." The room quieted down. He read off several notices that went unnoticed.

"Here's a bad accident involving one of the motor officers in the valley. Officer J. J. Lawrence went down and was unconscious for several hours, but is recovering now."

Pete grabbed that one. "Too bad he wasn't unconscious a little longer. They'd have made him a lieutenant!" The room broke up with laughter. Elf Ears' ears turned red, and he fumed.

"Felix, see me upstairs after roll call!"

After roll call, Pete went up to the watch commander's office. Elf Ears was waiting for him. "I've heard about your jokes at roll call Felix, and I don't like it," said Elf Ears. As he chewed Pete out for his comment at roll call, Pete looked at him and thought he really did look like an elf. An evil elf. "I don't want to hear one more word out of you at roll call! Do you understand, Felix?"

"Yes, sir!" answered Pete, as he walked out of the office. He knew he was in trouble and might even be transferred for his comments. Fuck this asshole, he thought, and went out to work.

The next day at roll call, the men were assembled when the lieutenant came in with his usual frown on. The room got quiet immediately. Roll call began. As the men's names were called, they answered up. Then he got to Pete.

"Felix?" No answer.

"Felix?" Again, no answer. Pete was trying to answer and waved his hand in the air wildly. Finally, Elf Ears repeated the name in a loud voice and looked around the room.

"Felix! Are you here?"

"Hmm! Hmm!" said Pete through the large piece of duct tape he had placed over his mouth. "Hmm!" he said again as he waved his arms in the air.

"Take that tape off your mouth, Felix," ordered the lieutenant. Pete pulled the tape off with a grimace of pain. "What are you doing?" demanded Elf Ears.

"You told me not to say another word at roll call, so I was just following your orders, Lieutenant," said Pete in a subservient voice. The men were laughing so hard that Elf Ears was stymied for an answer. After that, Elf Ears gave up on Pete and took up a waiting mode to try to catch Pete doing something for which he could be punished.

Pete and Noel had been living in Whittier, California, for about three years now and had a nice house in a middle-class neighborhood. Life was going well for the couple, and—although Noel had the same fears and dislikes about Pete's job, which were common to most cop's wives—they were getting along well. Pete rode into the garage of his house and parked his police motor and went into the house through the garage door into the kitchen.

"Honey, I'n hone," he yelled, imitating the Cuban accent of Desi Arnaz on the *I Love Lucy* show on TV. Noel came into the kitchen and kissed her husband hello.

"What are you so happy about, Jose?" she asked.

"I've been asked to be an instructor at the next motor school," he said excitedly.

"Oh yeah?" she commented. "Is that good or bad?"

"It's great!" he beamed. "It's kinda like being told you're one of the good guys."

"Congratulations," she said. "When do you start, and what do you do?"

"The school starts next month, and I'll be one of about six other cops on the staff. It's a kick in the ass."

"I'm happy for you. Don't get hurt."

"It's okay, Mom. I won't."

The LAPD motor school was one of the best schools around, and many other police departments sent their cops there to be trained. The only other police motorcycle training school was the CHP school in Sacramento.

Pete remembered his days in the school. He was amazed at how time had flown by. It had been almost ten years since he had joined the ranks of the BCMCs. He remembered the hassle the instructors gave the candidate cops at the school. Since then, Pete had gotten to know most of the men who had been instructors there and understood why they had done most of the things at the school. Still, there were always the things that were not pertinent to the training and were just done for fun. It was part of the spirit of the squad.

Pete found out that the school was run in a very informal manner. The older instructors gave the orders, and guys like Pete made it happen. Little had changed in the way the officers were taught how to ride since Pete and his class had gone through. So it was easy for Pete to jump in and teach. He liked to teach and had a talent for it, it seemed.

As the classes proceeded, it brought back memories of him and Ron and Bill and many others whom he had worked with over the years on motors. Bill Haymes had since been promoted to sergeant and had a squint job in Planning and Research Division. Ron Byron was still on motors but was looking for a place to go.

Why do they always have these classes in the winter? Pete wondered. The small group of instructors and candidates huddled around the fifty-five-gallon oil drum that served as a stove on the windy expanse of parking lot used as the training ground for the LAPD motor school. The parking lot was a part of the Los Angeles Zoo facility in Griffith Park and was a short distance from the area where Pete and his friends had taken their training. Of course, the new zoo had not yet been built then. This parking lot was huge and provided a good place to train the BCMCs of the future.

"We'd better get these guys moving, or we'll freeze to death," suggested Sergeant Drumm, the old-timer in charge of the school. He had been around since Harley and Davidson were crapping in their diapers, thought Pete. He was well-liked and respected by the troops because of his easygoing style and reserved nature. The fledgling motor cops were put through basically the same training that past LAPD motor cops endured for three weeks. Pete loved every minute of it and hoped someday he could do it again.

Pete decided to have some fun and obtained some blank cartridges used in training at the police academy. He loaded them into his gun that morning, waiting for the right opportunity to use them. That day a motor cop in uniform showed up at the school. This was not unusual because many cops came to watch and visit while the school was in progress.

The cop in uniform was a guy named Norman Kosinsky, a big blond Polish cop. Kosinsky helped himself to a cup of coffee from the instructor's pot and walked over to the edge of the asphalt training ground to the edge of a swampy area off the pavement. He stood with his back to Pete, who was standing about twenty feet away.

"Hey, Normie, hold up that cup and let's see if I can hit it from here," yelled Pete, as he drew his pistol. Kosinsky turned and smiled, as he held out his coffee cup to his left at arm's length.

"Bet'cha can't hit it," he yelled, accepting the challenge in a joking manner and knowing Pete would not really shoot.

Pow! Pete cranked off a blank round at the cup. Kosinsky staggered backward toward the swamp and nearly fell in.

"Jesus Christ," he yelled at Pete. "I felt the wind of that, you crazy son of a bitch!" Pete now expected the big angry Polack to either shoot back or beat the shit out of him. As Kosinsky came toward Pete, one of the other instructors intervened.

"It was only a blank, Norm. You're right, though. He is a crazy SOB, ain't he?"

They all started to laugh, and the class needed one anyway. Kosinsky even laughed . . . a little.

A couple of days later, another cop paid a visit to the school. This time, it was bad news.

"The Rocket is dead," informed the cop. Jim "Rocket" Evans had been killed in a motorcycle accident while chasing a fleeing suspect. Rocket and Pete had been friends. Pete had helped him move into his new home a couple of years ago. They had watched the first manned landing on the moon on TV at Rocket's house. Pete's thoughts ran back over the friendship, which had encompassed several years. The thoughts hurt, but the protective shield was in place that protects cops from too much trauma too close to home.

"We all know it might happen to us," Sergeant Drumm told the new motor cops who had just gotten the word also. Some of them knew the Rocket too. "The funeral is set for next Wednesday," the sergeant advised the men. "That's the reason we're having this school. So you won't end up like Evans, and several others we have known over the years. Don't take unnecessary chances chasing these assholes in the street. We know that fifty percent of the chases end in a traffic accident. It's usually the suspect hitting something or someone, but sometimes it's us!" The men were quiet and introspective. They were all experienced officers, but the experience of losing a comrade on duty is never easy. The old sergeant continued because he had to.

"If you kill someone in the line of duty, your ass will be on the line. Did you do it right? Was your action justified? The news media will be quick to criticize. When a cop gets killed, it's different. Do they care? Who was at fault? Will they hang the asshole that caused the accident? Mostly, no one cares but us and our families. To the people out there, we are doing our job. That job, to them, includes dying. They think it's a part of the job, and they accept it as routine. The bottom line is 'they don't give a shit'! So we have to. That's why we're so hard on you here. So you will make it. Not all of us do. Rocket didn't. Maybe it was his own fault. Maybe there was nothing he could do to prevent it. I don't know. Let's just make sure we leave this place with the best chance we can have to survive." The sergeant finished his speech, and the men were quiet. Cops don't show emotion to one another. They're just quiet.

About fifty percent of Pete's tickets were speeders. Pete liked to chase speeders. He thought it was the most prevalent cause of accidents. Most people think things like "running red lights" or "failing to yield the right-of-way" are the most frequent causes. But, as Pete always put it, "What makes 'em run the red or not yield? It's usually because they're going too fast!" Anyway, Pete liked the thrill of the chase, and most people who get stopped for speeding don't go to court. Why? Either you were speeding, or you were not. It's that simple. Pete always gave the violators plenty of slack before he cited them. He never (well, hardly ever) wrote anyone who wasn't going at least ten miles or more over the limit.

"Felix, do you want to work a speed complaint on Third Street?" asked the sergeant after roll call. Complaints come in from the field all the time. Mostly, they come from irate citizens about the traffic in their neighborhood. Most of them are investigated, and many of them are handled by assigning a "special detail" to patrol the area of complaint.

"The complaint area is on Third Street between Fairfax and Western. Speed is usually inbound early in the mornings. It should be an apple orchard for you," explained the sergeant. "Go out and write the shit out of them and turn the tickets in to me."

"Okay, Sarge."

The first day out on the complaint, Pete could see why people were complaining. The speed was terrific. Pete sat on a side street north of Third for a while and just watched traffic going east into downtown Los Angeles. The zone was posted thirty-five, but Pete guessed the normal flow at this time of the morning was closer to fifty. The street was two marked lanes in each direction with a parking lane on each side. During heavy traffic hours, the parking lanes were "no parking" eastbound from 6:00 AM to 10:00 AM, and westbound from 4:00 PM to 6:00 PM on weekdays. Not many cars used the extra no parking lanes for driving, mainly because they didn't notice the signs.

Pete set up shop and went to work. He sat in at both ends of the complaint area and chased speeding cars back and forth. Most of the tickets he wrote were for fifty or better in the thirty-five-mile zone. Pete was shooting them down right and left.

The second day on the compliant started about the same as the first. Pete sat in just south of Third on Orange Drive and watched traffic eastbound. A car sped by out in front of the traffic that had just left La Brea. Pete fired up his Moto Guzzi and started after the violator. He got trapped by traffic and had to wait for a few seconds before he could begin to chase the speeder. Pete could see him pulling away fast about two blocks ahead of him.

While Pete worked his way through the heavy traffic, he could see that unless he got out in front of the cars blocking his way, he would lose the violator. The right "parking lane" was clear. The other alternative was to turn on his red lights and siren and cross the double lines onto the other side of the street.

As most cops learn early in their careers, Pete did not trust red lights and siren pursuits. People don't see or hear when they drive. They just drive. Emergency vehicles, like fire trucks and ambulances, have to drive slowly while going "Code 3" just to survive in traffic. Pete was not about to go Code 3 after this guy, so he moved into the right parking lane and tried to get through that way.

As he approached the intersection of June Street, he noticed a Volkswagen Bug ahead in lane 2, the second from the center. The car appeared to be going at about thirty-five or forty. Pete guessed that he could wait and pass the VW on the right when the car had almost passed the intersection and could not possibly turn right. Now! Pete gassed the throttle to make the pass. At the same instant, the VW slowed and turned right. Pete's mind went into slow motion as he heard himself say, "Oh shit!"

The VW was about fifty feet ahead of Pete when it turned. Not a chance to stop. The rear wheel of the motorcycle skidded and screeched in Pete's ears. The VW loomed up in his face. *Bam!* The impact sent Pete flying through the air. Pete looked down as he passed over the top of the Volkswagen. Tumbling over and over in the air, he asked himself, When will I come down? *Thump!* I'm down on my feet, and rolling backward, noticed Pete with surprise. "Ooofff, ugh, oooh . . ." yelled Pete, as his momentum stopped; and he slid to a halt on his back.

Pete looked around in amazement. He was still alive. People were running over to him. He looked over and saw his beloved bike buried in the right rear of the VW. It just hung there. The driver of the VW was getting out of the car. Then, he just stood by his door and watched with his arms folded over his chest.

"Are you all right?" asked a face peering wide-eyed down at Pete. Pete tried to say something, but words wouldn't come out. That's funny, he thought. I've never been at a loss for words before.

"Get his belt off," said someone, and Pete felt tugging on his Sam Browne belt. The person didn't know how the buckle on his belt worked, so Pete tried to help. Funny, he thought, my right arm doesn't work right. Pain and stiffness in the wrist. Shit! Broken, I'll bet, he thought. Now the pain started in his ankles. Both of them. One of Pete's fellow officers, Hughie Milligan, appeared before Pete's eyes. He said something about the ambulance. Things are fogging up, thought Pete.

"What's your name, officer?" asked the ambulance attendant.

"Pete Felix," correctly answered Pete.

"What's your home phone number?" he asked. Pete thought and thought but couldn't remember it. How can I forget my own phone number? The ambulance ride to Hollywood Presbyterian Hospital lasted a few minutes. In the operating room, Pete heard the doctor saying that his boots should be cut off.

"Bullshit!" said Pete, coming out of his fog. "Those boots cost a lot of money. Just pull them off," he demanded through the haze. So they did. Pete fainted. When he woke up again, he was in another ambulance headed for somewhere. When he got to "somewhere," he went to sleep again. As the fog cleared again, he saw Noel's face looking down anxiously at his.

"Hi," said Pete. In the background, he saw other faces. Familiar faces for which he could not remember names. Then he felt the cold ice packs on his ankles and went to sleep again.

After an unknown number of hours, Pete returned to earth from wherever he had been. It seemed to Pete he was gone a long time. Little bits of memory came back to him, but they didn't seem to make any sense. He knew he had been in an accident. He remembered looking down at the top of the VW as he passed overhead like a projectile. Then things had gone into the fog. Now he was back.

He immediately felt the pain in his legs. Both of them. He looked down and surveyed his body. There was a huge plaster cast covering his right leg up to the hip. The left leg appeared to be wrapped in a splint. His right arm was in a cast up to the shoulder, bent at the elbow at a ninety-degree angle. Soon the doctor came in and advised Pete of his injuries.

"Well, you've broken your ankles at the joints, and your left heel is cracked. You've got a compressed fracture of the right wrist. Other than that, you're fine," said the thin young man with the title on his nameplate. "I did surgery on the right ankle and put a screw in to hold the bone in place while it heals. I did not cast the left one because then you'd be in a wheelchair for about six weeks. I didn't think you'd care for that."

"Thanks, Doc," said Pete. "I appreciate that. When can I get out of here? By the way, where am I?"

"You're in Orthopedic Hospital, and you can get out of here as soon as you can walk on crutches on your own. I've scheduled therapy to begin in a couple of days."

A couple of days! thought Pete. I can't even wipe my own ass, and therapy starts in a couple of days? Pete laid back and thought about his situation. Of course, he felt sorry for himself. He'd never been trapped in a hospital before. What kind of a madhouse is this? he wondered, as the nurses banged around; and people bustled in at all hours of the night and day, making all kinds of noise.

When Pete got more of his senses back, he looked around and saw that he was in a room with four beds, three of which were occupied. The man in the bed across from him, Pete learned, was a crippled truck driver. Dave had been a newly married young man driving a truck for a living. The accident had put his truck into the center divider fence of the freeway. He had been trapped in the cab, his left arm nearly torn off. In fact, a little more, and his head would have gone too. The injuries had left him paralyzed from the neck down, except for his right arm. Dave came to the hospital frequently for intensive care. Then he would go home for a few months.

In the other bed was a younger man. Pete estimated he was only about seventeen. He appeared to be part Chinese and something else, maybe Mexican or Negro. Pete was not too happy with Kung Fu/Jose, as Pete called him. He jabbered on and on about nothing. Pete worried about Dave. Dave seemed to have bright spirits, but Pete saw through the pain. Pete decided that Dave's future was not as bright as his spirits.

Noel came to visit Pete, as did his parents, who had flown in from Des Moines. It was now obvious to everyone, including Pete, that he would recover. The doctor had told him his recovery would take several months. Pete wanted more detailed information.

"I want to know how long it will take me to get back to normal, where I was before the accident."

"I would say about two years," answered the doctor.

"Two years! Two years?" he asked in disbelief. I haven't got that much time, he thought.

After that, Pete went into depression. He couldn't believe this was happening to him. He thought about his past life. He'd never been sick a day in his life. Two years? Bullshit!

"Therapy is the first step to recovery," they said. "Therapy starts as soon as possible after trauma," they said. A very nice-looking OBG (oldie but goodie) woman walked in and introduced herself to Pete.

"Hi, Pete. I'm Eve Levine, your therapist." Maybe he would recover after all, thought Pete. "Let's get you down to the therapy room for your first visit," the blond attractive lady with freckles said. Pete felt her warmth and friendliness and realized he was not just a lump of meat covered with plaster.

"Let's go, Chief," said Pete. They piled him into a wheelchair and off to the therapy room. On the way down, they were joined by another patient going to the same destination. This patient was a small boy, about seven years old with major birth deformities. His back and lower body had recently undergone corrective surgery.

When they arrived in the therapy room, Pete saw a large room full of other people and a lot of funny-looking exercise equipment. There were several other people undergoing therapy at the time. One man, about thirty, had a very large piece of his right calf missing. Another man had one leg fastened to the other in a skin grafting process.

The little boy cried out in pain as his therapy began. Pete looked around the room. He looked at the little boy on the table. He'd never be normal. The guy with the missing part of his leg—same deal. Poor Dave up in the room with his young wife. He'd never walk again or have a family. No one really knew how long he would even survive. Pete cursed himself for being so arrogant and for his self-pity. I'm going to get well, he thought. He knew that. When it's all over, I'll be back on that iron horse, Pete told himself. He knew it. He realized how lucky he was. God must have been looking down on him when he hit that car and tumbled through the air more than thirty feet, then to land on his feet instead of his head. How lucky can you get? Pete's attitude changed after that. At least until they got him up out of the wheelchair.

"Holy shit," Pete moaned, as the big black dude pulled on the thick leather belt with the handles on it that was fastened around Pete's waist. It had only been two days since Pete's surgery, and now they want him to stand up on two broken ankles? This ain't happening, he thought. But it was.

"Come on," said the black dude. "You can do it." Easy for you to say, asshole, thought Pete as the searing pain shot up his legs. He looked down. He was on his feet—sort of. Larry was holding most of his weight with his thick arms. Pete sat down again in the wheelchair with a sigh of relief.

"Now that wasn't too bad, was it?" said Larry the Therapy Dude.

"No, man," said Pete sarcastically. "There's nothing I'd rather do right now than dance with you!" The goal was explained to Pete. Once he could get around on his own on crutches, he could leave the hospital. To be able to use a crutch with his broken right arm, a specially designed crutch had to be fabricated.

A piece of wood was fastened to the crutch at a right angle to the length and parallel to the floor so that Pete's arm and elbow could rest on it instead of on his wrist. A small dowel was fastened to the end of the wood, so Pete could get a grip on the crutch. Two pieces of Velcro were then used to fasten the crutch to Pete's arm cast. The first time he tried to use it, he thought it wouldn't work. But after a little practice, he got the hang of it. He could only take a few steps at a time, all of which were filled with pain.

"Did you ever notice how pain hurts?" he asked Eve, his therapist, the second day on his new crutch. She laughed and patted his shoulder softly.

"Big brave cops can take it," she said. Why do people think we are different from other human beings? Pete wondered.

Generally, cops don't like to admit to any softness or empathy, even toward other cops. They must maintain the hard exterior shell of what they think protects them from harm, both physical and mental. Pete had trouble with that sometimes. Other times it was a necessity for survival. Most cops kidded one another about their personal problems. It was their way of saying, "I know you got 'em. Don't we all?"

Pete recalled the time when G. L. Wilhams had been broadsided by a deuce and had broken his back. Pete went to see him in the hospital. G. L. lay there wrapped in a plaster cast from his waist up over his shoulders, helpless. Pete hoped it would never happen to him.

The injured cop had not lost his sense of humor, though, and joked with Pete and said he appreciated Pete coming to see him. He also said that very few of the guys had done so. Pete asked why.

"I guess they don't like to think it could happen to them," explained Wilhams. "You know how cops are? They are invulnerable and think they can't be killed. If they come around here, it puts doubts in their minds."

"I don't understand, but maybe you're right."

"Hey, Pete, there's a crazy guy in here from Central Division who pulled a good one on the nurse. She left a bottle on his table for a urine sample. While she was gone, he filled the bottle up with apple juice from his lunch. When she came back to get the urine sample, the cop picked up the bottle and said, 'Looks a little weak, nurse. I'll run it through again.' Then he drank the apple juice. The nurse screamed and ran out to get the doctor!" The two cops broke up in laughter.

"Don't make me laugh. It hurts," said Wilhams, as he cringed in his plaster cast.

Now it was Pete's turn to lie alone in the hospital and think. His relatives had been there to see him. Ron had been in a couple of times, but Pete missed the guys he worked with. The nurse came in to get a urine sample from him. Pete wished he had some apple juice. She handed him a large pitcher for the urine sample and walked away, closing the drapes around his bed for privacy.

That was good because Pete was going to have to be creative to be able to pee in this container. Holding the metal pitcher with his cast right arm, Pete struggled to hold his penis with his good left hand and hit the pitcher. It was going to be a real chore.

As he lined up on the target, Pete saw black motorcycle boots walk into the room under the closed curtain.

"Just a minute," said Pete, as he was about to start peeing. *Swish!* The curtain was pulled open; and Pete saw the wrinkled, leathery face of Jim Stewart, one of the old-timers on motors.

"If you ain't the sorriest-lookin' son of a bitch," said Jim. He was shaking his head in disdain as he looked at Pete's predicament.

"Get the fuck out of here, you old fart," yelled Pete, as he tried to finish the task before him. The old man closed the curtain, and Pete placed the urine sample on the table beside his bed.

"I'll bet you got a kick out of watching me piss in a pitcher, didn't ya, asshole?" whined Pete.

"Here. I brought you a present, whipdick," said the old man, as he handed a box to Pete.

"Great! Cigars. You know I can't smoke in here, you dumb shit," complained Pete.

"Open it up and shut up," said Jim. Pete opened the cigar box and found it contained not cigars but a pint of good scotch.

"Hey, thanks, partner. You know, they don't open the bar around here very often."

"A stiff shot of this stuff with those fucking pills they give you at night, and you'll visit other planets," predicted the old man.

Pete felt good after the old man left. He guessed maybe cops weren't as hard as he thought. They just try to make people think they are. Even the old man.

As Pete lay there in thought, a hospital attendant came into the room to clean up. Pete hardly noticed him until he heard the attendant pouring his urine sample, he had struggled so hard to give, down the toilet. Pete could hardly wait to drink the scotch.

A couple of days later, Pete's commanding officer Captain Manger came to visit him. He had his adjutant, Sergeant Converse, with him. Neither man was well-liked by the troops. The captain had developed a reputation for being rather cold to most of the men. At least, the ones he didn't like. Pete wasn't quite sure where he stood on the captain's list. Pete had established a reputation for being a smart-ass at roll call. The incident at the safe riding awards with the previous motors commander had become something of a legend on the squad. Pete thought the captain probably would like to do without Pete's brand of humor, if he could.

The captain sat on a turned-around chair beside Pete's bed. The sergeant sat at the foot.

"How are you doing, Felix?" asked the captain.

"I'm having a ball, Captain. When they turn the lights out at night, me and these other guys in here all sneak out to the bar down the street."

The captain's brow wrinkled. Pete wondered why captains lost their sense of humor. Maybe it's required for the job? he thought.

"You know, we'll have to talk about this accident when you get back. You've had several others. This one may be another preventable," said the captain.

"No shit?" said Pete, his temper flaring. "Well, how about you and your sister get the fuck out of my room, and if you want to come back and 'cheer me up' again, call first!"

There was a short silent pause in the room; then the Captain and his companion got up and left. Pete lay there, stewing about the visit. He thought of several things. One, the captain was overdue in his visit. Two, any discussion of any fault in the accident could wait until Pete was out and back to work. He didn't need this. A few of the guys came to see Pete. He always wished there had been more, but he understood. The captain never came back.

Laying in a hospital bed was not Pete's idea of fun. Pete had never been sick a day in his life, Being out on the street as a cop was his life. In that environment, he felt free. Here, he felt trapped. His mind started to think about his future. Would he be taken off motors because of some permanent disability? Would he *be* disabled? Would he have to retire from the job? These thoughts tortured him while he lay almost helpless in his bed. He resolved to get out of there as soon as he could. He had to get out of there.

"Hi, honey," said Noel, interrupting his not-too-pleasant thoughts.

"Hi, baby, what's going on?" Pete was happy to see his wife. She had been in to see him every day and had done her best to cheer him up. She brought him news of the neighborhood and greetings from neighbors who wished him well.

"How come in the movies the nurses are all beautiful and sexy, and here, they look like shaved gorillas?" whined Pete. "And why is it the male nurse that comes to give you a bath is always an aspiring ballet dancer with plucked eyebrows?" Pete felt like pissing and moaning but knew it wouldn't do any good, and no one could help him anyway.

"I brought you a present," said Noel, handing Pete what appeared to be a small bottle wrapped in paper. Pete opened it with his teeth, as he held it in his good left hand. The paper peeled away, revealing a bottle labeled Listerine mouthwash.

"Gee, thanks, honey. I'm sorry if my breath is bad," said Pete, trying to show a little annoyance for his sorrowful situation.

"Read the label," said Noel. Pete looked closer at the label this time. In the upper right hand corner of the label was a smaller label that read, "Twelve years old." What the hell does that mean? thought Pete. Then he opened the bottle and smelled the liquid inside.

"Scotch," he declared. Then he realized that Noel had smuggled some of his favorite booze into the hospital. No one would question a bottle of Listerine in his drawer. It was kind of like sneaking a gun into prison, Pete thought. It excited him, and he had to laugh, in spite of the situation.

"Thanks, honey. I'll be sure to use this before I go to sleep tonight." Later, when Noel was gone and he was again alone with his thoughts and fears, Pete popped the sleeping pill the nurse had brought him and washed it down with a mouthful of "Listerine," making sure he gargled with it first, of course. The combination worked wonders for his sleeping ability, and he had a good night's sleep for the first time in several days.

CHAPTER TWENTY-EIGHT

BACK AGAIN

The doctor had said Pete could go home when he could walk with the crutches. That wasn't easy since Pete had to use the right crutch with his broken right arm. After about two days of practice, Pete was doing well. His therapist, Eve, helped him a lot, giving him encouragement and cracking jokes about "macho cops." Pete needed to be teased. It helped him keep going. He needed the humor too. After the tenth day of Pete's stay in the hospital, he took his "test" to get sprung from his prison. Pete was still in a lot of pain whenever he put his weight on his ankles, but he wanted out. Just before going down to the therapy room for his test, Pete took a big shot of Listerine to help kill the pain. It seemed to work well.

"Okay," said Eve, "let's see what you can do." Pete strapped on the Velcro that held his right arm to the crutch and grabbed the left crutch with his good arm. Larry supported him while he got out of the wheelchair. Pete cringed with the pain, when he stood on his left leg, the least injured of the two. He tried to cover up the pain by smiling as he hobbled forward on the makeshift crutch set up. One step. Two steps. Pete hoped they would not see the pain in his eyes and just look at his smile while he wobbled on. Three, four. Now the stair steps. The stair steps?

"You have to be able to go up and down these steps too," said Eve. When Pete looked at her, she instantly changed from the attractive, shapely woman he'd seen for the last ten days into the wicked witch he remembered from the *Wizard of Oz*.

"My little dog Toto too?" he asked. She cocked her head to the side.

"What?" she asked.

"Never mind," said Pete as he tried to put the crutch up onto the first step. After a little more wobbling and mind control, Pete apparently satisfied the Witch and her flying monkey that he was able to function on his own. Free at last, yelled Pete in his mind, anticipating his release from the hospital.

Pete had never been in a wheelchair before. The experience was humbling. He thought about all the people who would never get out of theirs. He knew he would get out of his. Pete felt lucky and thankful for his future. Everyone should go through this kind of experience, he thought. It's a good reminder to a person of how much better off you are than others who are less fortunate. Pete never forgot that lesson.

"I'm going to run to the store, honey," called Noel from the kitchen. Pete had been home about a week now and was still in the wheelchair most of the time.

"Okay, honey," yelled Pete. "I'll be fine." Pete heard the car drive away. He got up on his crutches and hobbled out into the garage. Pete had been waiting for just such an occasion. He was alone. He had planned this just as a prisoner would an escape. He hobbled out into the garage and looked at his 1971 Honda Four motorcycle sitting there, waiting for someone to ride it. Pete had purchased the new bike just months before his mishap with the VW. It wasn't even broken in yet. It sat there gleaming in the ray of sun coming in through the open garage door.

Pete didn't know why, but he had to ride it. He knew he would be well enough soon, but "soon" was not soon enough. He had planned this in his mind for days. How he would work the brake with his plaster-covered right arm. Once in first gear, Pete would stay there and go slowly around the block. Just once. That's all he wanted. He had to do it to prove to himself he could still do it. He'd been nearly helpless for too long now. He didn't care anymore. He'd planned this, and he was going to do it.

He carefully pushed the bike off the center stand. Pete had to maintain good balance during all these actions. If he lost it, things would come crashing down, and the game would be over. He didn't want to fail. Slowly, he pushed the bike out onto the driveway. Moving an inch or two at a time, he got the bike in position.

He had just swung his leg over the saddle and was studying the controls when Noel drove around the corner toward the driveway. As she pulled up and stopped, her eyes got big, and she jumped out of the car screaming.

"What are you doing? Are you crazy?" she yelled, waving her arms about.

"Don't try and stop me," said Pete in a determined voice. "I'm just going to ride around the block very slowly," he said. The engine fired up on the first try.

"You must be nuts," yelled Noel. "If you fall, you'll end up back in the hospital," she pleaded.

"I ain't fallin'," said Pete. "I gotta do this, so let me alone, okay?"

"I think you're a stupid idiot, and I don't care what you do," she yelled on the verge of tears. "I'm going in the house. I don't want to see this." She stormed off into the house. Pete let the clutch out slowly and started down the driveway. Once he got going, it was a piece of cake. He rode slowly around the block in first gear. When he came back up the driveway, he applied the front brake and came to a perfect stop. He carefully got off and put the kickstand down. As he picked up his crutches, Pete breathed a big sigh of relief. Now he knew he would make it. He was still a BCMC.

Pete struggled through the long boring days during his convalescence. It wasn't easy. The days were hot in August, and Pete lay there in bed reading and trying to scratch the itches inside his casts. It was driving him crazy. Finally, one of the motor cops that came to visit Pete gave him some hope.

"Get a fiberglass fishing rod and cut it off to about two or three feet. Make sure it's smooth and blunt on the end, so you don't poke holes in your skin. You can slide that beauty down inside your cast and get those itchy spots." It worked. It was Pete's salvation. It felt so good to scratch those itchy places under his casts.

"Honey," said Noel, "it's Ron on the phone." Pete took the phone.

"Hey, Nipplehead," yelled Pete, "what's happening?"

"Well, how do you like wiping your ass with your left hand, dipshit?"

"It's not fun," said Pete. "I'd give my right arm to be ambidextrous."

They continued to exchange insults for a few minutes and then said good-bye. Pete was planning his return to the motor squad as soon as he could. He was still worried about losing his spot because of his inability to ride. As his ankles healed and the casts came off, he started to feel better and more confident about his future. The scar on his right ankle from the surgery had healed well. His ankles were stiff, but he started to walk and exercise them.

It had only been a little over three months since his accident, and Pete was back to work on "light duty." Working the desk in the watch commander's office was not a lot of fun, but he was back to work. Pete's job was to answer the phones and the Gamewell callbox line and to check citations officers had written and turned in before they went to the traffic court for processing. If there were mistakes on the citations, Pete kicked them back to the citing officer for correction. In some cases, the corrections were made by Pete.

He soon learned that one of his jobs was to maintain and continue a list of odd names that appeared on tickets. Some people had really weird names, and others were just interesting. Pete reviewed the current list, which was quite long. He chuckled as he read some of the names. Dick Tracy was cited for speeding. General Washington had gotten written up. Nancy Lichdich? Pete wouldn't have touched that name with a ten-foot pole. Here's the best one of all, thought Pete. *Hedreth Nosegay!* Who would name a kid Hedreth? Pete wondered. The kid probably grew up and killed his parents to get even, he thought.

Pete still had a lot of pain in his ankles, but he wanted back out on the street. He had tried to get his motor boots on several times. This caused him excruciating pain. He knew that until he could get into those boots, he would be stuck in the office. After about a week in the office, Pete could stand it no more. He stuffed his swollen ankles into the boots and ignored the pain. The doctor at Central Receiving Hospital passed him for fitness, and Pete was back on motors.

Being back was a little more than Pete thought it would be. He could hardly walk in the motor boots. Getting on and off of his motorcycle was sheer agony. His ankles twisted and groaned every time he did it. He kept telling himself he would get better. In the meantime, Pete told himself to watch out. It's bad enough out in the street with all your limbs in good condition. In Pete's condition, he was fair game for anyone who took him on. Pete resolved to avoid any confrontations at all cost. Each night when Pete got home from work, Noel had to pull off his boots. The pain was almost unbearable. Noel knew it would do no good to try to talk Pete into staying off the bikes for a while until he healed more. She'd tried that before. Pete would do what he had to do.

"The asshole is suing me?" yelled Pete, while the papers had just been served on him. "The son of a bitch turns right from the wrong lane with no signal, fucks me up, and then sues me and the city?" The allegation charged Pete and the city with negligence and wanted the city to pay for the damage to his car and for his "pain and suffering."

The man who was driving the VW that had caused Pete's accident was an immigrant from Pakistan. In the original traffic accident report, Mr. Hassan had stated he was looking for a certain street, and when it came up unexpectedly, he had made a quick turn. "In other words," Pete had said, "this fucking camel jockey just turns without looking or signaling and nails my ass. Then he gets out of his car and stands there and watches all the other people try to help me while he doesn't do shit! Now he's suing me!"

Not long after the papers were served on Pete, he was summoned to Captain Manger's office. Pete had a feeling he was not going to like this meeting.

"Felix," said the captain, leaning back in his chair with his palms pressed together as if in prayer, "your accident has been found to be 'preventable' by the Accident Review Board, and you'll be giving up four days off as a penalty."

"When did the board decide this? Where was I?" asked Pete in amazement.

"It was done while you were off on medical leave."

"Don't I have the right to be there when you, guys, decide what I did was right or wrong?"

"No, that's not necessary," said Manger. Pete detected a nearly imperceptible smirk on the mouth of his commanding officer. It was payback time for the way he had blasted the captain at the hospital.

"Look, Captain, I don't mind taking the four days. It doesn't mean shit to me. But you, guys, have got to be crazy doing this at this time. Don't you realize the city and I are being sued over this accident, and if I'm handed a penalty for the accident now, it implies that I did something wrong? The lawyers for the camel jockey are going to have a field day with that in court. Don't you understand what this means? Why not wait until the court crap is over, and then you can give me ten fucking days if you want to? Just don't do this now!" Pete still couldn't believe what he was hearing.

"Sorry, Felix," sneered the captain. "That's not the way we operate."

"Let me see if I understand what you are saying here," said Pete. "The city asks for someone who is willing to go out and investigate a speed complaint on Third Street. The officer who does this will be putting himself in extra danger in doing so. I volunteer and go out and do the job I'm asked to do. When some dumb asshole from Timbuktu nearly kills me, you guys get together and decide, in my absence, that I did something wrong and give me days off. At the same time, I'm being sued, along with the city. The lawsuit could result in a loss to the city of God only knows how much money and I get the blame, right?" By this time, Pete's face was red, and he was approaching critical mass. It also was becoming clear to Pete that his chances of ever collecting any money for his pain and suffering were being severely hampered by the captain's decision. Other motor cops had collected large sums of money from accidents where drivers had committed traffic violations and had injured officers in the process. Pete saw his accident as no different. He had been chasing a speeder—doing his duty—and had been cut off by a traffic violator. What would this do to his chances? Pete was afraid to guess.

"I just heard that Sergeant Connors's accident that happened after mine was ruled to be 'nonpreventable,'" said Pete. Sergeant Connors was not one of Pete's favorite people. He was arrogant and a poor supervisor, and most of the men hated his guts.

"According to the report, he hit an oil slick and went down," said Pete. "The sergeant that was riding with him at the time said *he* smelled the diesel fuel two blocks away and saw the big puddle of it a block away. Looks to me like Sergeant Connors had his head up his ass and locked. The other sergeant slowed and moved into another lane to avoid the oil, but Connors runs into it and goes on his ass! That's 'nonpreventable'? What kind of a decision is that?"

"I guess it's an arbitrary call on my part," said Manger, with a slight smile on his face. Pete could see there was nothing to do but accept their decision and do the best he could with the case.

CHAPTER TWENTY-NINE

JUSTICE?

Pete hated the marble halls of the courthouse. They always suggested a mausoleum to him. He hoped it wouldn't be true for his case in the accident suit. Pete had hired Jim Lorimer, a lawyer whom he had known from several years before when Jim had been with the city attorney's office. Pete and Jim had become friends while Pete testified on many court cases involving drunk drivers. Jim had left the city attorney's office and was now in private practice.

Jim had received a copy of Mr. Hassan's report from his attorney. Mr. Hassan was being represented by his insurance company's lawyer, a former officer of the California Highway Patrol. Now there's a switch, thought Pete. Some guys will do anything for a buck! Pete's opinion of insurance companies was "they are necessary evils." Pete and his lawyer had their first conference with the ex-CHP representing Mr. Hassan.

"According to the Vehicle Code," the husky middle-aged ex-cop began, "an officer operating an emergency vehicle, like your motorcycle, must turn on the red lights and siren in order to be exempt from the California speed law. You admit you were speeding when you hit Mr. Hassan in the rear and you didn't have your red lights and siren on. That makes you partly responsible for the accident, Officer Felix." Pete couldn't believe his ears.

"That's bullshit," said Pete. "It's standard procedure to chase speeders without red lights and siren. If we did that, we'd never catch anyone speeding. They'd just see the reds and hear the siren before you could get a clock on 'em and slow down."

"That may be true, but the law is pretty clear," said the insurance lawyer.

"Then how come we don't know about it?" asked Pete. "We're the guys out there busting our asses, trying to prevent accidents, and we can't exceed the speed limit unless we have our red lights and sirens on? That's ridiculous!" A sick feeling hit Pete in the pit of his stomach. He knew he was about to be screwed. He could see it in his lawyer's face too. The opposing attorney pulled out a copy of the Vehicle Code, and they looked at the section pertaining to emergency vehicles. It was there.

"What does this mean?" asked Pete, after the conference was over and he and Jim were alone again.

"It means that the court would instruct the jury that both parties were at fault by certain percentages. For example, if you were found to be twenty percent negligent and the camel jockey was eighty percent, you'd lose the case."

"So what are my options?" asked Pete, feeling like he'd been hit again by the VW.

"I think the best we can do is take their offer to have the city pay for the guy's car; and his insurance will pay for your medical bills, and you get an award from workman's compensation," said Jim in a serious voice. Pete's heart sank.

"Who kisses me?" he asked. Jim looked at him inquisitively.

Pete answered before the question. "I usually get kissed after I get fucked."

They went back into court and settled the case. Pete got $10,000 from workman's comp. From that, he paid back the city for his pay while he was off injured (another pleasant surprise) and Jim's legal fees. Pete had about $2,500 left after all the bills were paid.

"Why do we do this?" asked Pete. Ron Byron and a couple of the other motor cops sat around in the coffee room, talking about Pete's problems. "The city doesn't back us, our own captain stabs us in the back, the people we try to save on the streets hate our guts, the blacks think we are an army of occupation, the politicians only like us when we save their asses, our wives think we are a bunch of male chauvinist pigs, the news media is just waiting for one of us to make a mistake so they can write us up and sell more newspapers, a dog chased my motorcycle today and tried to eat my leg!" The Beach Ball took a sip of coffee and kicked back in his chair.

"I love ya, Petey. Let's go into the locker room showers together and soap down," he said, with a smirking smile.

"I've been fucked by experts. Why should I lower myself to the amateur league?" said Pete.

"The answer to the whole question is simple," said Ron. Pete and the others turned to hear Ron's words of wisdom.

"It's because *that's the way it is.*" The chorus of BCMCs joined in and finished the statement in unison. They walked out to their motors laughing about all of the shit that goes on with the BCMCs.

Pete's thoughts wandered as he rode toward his beat. He hurt. He felt the cool night air blowing past his face. He listened to the rumble of the engine that vibrated beneath him. He knew he made a difference. He and the other cops on the street did good things most of the time. They helped people. They protected them. They tried. Sometimes they succeeded. Most of the time, they didn't. But they wouldn't stop trying. Pete wouldn't stop. He couldn't.

Pete knew his days on motors were numbered. The old breed was mostly gone. Retired. Working other jobs on the department. The seniority program by which motor officers gained their vacation times and beat selections was fading rapidly. The once-independent Traffic Enforcement Division was now being decentralized, and the motor squad was broken up and assigned to the various divisions around the city and stood roll call with the patrol cops. The TED motor officers were now responsible for any and all radio calls and accident investigations. In other words, the BCMCs were now just plain cops like all the rest.

Dang! This takes all the fun out of being a motor cop, Pete thought. His attention now turned to a different job on the department. He now had eighteen years on the job and wasn't getting any younger. His wife was never comfortable about his job after his big accident. Seniority was in the tank, and the "new breed" generally pissed him off. It seemed that all the fun was gone, and it was time to move on.

One of Pete's former partners had made the rank of lieutenant and was now working in the Records and Identification Division (R&I) and informed him that there was an opening in the warrant detail of R&I.

"So, sweets (Pete's nickname for Bill Haymes), what's this job all about in R&I?"

Bill explained that it was a plain-clothes job serving high-grade misdemeanor warrants and performing "Due Diligence" on them. As officers learned in the academy, warrants sometimes go invalid if no attempt to serve them is made. This is called performing Due Diligence in attempting to arrest the wanted person. It was a five-day-a-week job with weekends off and no night services. Pete thought it was a good place to do the rest of his time on the job, so why not?

So, in the fall of 1976, Pete left the motor squad he loved and took a new job that turned out to be a lot more work and more exciting than he ever imagined. But that's another story.

EPILOGUE

1995 — The middle-aged man was getting very drunk as he sat in front of his television and watched the City of Los Angeles burning *again*! Burning because a convicted felon on parole was thumped by the LAPD and later the cops were acquitted of any crime.

He thought about the 1965 Watts Riot. He'd been a rookie motor cop then. He thought about the tremendous effort the police department had made to heal the wounds left by it. What had it all been for? he wondered. They were making the same mistakes in this riot as they did in the Watts Riot thirty years ago! Don't we ever learn? he thought. How many times will they burn this city down? People get what they deserve when they let the politicians run the show, he thought.

"Come to bed, honey," said Noel. "You're just getting yourself all worked up over this. Anyway, you're retired. It's not your responsibility anymore, is it?"

Is it? he wondered. Pete felt a sadness for all the sacrifices that he and the other cops had made in their time on the job. What was it all for? Pete thought of Old John Sudinski, who had just died of a heart attack at the age of sixty-two. He thought of John on his soapbox that night when Pete was a rookie motor cop.

"Cops do help people. The people just don't know it," he'd said to himself. The job that cops really do will never be really known by anyone who has not been there, he thought. That thought made him feel better. He had a good job now as a minor executive in a good company, doing a job he enjoyed. A job that was important. He had his pension from the police department every month. He'd earned every penny of that day he crashed into the camel jockey, he thought. He now had a good job in a new career field in the motorcycle industry and was doing well.

He'd been a part of an elite group of men. A dying breed that no longer existed. But it still existed to the men who had lived it. It never went away in the mind of a BCMC.

Pete got up and walked slowly into the bedroom. He told himself he was satisfied with his life. He had to be. But people don't change, he thought. They never will. Neither will I, he said to himself as he dropped into bed. Why is that? he asked himself.

Because *that's the way it is*. He went to sleep and dreamed motor cop dreams.

THE END